MIAMI MOON

A JOSE CASTILLO MYSTERY

JORGE E. GOYANES

Fulton Books, Inc.
Meadville, PA

Published by Fulton Books 2017

ISBN 978-1-63338-340-1 (Paperback)
ISBN 978-1-63338-341-8 (Digital)

Printed in the United States of America

CHAPTER 1

Jessica was tired. She had been working the Tamiami Trail—or the Trail, as locals call it—since five in the afternoon. She worked the west end of it between the Palmetto Expressway and the turnpike because truckers were easy johns since they used both those main drags extensively.

She liked the truckers because they were in a rush to get their load delivered, no pun intended. She chuckled to herself. They had plenty of cash, and they usually had a bed or a small cot in their cabs, which sure beat the blow jobs and fuckathons in compact cars and sports cars.

It was getting close to midnight, and she was ready to call it a night when a plain-looking male pulled up in a small sedan and asked her what she would do.

"Well, just about anything, except animals, scat, or blood, amigo," she said while looking him over. He was about thirty years old, medium build, Hispanic-looking, well-groomed, which was always a good sign—and for fuck's sake, he had a child-restraint seat in the backseat.

Oh, baby, this is a recent dad. Mama is breast-feeding and probably is too tired to give papa some quim. He is probably so backed up he will shoot that load in about one minute. Easy money, here we go.

"Okay, papi, what do you want? Talk to me, baby."

"Miss, I like it a little rough, so that is why I asked what you would do." He was soft-spoken and almost shy, she thought.

"What's a little rough, papi? Spanking, whips, chains? What you got in the trunk of this car, papi?"

"Oh, Miss, just a little hairpulling, a little choking, that's all." He looked down at his hands, which were on his lap. He acted almost embarrassed.

"C'mon, baby, last trick of the night, but it will cost you a little extra."

"No problem, Miss, whatever you want." He was still looking down at his hands. He had a six-inch piece of rope that he kept making into knots and loosening them, making them, loosening them, making them, loosening them.

She went over to the passenger side and hopped in. She always looked on the seat to see if there were any weapons. Backseat look was next, and she looked in the glove box too. A girl could never be too careful.

"What's your name, Miss"? Mr. Shy was already trying to get his nerve up.

"Whatever you want to call me, señor, but my friends call me Brandy." She never gave them her real name.

She just wanted to make enough money to pay the motel rent, get her car fixed, and get out of town as soon as possible after being dumped and thrown out of her scumbag boyfriend's apartment. She was only thirty, but it was a hard thirty. She couldn't be a stripper because she was a bit out of shape, had some scars and tattoos; and truthfully, she had no rhythm and looked like an albatross when dancing. But she could suck the chrome off a trailer hitch and had the manual dexterity of a classical pianist. So here she was, giving hand jobs and blow jobs and the occasional laydown to make ends meet and survive, long way from Muncie, Indiana, to the mean streets of South Florida.

"What's your name, honey?" she asked while putting her hand on his right leg. He was focused on his driving, and he had driven them into Coral Gables. It looked like they were headed toward the Biltmore Hotel, which was built by Bowman and Merrick in 1926 just prior to the stock market crash in 1929. It became a national historic landmark in 1996 after extensive renovations of the old girl and is now a beacon of beauty in the middle of a bustling city.

"Just call me macho...bitch." Well, he was really trying to grow some balls, she thought.

I will have this guy finished in no time if I am submissive, Jessica thought to herself.

He pulled the car into the parking lot of the Biltmore golf course, which was right next to the hotel.

She said, "Are we getting in the backseat?"

"No, let's go over to the driving range by the ninth green. It's a nice night out, and I have a blanket." He was reaching in his trunk for the blanket, and she looked to make sure he was not grabbing any tools, knives, or rope.

They walked over to the range, and he laid down the blanket under a tree that was just off the cart path.

He proceeded to take off his clothes and instructed her to do the same.

Here we go, baby, Jessica thought. *Let's get this over and done with, and I can go take a hot shower and wash this day off me, grab a cold one, and rest my weary bones and muscles.*

"How do you want it, papa? On my back, on my knees?"

"Get on all fours like a bitch now!"

She noticed he was already hard and almost panting from the excitement.

He positioned himself behind her, grabbed her hips, and jammed it in as hard as he could. She was glad she had prepped herself with K-Y after the last john; this guy was a slammer. He grabbed her hair and pulled her head back with so much force that she actually moaned from the pain.

That seemed to incite him more. He pulled harder until she actually had to say, "Hey, you take it easy back there. That hurts."

She knew as hard as he was slamming her he would be spent soon. She thought she would just hang in for a few minutes, and it would be all over.

She felt her hair was loose again, but he grabbed her neck and started squeezing. *This guy really likes it a little rough. It will be over soon*, she thought.

She was starting to have a little trouble breathing. She tried to get out the position she was in, but he felt it and pushed his weight on her, and she was now on her stomach. He had wrapped his legs around hers, so she could not wiggle free, and his weight on her chest did not let her move at all.

She was staring to panic, which made him squeeze her neck harder. This guy was serious, and she did not know what to do for the first time. Most of the ones who liked violence got off as soon as you struggled or appeared to be helpless. This guy was slamming into her harder and was squeezing her neck to the point that she was now scared.

If she fought back, and he liked it, he would squeeze harder. If she caved in, she was afraid she would black out from lack of oxygen. Then what?

She decided to fight. She'd always been a fighter, and if this worked, he would shoot his load, and this would be over. Besides, she was a little heavier than he was. If she could turn the tables and get on top, she would have the upper hand, weight-wise.

She tried a hip swivel, and he was not moved or amused. This guy was in better shape than she thought. Her head was pounding due to the start of oxygen starvation; her thrashing was making her lungs heave, searching for air. He tightened his grip around her neck, and for the first time, she thought she might not make it through this.

She started to see spots in her vision. She could hear the pulse in her veins; it sounded like drums being pounded. She was starting to lose feeling in one of her arms. She tried to scream, but it sounded like a croak. She thought, *I hope I wake up from this, Mama. I promise I'll go home to Muncie and be a good girl. Promise, promise…*

She hoped she would wake up as the blackness descended upon her.

CHAPTER 2

Sam Sinclair was a creature of habit. Every morning, he would wake up at the same time, make his coffee, go out to get his *Miami Herald* from his lawn, and go sit out back and read the paper cover to cover while drinking his coffee.

This morning, he was wondering how far from the front door his newspaper delivery person would leave his copy. He thought *person* because every year, he would not know if his delivery person was a man or a woman until three weeks before Christmas. He would get the paper delivered with a personalized self-addressed envelope from the mystery delivery person for their "annual" tip. *That* paper always seemed to be right on the doorstep instead of by the sidewalk.

As he walked out his front door to get his paper, he noticed a girl sitting in a lotus position on his lawn. He thought, *What an odd place to wait for the school bus.* He assumed it was one of the local kids.

As he got closer, he noticed she was in her late twenties and she did not look good. He walked up to her and put his hand on her shoulder and said, "Miss…Miss…" And she fell right over. Then he saw the marks on her neck and saw those dead eyes—you couldn't miss those. He'd worked in a hospital ER and knew dead eyes when he saw them. He did not run back in to call the police. He knew she had been dead for hours. Rigor mortis had set in. When he tipped her body over, it stayed in the lotus position.

He knew his world was not going to be the same today. Cops everywhere, technicians everywhere, and of course, the reporters—they would be relentless. He called his brother in North Miami and told him to pack a bag and come down and help him keep the circus at bay.

CHAPTER 3

Detective Nate Devine had a formula for how his day was going to turn out based on years of experience working the homicide department of the Miami-Dade Police Department by gauging what the first case he would work entailed. If he was investigating a murder of passion, it would be a smooth day.

If he was investigating a drive-by, it would be a little rougher.

If he was investigating a gang *murking*, as the kids were calling murder nowadays, it would be quite a bit rougher.

But if he was investigating a murder and the signs of evidence, placement of the body, and modus operandi started to look vaguely familiar to other unsolved murders, the hair on the back of his neck started to rise, and his first thought was, *I have serial killer on the loose*—it was going to be a horrible, horrible day. Nate was hoping it would not turn out to be one of those days, but what little he could see was troubling.

Another case he was working on from ten days ago was of another prostitute who was dropped off in a front yard just off the Trail. That time, the body was positioned in a kneeling position with her hands clasped on her lap as if she was holding something in them. She had also been strangled. Nate did not need forensics or a visit from the FBI BAU team to tell him what every pore of his body, the hair on the back of his neck, and that good ol' cop barometer, the gut, told him: that this was the work of the same person.

His plate was full already with the Miami Beach hotelier who was found bludgeoned to death by his maid, the Russian owner of a South Beach nightclub who was found floating in the Miami River with his hands cut off, and now this, a dead girl dropped off and placed on somebody's lawn and carefully positioned in a lotus position. This had all the looks of a planner; most serial killers were planners. He needed this like his ex-wife calling him up for some more money to do some more remodeling. Not in the house that she got as part of the divorce but some more plastic surgery. His ex had more plastic surgery than the bumpers on his police cruiser.

His workload was pretty bad, but thank goodness for his assistant, Buck Taylor, who was as gay a caballero as you could find but was so anal-retentively organized that he made Nate's job easier. Buck had already canvassed the block and had everyone's name, address, cell phone, and e-mail address, one column for those who saw or heard something and one column for those who did not.

He was checking the day and times the garbage disposal trucks ran to see if it happened to be this morning. He was checking on the newspaper delivery persons to see if they saw anything, and he had hit pay dirt with that. He said the newspaper deliveryman saw a couple in a car parked in front of the house in question, but it looked like they were necking, so he did not pay too much attention.

Buck told Nate the delivery guy was coming by to give a statement and anything he could remember.

At this point, Nate could use any positive news. It was going to be an ass-biting week.

CHAPTER 4

Jose's Cruisers is my enjoyable business. I am Jose Castillo, and I restore classic cars for the well-off who can afford it. By enjoyable, I mean that I love working with my hands. I take pride and joy in restoring a vehicle to its former glory and, in most cases, make them better due to technology and improvements in the auto-parts industry.

My other business is Joe Castle Investigations, which is a one-man agency that specializes in surveillance, loss detection, and any case that requires stealth, discretion, and trial-proof evidence. While the agency offers me the occasional juicy case, most of the time, I am gathering evidence of someone who is trying to collect on a personal-injury case with a fake or manufactured injury, or the wronged party of a lover's tryst is asking for proof of the infidelity. South Florida has groups that actually stage accidents so they can generate medical bills, and everyone gets money. It's an epidemic of greed that is unprecedented.

Lawyers make money, doctors make money, clinics make money—and yes, investigators like me make money trying to figure out who is faking it and who is not. The driver of the car gets one thousand to stage an accident, five hundred to each passenger. The billing to insurance, clinics, and Medicare starts. It's a cash cow. People have stopped putting State Farm and Allstate stickers on their vehicles' rear bumpers because it's like a money magnet to crash teams.

On the infidelity front, the sad part is that Florida is a no-fault divorce state, so even if the wife is sleeping with an entire football team or the husband gets caught banging his sister-in-law like a screen door in a hurricane, one of them has to hire a fancy lawyer, or the marital house is evenly split unless there are extenuating circumstances. So the proof they are seeking is really a validation of their fears, suspicions, or instincts.

It is sad to show the cuckolded one the pictures or video of their worst fears. Once that happens, you can see the hardening behind their eyes, their jaw tightening, and their resolve either strengthen or their shoulders sag.

Every once in a while, you do get a missing-persons case, a kidnapping, or someone trying to right a wrong, and the interest meter kicks up a notch, and usually a fat fee follows.

I have done so many stakeouts that I purchased and outfitted a new Mercedes-Benz Swinger van with the latest electronics, thanks to my computer wonk, Jim Gafford. The van is tall-roofed and long-bodied, so you can stand up in it without hitting your head.

Jim installed a computer dock where I can slide my laptop into. He gave my system face- and voice-recognition software. He also added a radar and satellite array, fax, and scanner. Cameras with infrared on all four exterior corners of the van were also added. It has alarm and tracking devices both for protection of the van and for "painting" a vehicle in order to track it by satellite.

The latest gizmo Jim is letting me "test-drive" is a projection system that creates 3-D holograms. Haven't used it yet, but can't wait to try it.

The van has a kitchen, a bathroom with a shower, a gun safe, a Bose stereo system—and no, it does not have a bed. I string up a hammock and sleep in that if push comes to shove.

With the advent of Google Earth and MapQuest live, I can park a block away from a house and track comings and goings from that house on the computer in the van. But Jim has trumped even that. He hacked into foreign countries' satellite that is used by their security service and has let me "borrow" that for a while until he gets caught and has to steal another satellite's signal.

I use magnetic signs on the van from a cable provider, with all the extras on it. It appears like the real deal. Sometimes Jim comes on a stakeout with me. He calls the van the Mother Ship.

CHAPTER 5

Lisa had arrived at her usual corner on the Trail a little later than usual. She had a hard time getting a relative to watch her four-year-old. There was not a day care center open in the evening, and her roommate was nowhere to be found. She had to wait for her aunt to get home from her job in Hialeah in order to have someone watch baby Jesus. She wouldn't dare leave him with any of her crazy neighbors.

She hoped she had not missed any of her regulars, and with the light drizzle the way it was, she thought it would probably be a slow night.

Sharday, a transvestite whose real name was Luis and worked the same area, came over and said, "Girlfriend, I have some bad news. Two of the girls working the Trail have *gone missing* in the last few weeks."

Great, Lisa thought. It was enough to worry about the johns who liked it rough and enjoyed slapping you around, the ones who tried to get out from paying, or the ones who were just plain mean. Now there was worry about a couple of the girls going missing.

"I have a switchblade on me at all times now. You never know, girl." Luis was from Puerto Rico, and he was bilingual, so he usually got a little more action as a result.

"What happened to them?" Lisa was more than interested in that.

"Don't know, girlfriend. Had some cop come by and tell us to be careful. He said to call in any suspicious characters."

"Call in any suspicious characters? Hell, that would be all of our customers," said Lisa while eyeing a sedan that was doing a second slow drive by. She thought the driver was getting his nerve up.

The driver of the sedan pulled to the side of the street and motioned with two fingers at both of them to come over.

"Ay, chica, I think he wants a threesome," Luis/Sharday said to Lisa. "C'mon, let's make some money, honey."

As they walked closer to the car, Lisa had a strange feeling that this guy was always on the mark. She grabbed Luis by the arm and said, "If you have that switchblade, keep it handy."

When Luis and Lisa walked within two car lengths of the sedan, the driver got out, and they both saw the badge on the belt, and both relaxed momentarily.

He was black, about six feet four inches tall and wiry, but had broad shoulders.

"Evening, girls. Don't worry. I just need a few minutes of your time, and then I will let you get back to your capitalist ways. I am Detective Nate Devine with Miami-Dade Police Homicide."

"You got a sense of humor there, Officer. First, you call us girls when clearly I am not, and then you tell us we can go on making money like good little capitalists," said Luis while quickly raising his skirt to show a fairly large bulge inside lace panties. "My name is Luis, street name Sharday."

"Motherfucker, you raise that skirt one more time, and I will shove your own dick up your ass. I am here trying to give you some information and trying to keep the girls on this street alive, and I get sass from a transvestite. Nothing wrong with what your tastes are, but have a little respect. I'd call you a cocksucker, but you obviously are, so I'll just say you are one ugly woman."

Luis was going to say something, but Lisa kicked his shin. "Ay, puta, que haces maricona?" Luis squealed like a little girl.

"So your street pal tries to keep you from opening your big mouth, and you call her a whore and a queer?" Nate was running out of patience.

"Andale, Officer, you speak Spanish too. Mierda, what's this friggin' world coming to?"

"What the hell do you expect? I work in the unofficial capitol of Cuba. You don't speak Spanish here, you could be the only English-speaking person for miles. Besides, no speaka Spanish, nobody talks to tall black man. Comprende mariconcito?"

Damn, not only did he speak Spanish, he had the slang down perfectly. Lisa was impressed, and Luis was too. "What, you got a Spanish-speaking girlfriend, Officer?"

"I am not an officer. I am a homicide detective. My girlfriend is not Spanish. My one and only wife was, and my best friend is Cuban. So there is your show for the day, kids. Let's get down to business." Nate had enough of the games.

"There is someone stalking and killing girls on the Trail. It's not rumor, and it's a fact. I just finished with a crime scene of a second girl who was found in the same area, and we think there might be more."

"You know we cannot stop what we do, Detective, but we can be careful." Lisa was paying rapt attention.

"All we know right now is that he must like it a little rough because both girls were strangled to the point that their larynx was crushed. Their hair was pulled, and one had a scalp laceration. So we are asking you to spread the word and keep us posted if you hear or see anything. Here is my card."

"Gracias, Detective," said Luis while sticking his hand out to shake Nate's hand.

"Por nada, muchacho," retorted Nate while shaking his hand. "I meant what I said earlier Luis."

"What is that, Detective?" he said while putting his hands on his hips.

"You are one ugly woman." Nate was smiling as he said this.

"I might be, Detective, but I suck so hard I could make the top of your head cave in, babeee." Luis was chuckling like a Catholic schoolgirl on a backseat joyride.

Nate was shaking his head and chuckling too. "If I introduce you to my assistant, I might never see him show up for work again. Or I'll have to go to your bridal shower, and that would just kill me. I wouldn't know what pastel color to get you two."

"Bring him on. I'll show him how hot Latinos are."

"Got better things to do, fruit loops, like catch a killer."

CHAPTER 6

The 1961 AC Cobra that I had been restoring for the last six months was taking a bit longer than I anticipated. I had even tried to contact some old workers from the Thames Ditton, Surrey, England, factory where they were originally made in order to find any parts to help me finish this job. I even found some parts for the original 2.6-liter Zephyr engine through *Hemmings Motor News*, the bible of antique-car enthusiasts.

I had been feverishly working about eight hours a day on this car for the last two weeks. I wanted to get paid for all my hard work and materials so that I could build up the checkbook at Jose's Cruisers. Also, my fiancée, Kat, was on a photo shoot in St. Croix, so I had bit more free time than usual. My other business, Joe Castle Investigations, was hot and cold as usual. I had done a few surveillance projects for a personal-injury attorney after the Santana case. So one business fed the other and vice versa.

When I am usually finished with a restoration job, I get paid so well for those that I can take my choice of private investigator jobs. Obviously, I take less of the personal-injury cases as they are monotonous. Thank goodness that Mother is loaded with electronics, so I can play poker on my computer or catch any game from anywhere due to Gafford's "borrowed" technology.

Once this car was done, I would be collecting a nice five-figure fee, and it would be worth all the sweat expounded on this little muscle pocket rocket. Working on a car and restoring it to its original look is rewarding in more ways than one. Not only are you bringing back a classic beauty, but you can really appreciate the crafting of cars back when they were made by hands and not robots. The cars today are so sterile that you can put six sports sedans of different manufacturers side by side, and from one block away, you cannot tell any of them apart.

There is nothing like listening to a throaty exhaust coming out of twin muffler pipes opening up under the weight of your foot on the accelerator. Or that feeling when you are running your hand over the curve of a fender that came out perfect because of your hard work with sandpaper, paint, and some elbow grease.

I was admiring my work when a beep went off in the office, letting me know there was someone buzzing me at the front door and my security system was recording. I did not have any appointments for either business, but little did I know that the person on the other side of that door was going to send me on a job that would span international time zones, put me in peril more than once, and make someone mad enough at me that they would hire a hit man to come after me.

CHAPTER 7

"Hello, boss, I need your help." Standing in front of my door in a Hawaiian shirt, cargo shorts, and sandals was who else but Lesson. I had not seen him since we gave depositions in the Mrs. Santana slap-on-the-wrist circus that the state attorney put on for show after my last case. I am a firm believer that the karma wheel never ever stops turning until it comes full circle and either crushes the debris of past transgressions or tills the soil for new growth.

In Mrs. Santana's case, neither has happened yet, but I knew that eventually I would be able to see some karmic justice come her way.

"So, Lesson, stop beating about the bush and tell me what you need. And come on in, it's stifling out there."

I grabbed an Amstel Light out of the cooler I kept downstairs and decided to take a much-deserved break and listen to my big hulking buddy. I was secretly hoping he was having a car problem and nothing more. I had a feeling the karma wheel was headed his way after his stint with Mr. Santana. I offered Lesson a drink but he declined.

"Boss, I heard something at work, and it might be nothin', but it might be something too, I am not sure. That is why I wanted to tell you so that you could help me understand it."

I nodded and made a circular motion with my hand, which is my way of showing you to carry on.

"I work for Cookie's Gentlemen's Club on South Beach, which is owned by Sergei Volkov. I am a bouncer, and once in a while, I am asked to be Mr. Volkov's bodyguard."

I heard some stories about Volkov and how he had purchased his club for thirty cents on the dollar after squeezing the last owner until he had no choice but to sell. I heard from Nate that Volkov was connected with the Russian Mafia, but they called themselves something else. Volkov was allegedly a big player in prostitution, gambling, and smuggling. I would have to look into that.

"A couple of days ago, I was in his office, and he got a call that he said was important, so he asked if I would go pick up his lunch from the Russian deli. I was in the hallway when I went back in to ask him if he wanted me to pick up some cigars for him because, being the good employee I am, I wanted to make sure he had everything he needed."

"He had gone to the bathroom and was still on the phone, and I waited outside the bathroom door to ask him about the cigars."

Lesson spoke slowly, and I could tell he had practiced this speech in order to appear like he was not slow—which he was anyway, God bless him. I was trying to be patient.

"Mr. Volkov started yelling at someone in English about the package and that there was millions riding on this and if there were any problems, he would kill the idiots who screwed it up, their children, and their grandchildren."

"Did he mention what the package was, Lesson?"

"In a minute, boss. I am trying to keep the story in order so I don't miss anything."

"I was still waiting, but then I heard him say that he did not care about Homeland Security at all and that he had everything covered."

Uh-oh, this started the radar pinging in my head.

"He said there was no problem getting…here is where I think I did not hear right, boss. He said the seesum over here. The problem would be the crazy camel jockeys he was dealing with."

"Did he really say camel jockeys?"

"Yes, boss, he did."

"And seesum? Is that what you heard? Are you sure?"

"Yes, boss. I have tried to remember real hard. That is what it sounded like, seeee….sum, just like that."

"Well, I am sure Volkov speaks with an accent, and according to you, he was screaming half the time, so we will work on it. If you remember at any time that it sounded like anything other than this seesum, which I have never heard of before, you let me know right away." I could tell he was frustrated by not being able to zero in on what he heard; he does not like to disappoint people.

"So, Lesson, what makes you think you are in trouble?'

"Boss, after I heard the words *Homeland Security*, I got scared and got to leaving to go get Mr. Volkov's lunch. I know Homeland Security can lock you up for no reason even if they just think you are involved in any terrorist thing, you know what I mean, boss? I was almost to the door when he came out of the bathroom, and he yelled at me what was I doing back there?"

This was starting to look like a black hole.

"I told him I had come back to see if he needed cigars, but when I did not see him in the office, I turned around to leave, and that was when he came out of the bathroom. I think he believed me, but he was looking at me strange, like he was trying to believe me."

"So you do not think he suspects you? Has anything changed at work or at home?"

"No, boss, but Mr. Volkov called me this morning and said he would be out of town for a few days and that he did not need me and for me to take the rest of the week off and to come back on Monday."

"Before today, you had no idea he was leaving town?"

"Righto, boss. Besides, he must be going out of town, which is why he is not taking me. He only uses me for local stuff."

"Okay, be careful, and if anything feels wrong or you get a feeling about something, follow your instincts. Call me if you have any questions or, more importantly, if you remember what seesum really sounded like."

His cell phone started ringing, and he answered, just listened. His face turned white, and all he said was, "Yes…yes….okay…has anybody seen Fluffy? Oh gosh, thanks, Mrs. Torres. I'll be over soon."

I could not resist. I waited for him to hang up. "Please don't tell me you have a cat and that it's named Fluffy."

"She was, boss. That was my landlady I rent from in Coral Gables. She said my efficiency just blew up, and Fluffy was in it."

CHAPTER 8

I went with Lesson to what would be left of his efficiency to see if he could salvage any belongings. We had to deal with Frank McCoy of the Metro-Dade Fire Department whom I had met through Nate. He was another ex-marine who was a stickler for details. The other person with a badge was Roxanne Pleasant with Alcohol, Tobacco, Firearms and Explosives, more commonly known by the acronym ATF.

Roxanne was just the opposite of McCoy. She was sloppy, careless, and did not follow protocol; but she had a nose, instinct, gut feeling—call it what you want, but she could read people very well and had spent some time with the FBI's behavioral analysis unit in Quantico before coming to the ATF South Florida division. She was also six feet tall, all legs, redheaded, blue-eyed, and had pasty white skin. I told her the first time we met she reminded me of the American flag due to the red, white, and blue in her face. She told me to stick a flagpole up my ass. We have been friends ever since.

I shook hands with McCoy and saluted Roxanne. "Do not start that flag shit with me, you cockroach," she said while smiling.

"Here I am, saluting the colors of the flag of our great country, and you give me grief, Roxy."

"Bite my ass, Cubano. Now what the hell are you doing here?"

"I would love to bite and kiss that lily white ass of yours, but I am smitten, as you well know, my dear."

"Oh, you still have your girlfriend hypnotized, do you?'

"You mean my fiancée, don't you? Or haven't you heard we are engaged?"

"Poor girl. You buy a Santeria potion in Little Havana and slip that in her drink to get you to agree to marry you?'

"What's not to love, Roxy? Smooth Latin moves, suave and debonair, a gentleman, and dare say, a pretty good dancer."

"An insufferable ego, a smart mouth, a cynic, sarcastic to the end—sure, lots to love there, Cubano. Keep dreaming."

McCoy piped in, "Do you two want to get a room, or can we carry on an investigation here?"

"The faster we do this, the quicker we can move on, kids. Let's get to it." Roxy was putting on gloves and an ATF baseball cap with LED lights on the bill cap. She meant business.

CHAPTER 9

After an hour, Mac and Roxy were comparing notes by the temporary command center they had set up. I was waiting for their report when one of the officers guarding the perimeter came and told me that there was someone who had to talk to me right away.

They had cordoned off the area, and the newshounds were at the yellow tape strung across the street, yelling questions, taking pictures, and filming, all from a safe distance.

Inside the yellow tape and sitting on the bumper of an ambulance was none other than Lola Sanchez, the intrepid investigative reporter for *Miami Tribune*, the "hip" Miami newspaper. I saw that a pretty good-looking male paramedic was wrapping her ankle. She was acting like she was in pain.

"My, my, the things we do to get a story or even a phone number. Lola, you are shameless."

"I really hurt my ankle while I was beyond the barricades, JC, and this fine young specimen of a paramedic is making me feel much better." The poor kid was blushing. He did not know where to hide. He started wrapping her ankle faster.

"Did you hear that, Strauss?" I had looked at his badge. "She called you a specimen. That's what scientists call the rats they are studying. She gets a hold of you, it will be three days before she lets you out for fresh air."

"Oye, JC, can't a girl try to make a living without having a ball-buster like you around?" Lola had that lower lip sticking out; she had that pout down to a science. "Besides, you can't be jealous, are you? You have your little Southern kitten, or whatever you call her."

"Lola, you know her name is Kat. I am just trying to keep this young man from being led into a den of iniquity. I am also trying to keep him from being sexually scarred for life."

"Ay, there you go with those fifty-dollar words, JC. I am not taking a loan out with him. The only equity I have is these two babies right here in my bra." Thank goodness she did not grab them as she usually does. I am sure it was because on the other side of the yellow tape, the television crews were filming in our direction.

"Iniquity, Lola, iniquity. Man, how did you pass Journalism 101 in school, girl?"

"With a B+, and that does not stand for blow job, okay, chico? Now, tell me what is going on back there. I have not seen an ATF agent and McCoy working a case unless it's serious. I am guessing that little efficiency did not blow a propane tank while the owner was barbequing?"

I wanted to change the subject. Strauss was done taping the ankle. "All wrapped up there, buddy? No pun intended." Strauss had taken his sweet time with the wrapping; maybe he was not as shy as I thought. I took a twenty out of my pocket.

"Hey, Strauss, bet you twenty you can tell me the color of her panties?"

"Oh, sir, she's not wearing...uh, never mind. Got to go." Strauss had turned as red as the fire truck next to us, and Lola was giggling. She'd won another admirer over.

"Get his number, honey?"

"Ay, papi, I slipped my card in his medic bag. He'll be calling, trust me, since he saw that I am not wearing panties means that he saw the pearly gates. He'll want in, and he'll call."

"Pearly gates? More like Dante's inferno based on your track record."

"Stop changing the subject, JC. What is going on back there? Hey! Isn't that what's-his-name, the bouncer you helped out in the Santana case?"

Lesson had come out of his landlady's back door and was heading to what was left of his efficiency. Dammit, I was hoping she would not see him.

CHAPTER 10

"Okay, that is Lesson, This has nothing to do with the Santana case, and it has not been determined what caused the explosion, so just wait, and I will feed you the information once I get it. Promise."

"Oh, JC, my news nose is on fire. There is more to this than meets the eye."

"Well, better your nose than what's usually on fire, señorita."

"No, no, don't change the subject. You know how this works. You help me, I help you. Remember I helped you by running that story in the *Trib* to help you flush out the Fanzule kidnapper."

"I know, Lola, and who got exclusive photos and the first interview with the kidnapper? You. I helped you out too. Right now, I know as much as you do. I will keep you posted."

"Something is funny here. Of all the people to be in this mess, it's his place that gets blown up, but you are here. What is the deal?"

"You know, Lesson needs some guidance, and he sticks to me like glue since the Santana incident. I feel a responsibility to look out for him."

"Oh, violins are playing in the background. How sweet." Lola was beginning to get on my nerves. "Lola, you know how I feel about the karma wheel. What goes around comes around."

"Since when does a Cuban raised in Miami get off on this karma crap?"

"Read a lot, traveled a lot, my sensei is a Buddhist, so I started looking into that. Maybe you should try it." I motioned to one of the officers whom I saw was getting a cup of coffee by the command post.

"Officer, could you please escort one of the fourth estate's finest citizens over to the viewing area? She is all wrapped up and feeling much better."

Lola gave me a nasty look with those Asian eyes of hers. But she sounded like butter wouldn't melt in her mouth. "Why, thank you, JC, for your attention. A girl could always use a manly hand around." She turned to the officer and held out her hand to be escorted back to the cordoned area. What a drama queen, amen!

I walked over to McCoy and Roxy. "Do you have any preliminaries?"

"Nothing concrete until we get some samples to the lab, but based on the smell, it would be a good guess to say Semtex was used. Whoever made this also used gel to accelerate the fire after the explosion. They wanted to obliterate the dwelling and to make sure no one survived in the rubble." McCoy was still smelling some of the debris.

Roxy piped in, "This was not an accident. They tried to make it look like one by sticking it to the propane tank from the barbecue. This was done by a professional."

"Who is this guy, and who would want him dead?' McCoy was looking at Lesson and trying to size him up.

"He is a friend, a good soul, who just happens to have bad luck in finding the wrong people to work for."

Lesson was picking garments off a clothesline in the backyard. I had no idea people still used those.

McCoy was starting to wrap things up. He had two large tackle boxes with every compartment labeled and organized. "I suggest you get this guy underground, based on what Roxy and I have come up with so far. The pro who did this will probably try again. I will give this top priority in my lab. JC, call me in twenty-four hours for an update."

"Thanks, Mac. I owe you one." I shook his hand. I know it's corny, but it's one of the civilized things we do that separates us from the animals.

"No problem. Say hi to Nate for me."

Roxy was wrapping it up, but not like Mac. She was kneeling on the ground, stuffing everything she had used in a duffle bag.

"How do you find anything in there, Rox?"

"Simple. I dump everything on a table and grab what I need. By the way, who does the big gorilla work for?"

"Sergei Volkov. He owns a few establishments in South Beach known for—"

Roxy jumped up. "Are you kidding me? Volkov? I have been trying to nail that guy for something, anything, for three years now, and nada, zilch."

"Geezus, Roxy, your nipples are hard. Are you happy to see me, or is that the female version of a hard-on?"

"ATF knows this guy is dirty. I know it, but that man is slipperier than a vibrator with K-Y all over it." She was pumped up. "I need to talk to him"

"Thanks for the visual, sweetie. Okay, a couple of things. He is a bit slow, and he likes to think before he talks, so be patient."

Lesson was walking over with a trash bag full of his clothes. "Hey, boss, you have an iron I could borrow? I don't think my landlady is going to iron my clothes no more."

The guy gets his efficiency bombed, and he is worried about getting his clothes ironed. The meek shall inherit the earth, after all. "Lesson, talk to Ms. Roxanne. She wants you to tell her everything you told me that you overheard at work."

"She your friend, boss?"

"Yes, she is a good friend. She helps me out when I do my private-eye job." I winked at Roxy.

So bless her heart, she was patient, and he repeated the story that he told me verbatim. She said the same thing I had. "Seesum? Are you sure that is what you heard? Seesum? Thank you, Lesson. If you remember anything else, let JC know, okay?"

Roxy pulled me aside after thanking Lesson for cooperating. "I haven't a clue what he overheard. He has to have heard it wrong, but he seems pretty adamant about it, so I will make some inquiries, and I will tell you the same thing that Mac did. Someone wants this guy dead. Keep him locked up somewhere."

"Well, señorita, I believe a good defense begins with a good offense. I have a plan, and it does not include hiding him. In fact, I will do just the opposite. Let's stay in touch, Rox. Muchas gracias."

"Sounds like you are going to aggravate some people in your usual style, JC. I hope you don't get this guy killed."

"I will try not to, señorita."

CHAPTER 11

We grabbed as many of Lesson's items that were usable from the rubble. There was not much. I stopped off at a drugstore and told him to get what he needed. I told him that I would be on the phone, checking e-mails, and returning messages.

I made a call to an old buddy, Christopher Gerard Cataldo, or Chris as I called him. He was as Italian as they come. We met in the army, served together in Ranger School. He was an expert marksman, and I was his spotter for our first year there.

We were from different cultures, but our families had a lot of similarities. We had big parties with lots of family members who liked to drink, smoke cigars, and play dominoes. I was raised in Little Havana with the smells of Cuban coffee and lechon asado, and he was raised in Little Italy with the smells of espresso and spaghetti sauce, but we became great friends.

He had gone to work in private security after our stint in the army. Then he went "Hollywood" on me when he started working the movie-star detail in Los Angeles. He was usually seen with whatever actor, rock star, actress who was hot at the time, and he has even protected some royalty. I hoped when I called him he was still in town or even in the state, let alone the country.

Chris and I had saved each other's bacon more than once, in the army and after. I have helped him on some of his jobs when he needed an extra body or an extra set of eyes. He has helped me when I have taken on a big surveillance job. This time, I had a feeling I would be in need of some extra bodies for protection. My radar was telling me things were going to get a little ugly.

"Hey, buddy. Not a lot of people named Jose have this number. How's it going, JC?" He was a wiseass too; no wonder I liked him.

"Que pasa, amigo. How is your dance card in the next few days? Things might be getting a little hot down here, and I may need some help."

"Shit, some real work for change. I am tired of babysitting rock stars and spoiled movie stars. The gig I just got out from under, I cleaned up more vomit than I did tending bar in Brooklyn. Great, I will be down there tomorrow, get some fun and sun down in Miami. I am tired of the ghouls and bloodsuckers here in LA, man. Are the spare keys to your crib still in the same place?"

"Yes, I will get with you and let you know what is going on. I have enough hardware if things get ugly."

"God, I hope it gets ugly. I could use some action. I feel like a babysitter. I haven't smacked anyone in months, let alone shot anyone."

"Okay, buddy. Keep it in check till something happens. See you, mañana paisan."

Calling him in was the best thing I did. I would need him more than I thought I would.

Lesson came out of the drugstore with six bags worth of stuff. "Hey, how long do you think you are going to be at my place?"

"Sorry, boss, some things I got to have." Lesson had a sheepish look on his face.

"C'mon, buddy, let's get going. We need to plan for your return to work."

"Back to work, boss?" I could see the concern on his face.

"Lesson, trust me. At work, you will be the safest. I will go with you and talk to Volkov. Let's get some dinner, and we'll talk it over."

CHAPTER 12

I had nothing fresh or thawed, so I took two cans of mushroom soup, added some heavy cream and half a stick of butter with a half a cup of white wine and some chopped mushrooms, and put it on simmer. I took some Cuban bread that was leftover from breakfast, sliced it in half, added garlic, olive oil, shredded parmesan, and some finely chopped plum tomatoes before throwing it in the oven for a few minutes.

I had shown Lesson the guest room that was on the fourth floor of my unit, and he was taking advantage of the shower at the moment. The third floor was the master bedroom with a balcony that overlooked US Highway 41, known as Southwest Eighth Street, and otherwise known as Calle Ocho. The second floor was the kitchen and living room area. The ground floor was my warehouse and shop all in one. It had room for four cars or two cars and the Mother Ship, which was exactly what was in there now. Mother, the AC Cobra I was restoring, and my 1953 DeSoto sedan.

The right side of the building had a staircase, and the left side had a large elevator.

My cell phone rang. I saw it was Nate. I grabbed my phone to answer. "Hey, mandingo, what is going on with you?"

"Oye, Casanova, you home? I need to come by and blow off some steam."

"Come over, brother. Lesson is here. He will be happy to see you."

"No shit, bro. Guess it's never a dull moment at Joe Castle Investigations."

"I would rather it be quiet on that front. I need to finish this Cobra. It's going to be a huge bill. Jose's Cruisers could use the influx of cash."

"Do not forget your brother from another mother when you get that payday."

"I don't remember you working on this Cobra at all, my brother."

"Hey, I handed you a wrench while you were under the car the last time I was there."

"I will give you your share of that. Should come to about a dollar ten, less taxes, of course."

"See you in a few minutes, you cheap bastard."

I added another can of soup to the mix and made sure we had some Courvoisier, Nate's drink of choice. At least he would not stick me with a check this time.

Lesson came down from the fourth floor wearing a football jersey and sweatpants. He was a large man; he looked bigger than a left tackle for the Miami Dolphins.

"What do you want to drink?"

"Have some juice, boss?"

"Sure. Tomato or orange?"

"Orange is good, boss. Thank you."

I knew better than to ask if he wanted alcohol. Drinkers usually ask you what type of alcohol you have first; then they ask what type of mixer you have.

"Okay, Lesson, let's take a minute to talk about my plan for your work before Nate gets here."

"Nate is coming? Goody, he is okay with me. He tells it like it is."

"You are right, Lesson. With Nate, there is no guessing. He does tell it like it is."

"Okay, if you have any questions, just stop me. I will go to work with you and explain to your boss that you have hired me to investigate who bombed the place you were living at."

Lesson had raised his hand. "Boss, I don't have no money to hire you." He was waving his hands in a no-no motion.

"Lesson, we are just telling your boss you hired me. You do not have to pay me a thing. Just hear me out."

"But, boss, you said to stop you if I had any questions."

"Okay, you are right. The reason we are going in to your work with this story is so that your boss knows that someone is protecting you and looking out for you, so maybe they will stop trying to…to… well, kill you."

The look on Lesson's face was intriguing, to say the least. He was perplexed at first; then the look of realization came to him, and then his brow furrowed, and he was actually starting to scowl. "Trying to kill me? I do nothing wrong, boss."

"You did nothing wrong, Lesson. You and I will find out what is going on, but I need you at work for that. You need to be my eyes and ears at Volkov's. At the end of your workday, I or a friend of mine will pick you up at work and bring you back here, where you will stay for a while."

"Thanks, boss. I like your place, very nice, looks like those fancy places in the magazines I read."

The buzzer on the front door went off. I hit the security app on my phone, and it showed it was Nate at the front door. I buzzed him in.

"I didn't interrupt anything, did I?" Nate yelled from downstairs.

CHAPTER 13

I had set up dinner for three and poured drinks for all. Lesson had a spoon in his hand, waiting for Nate and me to sit. I gave Nate a hug, and he patted Lesson on the shoulder.

"Hey, Lesson, long time no see. How are you, pal?"

"Okay, Officer Nate. Gots to find a place to live, though."

I brought Nate up to speed on Lesson's troubles. And I told him whom he worked for.

"Volkov? Are you shitting me? I've been trying to get anything on that guy for five years. Nothing, not even a crumb. There's an unofficial bounty out on his head between a handful of law enforcement agencies. First one to nail him and gets something to stick gets a one-week paid vacation to Washington, DC."

"Geezus, if the media ever got a hold of that story, all the Pollyannas will be wetting their pants and calling it an abuse of power. Can you imagine if my friend Lola ever got a hold of that story? What is going on with you, my brother?"

"Hell, man, as soon as the heat goes up, the murders start. Don't know what it is about the summer, but it gets people riled up. I got a county full of homicides, a Miami Beach hotelier found bludgeoned to death in a sleazy motel in Hialeah, the owner of a South Beach nightclub who was found floating in the Miami River with his hands cut off, and of course, I have the Tamiami serial killer."

"Serial killer? It's official now, isn't it?" I asked.

"Well, my brother, I just came from a crime scene. All indications point to the same guy doing it. This would be the third one. The media hasn't put two and two together, but when they do, the feeding frenzy will start. I have a real sicko out there. He is taking the time to pose the bodies after killing them, and now with the third one, he is taunting us. Only a handful of people know this, but on the third body, he has written a message on the torso."

"Sounds like he is getting more brazen as he goes," I piped in.

"He sure as shit is, bro. All that is going to make him accelerate his agenda, whatever it is. I am working with Florida Department of Law Enforcement and the FBI. My department has behavioral specialists on staff, so all of them are trying to put together a profile."

"Anything I can do to help, let me know. I know I am just a one-man operation, but you never know," I tried to pick up Nate's spirits.

"Thanks. We have a small army working on this. As soon as I get a profile package from my team, I will send it to you. In the meantime, tell me a little more about Lesson and Volkov and what you are planning to do."

"Sure. Anyone need seconds?"

"Okay, boss. I take more please."

"Coming right up, Lesson. How about you, Nate?"

"I'll take another shot of Courvoisier."

I brought the bottle over to the table after I served Lesson some more soup. I was thinking that I better load up on groceries.

"This is my plan, and I hope it works. I will take him back to work tomorrow even though he is not supposed to return until Monday. I will explain to his boss that Lesson will be dropped off and picked up when he is done working, that he has hired me to find out who put the bomb in his apartment. Hopefully, Lesson can find out some info on this meeting or this seesum, whatever the hell that is. I do not think Volkov will fire him because he needs to know exactly what Lesson knows. And since I will be investigating the bombing, maybe there won't be any more attempts on Lesson."

"JC, that is a hell of a stretch there. Are you sure you won't get Lesson in the line of fire as opposed to stashing him somewhere till it's safe?"

Lesson was finished with his dinner, but he was listening to Nate and me.

"It might never be safe. I think that it's better to be proactive. If they want to harm Lesson, they will not stop, so why not take the offensive approach? That is why I have Chris coming down to help me."

"How is that old sharpshooter doing? I haven't seen him in ages."

"He'll be here tomorrow. I will pass on your regards."

"Be careful, my friends. You get anything I can use on Volkov, hook me up right away. Kat still doing that shoot in the islands?"

"Yes, she is. I sure do miss her, but I am glad she is not around right now. I have a feeling things could get ugly."

"Ya think, bro? You've taken in a guy that was bombed out of his house. He works for a Russian hoodlum who might or might not want him dead, and you are going to tell the guy that probably initiated the bombing that you are investigating the attempt on Lesson. You are inviting a quote-unquote bodyguard to help you out who is suspected of being a gun for hire. Make sure your insurance is paid up, and I can always pick up Kat for you at the airport in case you are in the hospital or the morgue."

"What are good friends for? To give you that confidence and spur you on. Thanks for the positive vibes, Nate."

Lesson had not said much, but he meant what he said. He said to Nate, "Don't you worry about JC. I got his back."

"'Nuff said, brother. Good night, all."

CHAPTER 14

Sally had just finished with a quickie blow job in a pickup truck when she saw a sedan parked across the street from the cemetery on Forty-Eighth Avenue. The driver was motioning to her. She was hoping it was not going to be another backseat quickie. She could use a mattress, a shower, a soda pop, and a cigarette (in that order) after another paying customer.

She walked over and relaxed a little when she saw the child seat in the backseat. Another married guy needing a little attention 'cause mama was busy with the baby or too exhausted from working a full-time job then having to come home to attend to dinner, papi, and the baby.

"Hey, babeee, how much for an all-nighter?" He had a Hispanic accent.

"What you got in mind, mister?" She was hoping this was going to be a motel special instead of a choke and puke. She needed a break, a little air-conditioning.

"Let's go get a room, some beers, and make a nice, long night out of this, honey."

"Okay, papi, but this will cost you three hundred for the night." Sally figured she would go for broke. He was ready, horny by the look in his eyes; and worse comes to worse, he could say no.

"I'll pay you four hundred, but we will do what I want, where I want, and I am going to keep you all night."

He looked to her like he was salivating; he was that hot for her. He was grabbing his crotch and kneading it with his left hand. In his right hand, he had a piece of rope about six inches long, which he was making into a knot then loosening it over and over with just one hand. Strange, but what hadn't she seen in this racket?

I might be able to get a little more out of him, she thought as she went around and jumped on the passenger seat.

"Let's go, papi. Can't wait to hit that mattress."

"First, we are turning in here, missy." He made a turn into the cemetery.

"What the fuck are you doing? Are you one of those necrophiliac weirdoes?"

"No, babeee, we gonna start here. We finish at the Nest motel." The Nest, where they had a hedge around the complex and even between the parking spots for privacy. It was perfect for nooners and lovers' trysts. Even the office was blocked off from the street so pictures could not be taken of anyone checking in.

Okay, she thought, *this guy has done his homework. He really is married and wants to keep a low profile.*

He pulled around to the back of the cemetery behind the only mausoleum. He had done this before, she thought, and relaxed a bit more. He parked the car, turned off the engine, and stepped around back to the trunk. He opened it and started taking out a blanket.

Sally had stepped out of the car and was watching him. He was so ready his hands were shaking. He took the blanket, laid it by a tree, and started taking his clothes off. He was erect already. She had done a lot of weird things in this profession, but this was a new one on her.

"On your knees, bitch. Time to ride the tiger."

She slipped off her sundress and slipped out of her thong and assumed the position.

She noticed him reaching for the corner of the blanket and noticed his hand went into a pocket! The son of a bitch had sewn a pocket in the blanket. Dammit, she had missed that. She was relieved to see him pull a tube of K-Y lubricant, a condom, and rubber gloves out of the pocket. He squirted some on his hand and rubbed some on her cheeks and on the inside of her thighs. At least he was a clean freak.

"Any ass play is extra, okay, papi?"

"No problem, honey. I got you covered." He grabbed her pelvic bones and thrust his member into her mound as hard as he could.

"Easy, baby, we got all night." This guy was going to be like a bucking bronco, she thought, as she sunk her nails into the blanket for stability.

He tucked his hand under her stomach and brought it around as far as he could around her waist and pulled her even tighter as he thrust into her. With his other hand, he grabbed her hair and started pulling it.

This guy must have taken a Viagra or something, she thought. He should have finished by now, as hard as he was thrusting.

"Hey, easy on the hair, pal." He was really pulling her hair hard.

"Okay, babeee, I let go of your hair." He did, but he wrapped his hands around her neck.

Man, he had strong hands, she thought, as he started to put pressure around her throat. *He likes it rough. Good, they usually shoot that load as soon as they get the upper hand.*

She started to moan a bit, hoping that would get him going in the right direction, but it just made him tighten his grip on her neck more.

"Time to take you to the promised land."

Thank goodness, she thought. 'Bout time this guy finished; she was starting to get worried about the pressure on her neck.

She barely squeezed, "You are hurting me," out of her throat when he did finally let go of her. *What a relief,* she thought. *Let's get it over with.*

He quickly grabbed her in a sleeper hold.

She panicked because she remembered when she was a kid, her brothers would wrestle with her; and her little brother, who was smaller than her, would use the sleeper hold on her and make her lose consciousness every time.

She remembered not to fight it because that would make it worse and she would pass out faster. She could feel and hear her pulse in her head. It felt like a muffled bass drum—*thump, thump, thump.* Her eyes started to tear, and her sight became blurry. She slowly closed her eyes, and darkness engulfed her. Her last thought faded as fast as her sight did.

When he finished choking the life out of her, he disengaged and took his condom off and proceeded to stroke himself to orgasm, being careful not to get any DNA on her.

He hurriedly dressed and threw her in the trunk. He wanted to get her to the hotel room so he could pose her body before rigor mortis set in.

As he pulled into the Nest Motel, he smiled at the thought of how convenient the location was, just a block from the cemetery; and with the privacy hedge, he could carry the body into the room with no problem. He paid for two days and asked for no maid service.

He cleaned her body, posed her in the position, and held the pose by using industrial size Saran Wrap. He would be back the next night, unwrap her, and leave her on someone's lawn. He admired his work and chuckled at what he had written on her back with a magic marker: *keep lOOking, you'll never find me.*

He thought the capital *o*'s looked like eyes, nice play on words. He was proud of his work, taking another whore off the planet.

CHAPTER 15

I've been called a bastard in many a situation, whether photographing a pair of lovers coming out of a motel, or catching a supposedly injured person who received a settlement playing golf, or unfortunately, in too many cases, a woman calling me that name because of a relationship issue.

Little did those people know how close they came to the truth. My mother worked as a phone operator in El Capitolio, the capitol building in Havana. She had moved there after graduating from Cuba's equivalent of high school against my grandmother's wishes.

Mother was headstrong, independent, smart, and a good-looking woman. She was tall and had long black hair. She was way ahead of her time. I remember her sitting me down when I was a young teen and talking to me about peer pressure and about drugs and alcohol. She told me that if I was curious about anything, ask her, and we could try anything at home under her supervision.

At the capitol, there were politicians, of course, army staff, and many of Cuba's well-to-do milling around for government business and private concerns.

I started asking about my father when I was six years old. At the time, my mother told me that he was not around, that he would never be, and that she would tell me more when I got older and showed some signs of maturity. At age fourteen, she told me that on my birth certificate, she had given me her family name instead of his because she did not want to be reminded of a weak moment in her life.

While she would not give me specific details, she only told me my father was an officer in the army and that he had not been forthright with her. She did not tell me his name because he had bailed out on her when he was told she was pregnant.

I was fortunate enough to be raised around my mother's brothers, who were good role models. They were in the army or were policemen in pre-Castro Cuba. They instilled discipline and order in my life once our family's emigration to the United States became complete after the overthrow of Batista's government on December 31 in 1959 by Fidel Castro's rebels.

Not having a father around was not a big deal, out of sight, out of mind. The point is I do not take offense in being called a bastard because I am one and sometimes I act like one. It's just my nature, a defense mechanism I have built up over the years.

I was getting ready to play the pain-in-the-ass bastard card with Lesson's boss, Volkov.

The next morning, while driving Lesson to work, I ran my plan by him and told him to play along that I was pretty sure nothing would happen to him.

"Pretty sure, boss?" He looked a little worried.

"Yes, I am, always looking to right a wrong or put a bully in purgatory."

"That one of those fifty-dollar words Ms. Kat is always saying you use?"

"Purgatory? Yes, Lesson, I like to punish those that think they are above the law, whether it's laws made by society or laws between mankind."

"Don't know of laws between mankind, boss. Is that written somewhere?"

"No, Lesson, just simple, basic commonsense things like, don't steal, help those that are weak, young, sick, or defenseless. Treat others how you would like to be treated. Try to leave a nice footprint on earth before your time is up on it."

"How can you leave a footprint on earth, boss? I don't get it."

"What I mean by that is to leave something good for people to follow, to remember you, and to inspire others. Easy to say, hard to do."

"I see, boss. So people remember you as a nice guy."

"Not for that, my friend. Just try to set an example. People need to see someone do things before they will try it, or some people have to be shown the way."

"Sort of like school for grown-ups, huh, boss?"

I chuckled at that, easily put, nice context. We were crossing the MacArthur Causeway into South Beach, and I saw the cruise ship terminal on the right with gigantic ships that looked like they were from the future. Some were coming in to port (back to reality for those on board); some were heading out, leaving their cares behind, on to exotic locales.

"That's funny, boss?"

"No, Lesson, you just said in three words what I said in forty, and you got right to the point. Maybe Kat is right. I should use fewer words."

"It's okay, boss. I learn new words when I am around you. I will remember *pur-ga-to-ry*." He stretched the word out.

"Speaking of purgatory, don't be surprised at anything I say while we are in there with your boss. Act cool, calm, and collected just like if you were on security detail. And one more thing, stop calling me boss."

"Oh, boss, my grandfather taught me to treat those that are older with respect."

We were pulling up to a colorful condominium that was built on the old dog track property on the southernmost end of South Beach.

"I am not that much older than you, so just call me Jose or JC. And you see, your grandfather left a footprint through you. He instilled in you to treat the elderly with respect."

"I get it, boss—I mean, JC."

"Let's go annoy your real boss. It's time to stir some shit up!"

CHAPTER 16

Volkov's offices were in a monolithic building. The ground floors were chez trendy shops with the latest overpriced goodies from Europe. There were bistros that charged you twenty dollars for a hamburger and fifteen dollars for a cocktail. Two years later, they would be closed, and a new incarnation would take its place until that joint lost its luster. The second floor contained offices that were utilized by professionals.

Volkov had a real estate office on the ninth floor, and on the top floor, he had the current hot spot called Cookie's, which was frequented by recording artists, basketball players, and their wannabees and hangers-on. Below the top floor, he had his private office, which was where Lesson usually worked unless he was sent upstairs to help the bouncers when things got a bit crazy.

I pulled up to the valet and asked him to take special care of my DeSoto. He was about eighteen and kept looking at my car like it was a flying saucer or something out of this world. He got in it and had both hands on the wheel and kept looking around for something. I figured he was looking for a push button based on all the late-model cars he must have parked on a regular basis. I was sure he had never encountered a steering wheel that big or seen a shift selector panel with *R, L*, a space, then *N*, followed by the *D* on the end instead of *P, R, N, D, 1, 2, 3.*

"Hey, kid, want me to park it for you?" I had to ask; that was my pride and joy.

"It's okay, mister. I think I can figure it out." He tried to look confident.

"Just ease on the accelerator. She might appear to be a big boat, but she has some guts."

When Lesson tried going into the employee elevator, he was stopped by a security guard when he saw me behind him.

"Hey, Lesson, who is the guy with you?" His badge said *Desronvil*, so I knew he was Haitian.

"Ummm, he is my friend and a private eye I hired."

The guard looked me up and down and said, "I have to call upstairs to get him approved." He went into a closet-like cubicle, closed the door, and picked up a handset.

He opened the door, stuck his head out, and said, "Go on up. They be waitin' on you."

Lesson tucked a plastic card into the control panel, and a metallic voice said, "Access all floors. Which floor, sir?" That showed me security was state of the art and that there must have been face-recognition software installed in the system.

Lesson said, "Nine, please," to which the voice replied, "My pleasure, Mr. Liu."

I looked at Lesson and said, "Mr. Liu, really?"

He was going to answer, but we arrived at the offices. As soon as the doors opened, two shotguns were shoved through the opening doors. Lesson was allowed out, but the two goons holding the shotguns came in to the elevator, pushed me against the wall, and frisked me. One of them took out what looked like a garage-door opener and ran it from the top of my head to the tip of my shoes. I assumed it was a device to check for electronic bugs.

"Nothing in me except for the plate on my head." No comment from the goons. "No sense of humor, huh?" Their gadget started beeping.

They had taken my Ruger LCP from my holster already. My PI badge was metal. I gave them that too.

Once I was cleared, they let me out of the elevator, and the view was spectacular: downtown Miami on the right; the Port of Miami and the ocean as far as the eye could see on the left.

Standing by his desk was who I guessed was Volkov. He was wiry, tall, gray hair in a ponytail, had coal-black eyes, and was immaculately coifed as those with large sums of money usually are. He was wearing Gucci bedroom slippers, a smoking jacket, and what appeared to be satin pajamas underneath. I guessed he was close to sixty.

I said, "Geezus, the second coming of Hugh Hefner right before my eyes." I couldn't resist.

"Mr. Castillo, your reputation precedes you, a smart-mouth and no respect for authority," he said this with a heavy Russian accent, just like a bad guy in a James Bond movie.

This told me what I suspected: they did have face-recognition software as part of their security setup, and their intel database was top-of-the-line.

"Good, you know about me. And I do respect authority, but the catch is that there are few authorities that deserve my respect. Money does not impress me; and bullies, even less."

"Yes, yes, Mr. Castillo, you who came from such humble beginnings backed by the Castillo family fortune that mysteriously appeared in Miami after your family left Cuba when Castro took over."

Damn, this guy's intel was impressive.

"I never used my family's money. I went to college on a schol-arship and into the army after that, and I made my own way. I may not be rich, but I have everything I need, and I am comfortable and independent. But we are not here to talk about me but about Lesson's safety."

"Safety? Lesson is in good hands here, Mr. Castillo. What could possibly be wrong?"

"I guess you did not watch the news yesterday, but Lesson's humble abode was firebombed, so I am here to let you know that I will be looking out for him and that I hope that no harm comes to him while in the line of duty for you."

Volkov was looking at me for a minute before he sat down behind his desk. "Mr. Castillo, please have a seat. Lesson, you can report upstairs. We have a big reception tonight and I need you there."

"I turned to Lesson, Chris will be picking you up when you are done. Call him when you are ready. He will be five minutes away."

"Thanks, boss…ummm, I mean, JC, thank you." Off he went to the back of the office, so I figured there were stairs and a back way in.

"Okay, now that our protégé is gone, let's get down to basics, Mr. Castillo. You are here to show that Lesson is being watched and protected by you and at least one associate. You have nothing to fear. Lesson is a valued employee, and I have no animus toward him."

"Wow, *animus*. I have met my intellectual equal. There's someone I can use my college-education vocabulary on."

"Mr. Castillo, I am sure there are psychiatrists that can help you with your antisocial disorder where you have to buck authority, respect no one, and make fun of all. But I am getting tired of your attempts at humor, your lack of respect, and you are wasting my time. I make more in one hour than you do in an entire month."

He was starting to twitch a little out of his right eye. Good, I was getting to him.

"Again, money does not impress me, and there are very few people I respect. It's a short list, and you are not on it."

"You may drop off Lesson at work and pick him up, but you will not be allowed in this building. Any questions you have, please contact HR, and they will handle it."

"Okay, Volkov. Make sure that no harm comes to Lesson in and out of your employ, no accidents, or I will make sure you pay for it."

He started laughing and holding his sides; I thought he was going to fall out of his chair.

"Castillo, I have been threatened by many. I am still standing, as you can see. Best of luck. Now, get the hell out of here."

No sooner had I stood when the two goons showed up behind me. One of them made the mistake of getting close enough to put the muzzle of a gun behind my back. I pivoted, elbowed the gun out of his hand, chopped him on the neck, causing him to black out. I turned on to the other goon and double chopped his neck while sweeping his feet out from under him. He hit his head on the marble floor, and he was out like a light.

There was a big commotion by the elevator, and four guards with automatics came rushing at me. I put my hands up.

"Very impressive, Castillo. Now what?"

"I came in here to discuss business, and there was no need to muscle me. Do yourself a favor. Next time you have someone pull a gun on me, have them use it because I will not be as lenient as I was now."

"Get this worm out of here right now, gentlemen." He was standing up and tapping his desk with a cigar. Damn, I could think of a better use for that cigar than to be used as tapper on a desk.

"Worm? Worm? You have to get an upgrade from bad guy two point—oh, Volkov, worm…really?"

One of the guards made a move toward my arm, but I stared him down. "You don't want to do that. Besides, I am leaving. I have a feeling we will cross paths again, Volkov. Keep it real."

"I do not think so. We travel in different circles, and those circles are in different paths."

"Well, yesterday you did not know me from Rasputin, but here I am right in your path. We shall see how our paths traverse."

"You wish, worm. You wish."

Now he was getting under my skin. My Cuban temper was starting to raise its ugly head. I had a feeling things were headed on a collision course with this guy with bad endings for all.

"I'll be around. I am like a pit bull with an attitude."

"Castillo, you do not know who you are dealing with. I will crush you like a bug. I belong to the Vory. That's *v-o-r-y*. Look into it, and maybe you will slow down a little."

He was waving for his guards to take me away, but none of them moved. Guess they saw what happened to their associates who were just coming around on the floor, and they did not sound too good.

"Let's go, boys. Show me downstairs so Volkov can light his pipe or drink his Port or watch Masterpiece Theatre or whatever the hell he does in that getup."

"Get him the hell out of here right now!" Volkov yelled. I finally got to him.

I did what I intended to, got under his skin. Little did I know how much it would cost me later on.

CHAPTER 17

As soon as I got to my car, I headed to my shop and placed a call to Gafford. "Hey, Jim, do me a favor and look up *vory* and see what you come up with this guy. Volkov, whom I just left, said he was a member or something in it. Never heard of it, and I read a lot."

"Okay, compadre, right on it. By the way, I tweaked the holoportation software program on Mother, so we have to give it a try one of these nights."

"Did you change the oil too while you were at it?"

"JC, you know I do not get my hands dirty. That's your job."

"Talking about car repairs or detective work?"

"Hmmm, now that you mention it, it could be either one."

I arrived at my shop and was excited to see a DHL box by my door. I picked it up, and the send address was Thames Ditton, Surrey, in the UK.

My connections in jolly ol' England had come through for me. My dear friend Janet Harrison, whom I met while I was studying at Arthur Findlay College in Stansted Hall, was able to go to the village of Thames Ditton on my behalf. She was able to track down some of the retired workers from the AC Cobra plant who were in that town until its closure in 1984.

She must have been dogged and determined as usual because not only did she score me a Cobra manual but some phone numbers and e-mail addresses belonging to some of the retired workers from that plant as well. I would now have a pipeline into old Cobra parts so I could finish my restoration project sooner.

I was fortunate to take some seminars at Arthur Findlay College at a time when I was studying spiritualism and the art of mediumship. I started by going to Cassadaga in Florida, which is the second oldest spiritualist community in North America with Lily Dale in New York being the first, which I also visited. That is where my interest in Findlay College came from. I met some folks at both Cassadaga and Lily Dale who suggested I go to Findlay if I wanted a rounded curriculum on what my interests were at the time.

My phone buzzed with a text from Gafford: "Check my e-mail for info on vory. Grab a cold one, plenty to read, buy more bullets. It was nice knowing you, and where do you keep the title for Mother?"

And people call *me* a wiseass.

CHAPTER 18

As soon as I made my way into my front door, something did not feel right in my condo. My alarm was on, and I had to key in the code to shut it off. But something didn't feel right, like a presence or a vibration that was not usually there.

I placed my package on the floor and reached in my waistband for my trusty Glock. The first floor of my condo is the shop where I restore cars, and just the AC Cobra was there since Gafford had borrowed Mother for the software install and the DeSoto was at the detailers, so I had a clear view of the first floor.

There was an elevator on one side and stairs on the other; I took the latter. When I reached the second floor, the kitchen was clear, and so was the living room beyond that. Something still did not feel right. I go by instinct more than I should, but I rarely ignore it when my "radar" is on fire, like it was right now.

The third floor has the master bedroom, and that was clear, even after checking under the bed and the bathroom, which has a shower, a tub, and a Jacuzzi. This left the guest room. I took a few breaths to steady myself, passed the hall closet, and went into the guest room with the Glock locked and loaded. Nothing there. I checked the closet, nothing. I am rarely wrong, and I was beside myself for being wrong, I headed back to the master bedroom to shower and change. I left the Glock on the nightstand.

I turned on the shower, took my clothes off, and went back into the walk-in closet between the bedroom and bathroom. I was able to see through the door slats the entrance to the bathroom and totally blocked from seeing the balcony doors. In about a minute I heard the sound of a doorknob twisting, which could only be from the balcony since I could see the door on the bedroom and a view of the bathroom door, and neither of those were moving.

I grabbed a Ruger SR22, which is a little compact gun with a huge kick. At the time I was twisting the doorknob on the closet, I saw a shadow coming from the balcony area dash into the bathroom. I slid out the closet door and immediately slammed into the body coming out of the bathroom. We banged heads, and I heard a familiar, "Ay, marrone."

"You asshole, you could have gotten shot," I yelled as I peeled myself from the top of Christopher Gerard Cataldo. He had gained a little bit of weight since I last saw him, but he carried it well on his six-foot-one frame. His light-brown hair had thinned a little bit. His ace in the hole was his blue eyes. According to him, the women couldn't resist them.

"Just checking your instincts, buddy," he said in his thick New York accent. "You checked everywhere but the balcony. You're slipping. Now put some clothes on before your neighbors think you are all of a sudden hitting from the other side of the plate."

"How did you get past my alarm?" I asked as I put some shorts on.

"Oh man, you know I run with the stealth types, latest gizmos and spook stuff. I can bypass most commercial security systems."

"You and Gafford should have a fine time comparing spook gadgets."

"How is that retro hippie doing? He is one of the few people I know that looks like he just stepped out of Doc Brown's DeLorian from the seventies, yet he is only, what, thirty?"

"He is doing all right. Speaking of spook gadgets, Gafford's got Mother, and he's jazzing her up with the latest. You'll be impressed."

"Takes a lot to impress me, but all right, where's Kat? She wise up and dump your sorry Cuban ass yet?"

"Nope, still got her fooled. Thinks I'm the greatest thing since sliced bread. She's in the islands doing a shoot for a swimsuit issue."

"Well, you should market some of that potion you are feeding her if she still feels that way, or pay your Santeria priest more money to keep her fooled."

"You know, I haven't seen you in two years, and you are just full of love, Chris. No wonder you don't have any friends. Let's head downstairs for some lunch."

"I almost had you, paisan."

"After your stunt today, I don't know. You almost got shot."

"Nah, I would have disarmed you first. I'm keeping you on your toes while I am here. You've gotten soft, and years ago, you would have checked the balcony.

"Hey, I made you think I was in the shower, didn't I?"

"Yeah, you are right. I'm getting soft too. There's not much action protecting these Hollywood types. Worse, we have to do is bounce some paparazzi off the asphalt every once in a while and keep the starlets' recreational drug suppliers away. One of the reasons I came here besides you is I'm hoping for some action. I need that edge again."

"You will get some action. Let me bring you up to date on Volkov and his Vory, whatever that is."

"The Vory? Are you fucking kidding me? Whatever you are paying me just doubled."

"That will be interesting since I am paying you nothing. I guess it will be double *of* nothing." I chuckled at my wordplay.

"Very funny. Wait 'til you get a load of what you are up against. We might need reinforcements."

Damn if the son of a bitch wasn't right too.

CHAPTER 19

I downloaded the info from Gafford, showered, and took Chris to lunch in Little Havana. We walked since it was not too far, and I wanted to show him some of the improvements in the neighborhood I grew up in.

The Tower Theater had been restored to the original design from the sixties. Now they showed Latin movies as opposed to what I saw there as a kid. The city of Miami had created Domino Park, where old Cuban men played heated domino games for hours on end while reminiscing about what they were like when they were young back in their homeland. The smell of Cuban cigars and Cuban coffee permeates that corner like no other in Miami.

Some of the shops have been reborn as minigalleries featuring Latin artists. Some of the restaurants have live music on the weekends. You can hear salsa on one block, reggaeton on another, cumbia on another. The sounds of the Caribbean and Latin America are pulsing through you as walk along the streets of Calle Ocho.

Of course, there are cigar bars a plenty, which make the old Cuban men chuckle about the fancy smoke shops. They are used to buying their cigars at the supermarket, and for those who want a little fancier smoke, they go straight to the mom-and-pop cigar shops and have theirs freshly rolled.

I took Chris to Catharsis Restaurant, which is on Sixteenth Avenue and Calle Ocho. Chris ordered the lobster ravioli, which was succulent and would melt in your mouth; he did give me a taste. I ordered the churrasco, which is a charbroiled flank steak marinated in chimichurri sauce, which consists of parsley, garlic, peppers, and olive oil. It came with sides of white rice and black beans.

We finished that off with a dessert of tres leches; it's a cake that is made with condensed milk, evaporated milk, and heavy cream. Obviously, we were not watching our girlish figures. And of course, a couple of demitasse cups of Cuban coffee.

We went outside to light up a couple of Rocky Patel 1961 Toro Naturals. I have a box of which I save for special occasions, and this was one of them.

"Wow, '61s, I'm impressed. Thanks, buddy." Chris was rubbing his midsection and smiling.

"Well, lunch and that cigar is going to be the extent of your pay, plus room and board, of course. Oh, you also have the privilege of watching a world-class detective at work."

"Yeah, world class. That is why you had to call me in. Let me tell you what little I know about the Vory, and we will compare that with Gafford's notes."

We ordered more Cuban coffee with some ouzo shots.

Chris leaned back and started, "They are the new version of the old Russian Mafia that started back in Stalin's jails. They were very strong in the 1920s and '30s. The Vory died out after World War II, but it appears they are making a comeback. They are the elite of the criminal underworld, which in addition to the Russians, now have members from Poland, Czechoslovakia, and other former Warsaw Pact nations."

"What makes them any different than any other organized crime syndicate?" I was starting to get curious.

"The original Vory died out because they were too strict. You had to have done jail time, you could not have a family, and all your income had to be from ill-gotten gains. You could not have a home or apartment. You could not talk to or assist the authorities whether in jail or out in the real world. And last but not least, all your criminal accomplishments had to be tattooed on your person."

"Wow, no family. I find that hard to believe." I really did; I had never heard of the Vory until now.

"The modern Vory started a comeback after the breakup of the old Soviet Union in the 1990s. They have eased up on the no-family restriction, the owning of property, and you can have dealings or agreements with the authorities. Makes sense in this day and age.

"Imagine, there are one thousand members. Each of them is a major player in their part of the world, and they have armies of underlings behind them. So it's like dealing with one thousand capo di tutti capis or boss of bosses, as they used to say in Little Italy when I was growing up."

"Dammit, Chris, they really said armies of underlings? I better check my underwear for a brown stripe. Let's get back to the shop and see what Gafford sent us on the Vory."

"Sure, but first, did you notice the town car across the street with the tinted windows? It pulled up when we went into the restaurant. No one has come out of it since, and the engine is idling to keep the air running in this stifling heat."

"Yep, can't see in the windows. I'll be right back. I have an idea."

I went straight to the kitchen, where I knew all the staff. "Oye, muchacho, nescecito un platano." The sous-chef looked at me like I was a madman. He grabbed a plantain and threw it to me underhand.

When I got outside, I said to Chris, "Hey, go over across the street and stand in front of that store and act like you are looking at the artwork. After a minute or so, drop your cigar, pick it up, and head back over here."

I went back in the restaurant through the kitchen, out the alley, and around the block. I had grabbed an apron when I dashed through as the sous-chef was nodding his head, saying, "Ese Americano esta loco."

I grabbed a hat from the head of a panhandler who was at the corner and threw him a fiver for it. I looked like kitchen staff out on a smoke break. As I turned the corner, I was behind the Lincoln by three car lengths. Chris saw me out of the corner of his eye, and as I approached the Lincoln and was about a car length away, he dropped his cigar.

I went behind the Lincoln, jammed the plantain in the tail-pipe, and crossed the street and went inside the restaurant. Chris had started walking toward the Lincoln and cut right in front of it to get their attention as he crossed the street and sat down where we were having our ouzo and stogies earlier.

I went back inside and gave the sous-chef the apron and threw the cap in the trash. I washed my hands, went outside, and sat back down.

"Let me guess, paisan. The old potato in the exhaust trick?"

"Yeah, except we use plantains down here. In a few minutes, the exhaust will back up into the engine and shut that baby off. We will see how long they can sit in ninety-five-degree heat without air-conditioning."

We ordered more coffee and ouzo and just sat and waited. I dropped a spoon, and while I was on my knees, I looked across the street at the underside of the Lincoln where the catalytic converters would be in the exhaust system. I knew from my work on cars at Jose's Cruisers that they are positioned in the middle of the under-carriage just past the front seats.

They were starting to glow from the heat as the exhaust was backing up into the engine. Not only would the engine and the air-conditioner stop working, those catalytic converters would be at about fifteen hundred degrees soon.

Five minutes later, we heard the pinging of the engine as it was in full overheat mode. No one came out of the car. Three minutes after that, the engine stopped, and I told Chris to get his cell phone ready.

In a couple of minutes, four hulking goons stepped out of the car. We snapped pictures of them. They were wearing jackets in this heat, which told me that they had weapons under those jackets.

One of them saw us taking the picture, and he said something to the others, and they strolled over.

Big bastards—Euro goons, if you ask me—lily-white skin and those Slavic foreheads. The only skin we could see was on their hands and necks, but what skin we could see was full of ink.

In an accent that was even heavier than Volkov's, the head goon said to us, "Did you take our pictures?"

"Oh no, Yuri. We were taking pictures of the storefronts across the street." I saw that he was flaring his nostrils already.

"My name is Sergei, not Yuri. We must have your cell phones."

Chris had positioned himself closer to the two goons on his right. Sergei was in front of me and the other goon to my left.

I knew Chris had a gun in his ankle holster, and I was carrying the same—too hot for jackets. But we did not want a shoot-out in Little Havana in broad daylight. Besides, I suspected these four had semiautomatics or worse under those jackets.

"Calle Ocho is a one-way street where we were at, and I saw a Metro Dade police cruiser coming our way. I threw my cell phone up in the air, and as Sergei and the goon with him reached for it, I ducked under their arms and jumped out into the street. The Metro Dade cop had to jam on his brakes so he would not run me over.

The cop put on his lights and got out of the car, and he was none too happy.

"Mister, are you crazy?" I saw his badge read *Gonzalez*, and I spoke to him in Spanish and quickly explained the situation. I said, "If you need a reference on me, call Nate Devine in Homicide."

He walked up to the group and said to Sergei, "I understand this gentleman wants his cell phone back."

"Officer, that is my phone. He is mistaken." If Sergei was the leader of this outfit, they were in trouble; he was not the sharpest knife in the drawer.

"No problem. Let me see the phone." This cop was pretty smart. He started playing with the screen. I knew what he was doing.

"Hmmmmm, this phone has a picture of this gentleman, and it looks like another picture of him and a blonde lady."

"Sorry, Officer, my mistake. I make apologies. We go."

"Not so fast there. How about some IDs, gentlemen."

The four pulled out driver's licenses and concealed weapons permits. Sergei gave the cop a business card and told him to visit Cookie's nightclub anytime, and he would be comped.

"No, thank you. That could be mistaken for a bribe. You gentlemen move along. I know where you work."

The sight of four hulking pasty-skinned giants with neck tattoos and wearing jackets walking down Calle Ocho in Little Havana in 95 degrees and 103 heat index was priceless.

I whistled, and when they turned around, I took a picture of them with my cell phone and waved. One of them gave me the finger. Have to keep my wiseass reputation up, you know.

CHAPTER 20

Gafford was waiting at the shop with Mother when Chris and I arrived there after lunch. Gafford's eyebrows went up when he saw Chris.

"Dude, haven't seen you in ages, my man. What are you doing here?" asked Gafford when hugging Chris.

"Wanted to get away from Tinseltown. Besides, JC is getting in a little deep here and needs a little hand-holding."

"C'mon, dudes. Let me show you how I pimped Mother up." He was like a kid showing off new toys.

"Installed a keypad so you have to key in a code to start her, and she can't be hot-wired. I have perfected the software in the holoportation system, so it works in daylight too. The only problem is range, can't wait to try it to see what its range is."

"Where's the espresso maker?" Chris asked.

"Hey, dude, if I had room, I would put one in," retorted Gafford.

"Man, JC, you got enough money in this baby?"

"Gafford installs the toys at cost, and I let him use Mother on occasion when he wants to show a prospective customer some of his work."

"Okay, last thing I put in is an add-on to the corner cameras I had already installed. We now have wireless minicams that we can install up to one hundred feet away from Mother, and she will pick up their signals in real time."

"See what I mean, Chris? It's a nice trade-off. I have a case that might have need of those cameras. I have just been hired by a young lady who comes from money, and she is trying to make sense of her parents' marriage. Her family owns Pavarro Farmacias.

"She is trying to keep her family together, and her mother thinks her father is having an affair, so she wants me to spy on him and to prove it or disprove it so her family can move on. A divorce between her mother and father would wreck the family and throw the whole family business into court. That would require her to get back into the business and take sides between her father and mother."

I looked at Gafford. "You can come with me on the first surveillance and work the cameras."

Chris piped in, "What, do we have an apprentice gumshoe now? What are you going to rename the agency, J and J, Joe and Jim, Brains and Brawn?"

"I don't want a PI license. I'm just trying to help a friend and try out new equipment." Gafford was still twirling that ponytail.

"Okay, Jim, let me know when you want to do this dry run. Meanwhile, I am going in and reading up on the Vory info you sent me. Later, buddy."

Little did I know at the time that Jim's attempt to upgrade Mother would allow me to catch a killer.

CHAPTER 21

Chris's description of the Vory was pretty well spot-on based on what Gafford sent me. Gafford's info had much more detail since it was in an e-mail, and Chris had just told me what he knew.

The *Russkaya Mafiya*, or the Russian Mafia; the *Bratva*, or the brotherhood; the thief-in-law or *vor v zarkone*, which is probably where the name *vory* originated, stands for a criminal who obeys the thieves' code. They have the highest ranking in the criminal underworld. Back in the origins of the group, they were not allowed to have a family, own property, and had to obtain all their income through thievery only.

My first thought was, *No wonder they faded into oblivion.* But now it appeared we had a new Vory with modern sensibilities and a more relaxed approach to membership and qualifications.

I copied McCoy and Roxy on the Vory info. I figured any bit of help would, well...of course, help.

I put in a call to Nate. I was shocked when he answered right away.

"How's it hanging, my brother?"

"Low and slow, my Latino brother. Another day in fucking paradise. You know, no wonder the Bermuda Triangle is just off our coast. I think Florida gets more wackos, miscreants, con men, reprobates, and scam artists per capita than any other state in the union."

"I agree with you, Nate, but why? Just want to make sure we are on the same page."

"Hell, bro, they just seem to gravitate to Florida, and specifically South Florida, which to me is anything from Orlando south to the Keys."

"Okay, so far on the same page." Nate sounded frustrated. He needed to vent, so I let him.

"Here is the deal. The hotelier that was bludgeoned to death had ties to Volkov. You're shocked, I know. Volkov wanted to open up a nightclub in his hotel, and the deal never happened."

He was right; I was not shocked. But the next thing he said did shock me.

"The owner of the nightclub that was found dead and handless also had a run-in with Volkov. He was made an offer to sell to Volkov, and he refused. Strange that they turn on their own kind, but there it is."

"Damn, Nate, this Volkov is involved with people that harm happens to befall them. Got anything on him?"

"Nothing but impenetrable alibis, my brother. Crime lab is coming up with nothing. No one is talking anywhere."

"If Lesson gets anything on Volkov, I will let you know. I got him back to work, and Volkov knows not to mess with him since we are looking out for him."

"By we, keemosabe, you mean you and Chris?"

"Yes, but I have help coming. Chini is on his way."

"Chini! Last time he was here, there were a lot of unexplained corpses floating in Biscayne Bay. You bring that trigger-happy mercenary down here, you best keep a tight leash on him. I know he has a twisted way of justifying killing scumbags and those that deserve it, but this ain't the Wild West like it was in the '80s when the cocaine cowboys were shooting it up here."

Nate was in full cop mode; I had to get him to see it from a different angle.

"Look at it from a civilian point of view. I have Chris, Chini, Gafford, and to a certain extent, Lesson. We don't have the manpower you do, but we have the time and, in some cases, better technology than you have. So if I can get anything on Volkov, you know, I will pass it on to you."

"Sure, JC, as soon as you filter it and take what you need and give me some scraps. I know how you work, on the edge as always and playing by your own karma code."

"Absolutely right, my friend. I am not encumbered by the laws and bureaucracy that you are handcuffed with, no pun intended."

"Just keep an honest cop in the loop. Throw a brother a bone if you can."

"You know I will, and I always have—after filtering, of course." I had to keep that on the table.

"Speaking of bones, we just got popped with victim number four, left in a kneeling position like she was praying. She was left a block from the Trail on someone's front yard. This guy is escalating and getting more brazen as he goes along."

"That is four in a few weeks, Nate. Any headway?"

"Not yet, but I think something is going to break soon, whether he slips up, gets too confident, or the law of averages catches up with him."

"How about the old karma wheel catching up to him?"

"You know a cop can't count on that. We need facts, witnesses, and proof. You stick to your Bruce Lee karma shit. I will catch them and bag 'em the old-fashioned way."

"It's not Bruce Lee. It's instinct, fate, karma, gut feeling, spiritualism, just following common sense and your inner voice."

"Good Lord, JC, when are the angels going to play their harps and sit on your shoulder? It's a mean world out there. Stop sounding like a guru and start growing some scales, man."

"Throw this in your intel report for Volkov. Tell your analysts to look into Vory. That's v-o-r-y. It might help you in understanding and give you an insight into how he operates. I'm keeping my actions based on reality, Nate, not never, neverland."

"No disrespect meant, my man. Just want you to know we are dealing with bad men here. Take care. Keep it real. I'll be in touch."

"Be well, my brother from another mother."

"Sho' 'nuff, peace!"

CHAPTER 22

In the evening after Chris and I dropped Lesson off at Cookie's, we decided to stay in South Beach. We went to a sushi joint on South Ocean and sat at a table right on the sidewalk. That way, we could watch all the eye candy, tourists, posers, and wannabees who would be walking right within an arm's length from our table. If the breeze blows the right way, you can smell the perfumes and colognes mixed with the salt air of the ocean from those walking by.

That is one of the many things that you will not see walking down the street on a Saturday night in downtown Peoria. The traffic is bumper-to-bumper because there are those cruising with the windows down even when the humidity and heat is so palpable you start to feel it the minute you step outside of your air-conditioned hotel room or car.

There are limos full of partiers cruising, lowriders, cars with stereos that have more bass than a rap artist's recording studio. The neon lights come to life as soon as the sun fades in the west. The Latin beat starts blaring from the different alcoves. The hostesses who entice you with the restaurant menus look like they could be on the cover of *Ocean Drive* magazine. And of course, the beauty is that if you like people watching, you can see just about anything and everything, and it's all free.

Afterward, we walked down to Larios for a couple of mojitos then did some more walking and finished off our Punch Grand Cru cigars while listening to a flamenco guitarist who was playing on the front steps of a newly remodeled art deco hotel. With a couple of Cuban coffees and some Grand Marnier accompanying our stogies, it was a fitting ending to the evening.

On the way back, as we were driving on the MacArthur Causeway toward the city of Miami, Chris asked what the plan was with Lesson.

"Here, it is subject to change at anytime. One of us drops him off, and whoever is available picks him up after Cookie's closes at 5:00 a.m. If I am on a case, you or Chini can take turns."

"Okay, JC, how long do we do this for?"

"I figure until Lesson finds out what it was that he was not supposed to hear, or the feds break the case, or we spook Volkov."

"Good luck with spooking Volkov. That guy probably gives shakes to the Grim Reaper."

"Don't worry, buddy. Gafford is setting me up with some equipment where I might be able to listen in on Volkov's office."

"You are crazy, JC. Don't you think that he has his office swept for bugs every day?"

"I'll show you what Gafford has planned when we get back to my place."

"Oh boy, what an exciting evening. You for my dinner date and more techno geek stuff to drool over when we get back. This is not what I was looking for when I came down here."

"You know, call it what you want, but I have a feeling we are going to be pushed to our limits very soon."

"Oh goody, a feeling. Are you breaking out the Ouija board when we get back to your place?"

"You know, there's karma for you, Chris. I am a wiseass, but I am surrounded by them too. You, Nate, Gafford, and Kat give it to me as good as any."

"Paybacks are hell, paisan. If you dish it out, you better be able to take it."

Once we arrived at my place, I showed Chris what we had for Lesson.

"We have equipped him with a Zmodo spy pen camera that records video and audio."

"Oh, I've used one of those to catch a paparazzi that was trying to blackmail a starlet. But Lesson won't be around Volkov all the time."

"You are right, so we have leased an office across from Volkov's wing. Our office is only fifty yards away, so we have tinted the windows and have a parabolic microphone aimed right at Volkov's office windows. He can sweep his office all he wants, and he won't pick it up. Gafford has an infrared and thermal monitor on the mic, so it will only record when someone is in the office."

Chris was scratching his head, which he does when he is thinking over a problem.

"Okay, JC. What about when he is not in his office?"

"Good point, goombah. Remember, I am in the car-restoration business, so I know a lot of folks in the industry. I will be paying a visit to the guy that works on Volkov's limos. He owes me a favor, and all I need is two minutes to plant a bug and tracking device where no average joe will find it, no pun intended."

"Other than a bug on his bidet or mattress, you have all bases covered, JC."

"I don't think he will be talking about business in either venue. That would be really hard to tape. Good night, bro. I will take the first trip to get Lesson at five."

"Thanks, pal. I am still on West Coast time. Should be acclimated to East Coast time by tomorrow at the latest."

"Great. I have a long day tomorrow, so you can take him to work tomorrow night, and I'll get him at five when they close."

CHAPTER 23

The next day, I put in a few hours on the AC Cobra. I had the interior put together, and all I had was the paint and some body moldings left to track down. I was really starting to like the way she was working out. When you buy a car, some turn out to be *he*s and some are *she*s. I can't tell you what the formula is, but after you've fallen for your car, you will know. Kat calls her SUV *Janie*, which for a rugged all-wheel drive, is interesting.

My '53 DeSoto does not have a name, but it's always been a *he*. Too much power under the hood, too much throaty exhaust for it to be a girl.

At noon, I went to my dojo and worked out for only an hour, much to the chagrin of my sensei, Harold Rothstein.

"Well, well, look who decided to grace us with his presence, Mr. Big Shot, Jose Castillo. So kind of you to practice once a week. You'll go far, you lazy bastard."

"Love you too, Harold." I gave him a bear hug, which didn't take much considering he weighed 150 pounds to my 225. He was lightning fast, and I had seen him take out larger opponents in many a competition, including me.

"I am pretty busy and getting busier. I am working out at home on the speed bag just to keep my edge. Promise, once I slow down, I will be in three times a week as usual."

Harold was putting his locks in a ponytail, which meant he was done with a class or an individual lesson.

"We have a meeting in three months. Hope you are ready well before then. We are going up against those jerks from Palm Beach," Harold said in his nasal New York accent.

"How is your sister doing these days? I heard she is popping out babies like a Pez dispenser," I said, hoping to change the subject. I had dated her back in my college days at the university of Miami.

"She is glad she didn't wind up with you, that's for sure. Married a nice Jewish boy from North Miami Beach, and Abuela Rothstein has more grandkids than she ever dreamed of."

"See, a happy ending. Your mom liked me, but she didn't want a goy for a son-in-law."

"You were all right. It's all that pork you Cubans eat, and family picnics would have been a friggin' war."

"Too funny. Catch you later, pal. Say hi to Amy and Mom for me."

"Hasta luego, amigo. See you sooner, like three times a week."

"Nag, nag, nag. Oy vey, what a Jewish mother."

"I got your oy vey right here," said Harold while grabbing his crotch.

"Hey, you need tweezers to grab that?" I couldn't resist.

"I am so glad my sister didn't marry you. What a sarcastic prick."

"Takes one to know one. See you." And off to class I went.

Harold was right about my lack of discipline. I took my lumps in class. I was rusty, and my reflexes, which are my strength, were not very sharp. I needed to come in more often.

When I arrived at home, there was an e-mail from Kat. She wrote for me not to call her past ten since she'd had a long day. I was missing her more each day. The e-mail also said she should be done in a week or so. I wrote her back mentioning it was a good thing she was out of town since I had Chris there and Chini was coming soon. I did write that I missed her and to call me when she could.

I took some time to work on the Cobra and turned in earlier than usual so I could pick up Lesson at five a.m.

I was a few minutes early, and Lesson was out at five-fifteen.

"Anything to report?" I didn't even wait for him to get in the car.

"Nothin', boss. Every time I was around him, he was talking in Russian."

Lesson was right. When we listened to the audio, it was all in Russian, but I could pick up twice what sounded like *seesum*. So much for that genius plan. Now I had to get a Russian interpreter.

No matter how much you plan, always plan for the unexpected.

CHAPTER 24

The next day started out the same. Chris took Lesson to work, and I continued to work on the Cobra.

Chris came in to tell me that he was going to the airport to pick up Chini. "You sure I can't take the DeSoto?" he asked. I had rented a van for Chris. He was not too happy driving a van, but it was all they had available at the time.

"No one drives the DeSoto, amigo."

"Not even Kat does?"

"She hates driving that car. She says that the steering wheel is too big, and she says it handles like a tank."

"I wouldn't mind driving that DeSoto. I feel like a soccer mom driving that van you got me."

"Take it up with the complaint department. It's up on the fifth floor."

"You're number one with me, pal," Chris said as he showed me the finger.

A few minutes after I went back to work on the Cobra, the bell rang. I was not expecting anyone but saw the UPS truck from the side window.

The UPS driver had his hands full. He was wrestling with a hard-shell golf travel bag. It was wrapped in cellophane like they wrap the luggage at airports now to keep the luggage from being opened and pilfered. When I saw the Tampa mailing address on the label, I knew it was sent by Chini. Little did the UPS driver know how much firepower he had in that container. I signed for it and did not open it, I knew how Chini worked, and I bet he had that bag booby-trapped.

I went back to working on the Cobra and was getting ready to install a chrome headlight ring when the bell rang again.

I knew it was too soon for Chris to get back from the airport with Chini, so I took a hammer and put it in my back pocket.

When I opened the door, there was a gentleman who asked for Mr. Castle, so I knew he was looking for my other business, Joe Castle Investigations.

"I am Joe Castle. I am working on a car, if you don't mind coming in while I clean up."

"Oh, no problem. Take your time." He was hard to figure, no accent, no hint of where he was from. He appeared to be in his forties. He was dressed plainly in casual slacks, a dress shirt, plain loafers, and a Guess watch. No other jewelry, very plain. I had looked over his shoulder at the car he was driving, and it looked like a rental. His hands were a little rough and had some scar tissue on his knuckles.

"Come in to my office. I will be right back."

"Thank you, Mr. Castle. I've been told you are a man that uses discretion in your work." He sat and reached for a magazine from the table next to him, but he stopped and leaned back just before he grabbed the magazine, like he'd remembered something, acting like a cool customer, no rush, no cares, and crossed his hands on his lap.

Of course, coming to see someone like me means there's something you care about, and it might not be going as you would like.

"I will be right back. Help yourself to a cold one from that vending machine." I had a working antique Coca-Cola vending machine in my office that had soda, water, and beer in it.

When I went to the back of the shop to clean up, I switched on the camera I had in the office. It showed Mr. Calm just sitting, and he still had his hands crossed on his lap.

My *radar* was on; something was not right about this guy. When I have *that* feeling and I have ignored it, it has cost me. So I went into the office with clean hands and a cleaner mind. What was my radar telling me to pick up?

"You did not get a drink. Are you not hot?" I tried to be sociable.

"No, no, I am fine, thank you. I just want to see if you can help me."

"Well, what do you need?"

"It's about my wife, you see. She is twenty years younger than I am, and I suspect something is going on, so I just need you to tail her on specific days and times." He was still calm, hands still on his lap.

"I see. What do you want me to do, photograph her? Videotape her?"

"I need some peace of mind. She might be doing nothing, but I need to be sure."

"This can be expensive. Round-the-clock surveillance will require more than one man."

"Mr. Castle, while money is no object, I actually only need her watched when she goes to the gym, so it is not round-the-clock. One man will suffice. On those nights, she is gone for about three hours, which is a little long, I think. I have met her personal trainer, and I heard through the grapevine he is a womanizer and looking for a meal ticket."

I decided to stop being sociable. "You know, you have not even told me your name. You did not call for an appointment. You don't have a wedding band on, and yet you say you are married." It also dawned on me what was bugging me about him: he had not touched anything. The magazine he backed off from reading, no hands on armrests, no cold drink. No fingerprints.

"Mr. Castle, here is what you need to know. I will give you a picture of her, her car, and license plate, tell you where the gym is and the two days I need you to watch her, and give you ten thousand dollars in cash for that. Interested?"

Holy smokes, I thought, *ten grand for two days?*

"Definitely tempting. Can I think about it for twenty-four hours?" I had to think this through.

"Sorry, one-shot deal. Take it or leave it. If you say yes, there will be a courier at your door at 8:00 a.m. He will hand you a package with everything you need, including the ten thousand in cash."

"I will take it. I usually sign a contract for services. Any problem with that?"

"Yes, there is. It's a cash deal, no taxes on both our ends. No contract, no receipt needed, no paper trail."

"How will I contact you?" I felt uneasy having no control of this guy.

"I will have a way for you to contact me. It will be in the package. Good day, Mr. Castle."

He got up and did not intend to shake hands.

"Well, since I do not know your name, I will just call you Cash. Have a good evening, Mr. Cash."

"You do the same, Mr. Castle."

As he left out the front door, I made sure my corner cameras got a shot of his license plate. I did not think I would get anything, but it was more than I got from Mr. Cash.

I sent an e-mail to Gafford with the license plate number and asked him to run it and see what he came up with. I went back to working on the Cobra and waited for Chris and Chini to show up.

In a few minutes, I received a text from Gafford that the plate was legit, and it belonged to a rental car company. I texted him back to try and find out who had rented it, and I needed to know by the morning. I also sent him a video file showing Cash's face and asked that he run his facial-recognition program and see if he got a hit.

"Already on it, massah," was his response. I'm surrounded by smart-asses.

CHAPTER 25

I heard the beep from the front door opening, and in walked Chris and Chini. Chini had one suitcase, and Chris was carrying what appeared to be two shopping bags from a duty-free store. Chini was five foot six, still had a crew cut, and reminded me of Bruce Lee, not only in his demeanor but his looks too.

"You guys knock over a liquor store on the way back from the airport?" I inquired.

"No money in that. It's all in bonds and banks, man," Chini said as he put his bag down. He came over and gave me a hug.

"Oye, brother, long time no see. How's things in Tampa?"

"Calmado, quiet, just the way I like it."

Chini had been a sharpshooter in the Rangers. That is how we met. He could shoot the ass hairs off a gnat at one hundred yards. He taught me more than my own instructor. He showed me how wind and temperature can affect a shot and how to calculate those factors into a kill-shot trajectory.

He had a Cuban father and a Chinese mother. Chini was raised in Tampa. He had relatives there because there had been two generations of Gonzalezeses working as cigar rollers at the tobacco factories in Ybor City. His name was Abelardo Atienza Gonzalez; hence, we called him Chini for short.

I loved taking him to Cuban joints in Miami just to see the look on people's faces when they heard perfectly spoken Spanish from a guy who looked like Bruce Lee.

The thing was that he was for hire, and he would do any job if the money was right as long as the target was not a woman or a child. He did not have any qualms about what he did. He said to me one time over beers, "I don't ask. I just do it. I figure if I refuse the target, they will get someone else. At least with me, it will be a clean kill, and the target won't suffer. They will be dead before their body hits the ground."

Rumor was he was paid a million dollars a job, and he asked for his payment in Krugerrands. I could and would trust him with my life. You see, I was his spotter in the army in my last year there. A spotter and the shooter form a bond because they have to work as a team. He had to trust my judgment, and I could make him miss if I didn't lead him to the target properly.

His golf carrier was still downstairs, and he went to it and cut the wrapping off. I went over to see what he had cooked up as far as a booby trap. He opened the case, and there was a solar panel about four inches square, which, as soon as the light hit it, started flashing, and I saw a timer counting down from ten seconds. There was a cell phone plugged into the solar panel, and Chini picked up the phone and put in a four-digit code, and the timer stopped at 003.

"So a light-sensitive trigger amigo? Very ingenious, and you can change the code anytime you want using the cell phone keypad. What happens if they open it in the dark?"

"You would ask that question, JC." It is very light-sensitive. Even a light from the other room will trigger it off."

"And I am sure there is a small block of Semtex on the other end of that wire."

"Si, amigo. Semtex made with no detection taggant, so it's hard to trace."

"Mano, I thought I had connections. You are the bomb, no pun intended."

Chris finally piped up, "Before you two get hard-ons talking about explosives, let's drop Lesson off at work and get something to eat."

"Food and broads, that's all this fuck thinks about. See, nothing's changed, Chini."

"Hey, I'm Italian, waddya expect?" Chris was grabbing his crotch and rubbing his belly.

"Chini, you see how refined CGC has become since going to Hollywood? A real class act."

"Hey, ma fangul, if I grab my crotch in Hollywood, they'll be starlets and wannabees on their knees thinking I want a blow job, and half of them will be queer. If I rub my tummy, the frustrated wannabe mommies will be spread-legged like windmills in Holland thinking I want to make babies. I can grab my crotch and rub my belly here, and no one gets the wrong idea."

"Okay, Chini, you go freshen up. I will go clean up, and we will hit the town. We'll start in Rincon Argentino. It's a steak house in Coral Gables. We will work our way over to South Beach for eye-candy watching and dessert after that. By the way, rack your brains. We need a Russian interpreter. I'll explain over dinner."

CHAPTER 26

Nate walked into the room and immediately got everyone's attention by saying, "Hope you rocket scientists have some solid leads for us locals and dignitaries from the Federal Bureau of Investigations." He dragged out the FBI's name, making sure they knew that he knew they were there.

The room was filled with at least thirty people: some FBI, some Florida Department of Law Enforcement, and a lot of department heads from Nate's own Miami-Dade Police Department. Frank McCoy from the fire department was there, so was Roxy Pleasant from ATF. There was a pair of suits with sunglasses, white shirts, and black ties in the back of the room. Nate made a mental note to make sure to point them out.

Nate took the podium and tapped the mic with his pen to make sure it was on. "Ladies and gentlemen, we will bring all of you up to date with what little we do know and what little forensic evidence we do have. But first, is there any one that did not sign in?"

The two suits in the back raised their hands.

Nate pointed at them. "Gentlemen, identify yourselves please."

"Dale Wesson here, Homeland Security," the taller one said. He was probably six feet six and had blond hair cut in jarhead style.

"Chip Smith, same." He was much shorter, probably five feet five but stocky and built like a bull. He was as bald as a cue ball.

Nate started chuckling. "Okay, boys, I get it—spookville, national security, black ops. Smith and Wesson, Chip and Dale? Let me guess, your boss's name is Agent Zed, right?" Some in the room got it and laughed; some didn't.

The two spooks gave Nate thumbs-up, like, *Okay, you got it. Carry on.*

Nate grabbed the mic and adjusted it upward to compensate for his height. "Here is the order of our speakers' boys and girls. Julio Alonso, medical examiner, Miami-Dade. Laura Zane, senior profiler, Miami Dade. I will go last. We have representatives from Miami-Dade Fire Department, Florida Department of Law Enforcement, the FBI, and the ATF. Any questions, please raise your hand, and we will go from there. Dr. Alonso, step up to the plate."

Julio Alonso took the podium with a folder in his hand. He was wearing bifocals, stood about five eight with salt-and-pepper hair and beard, which made him look professorial. He brought the mic down almost a foot and nervously cleared his throat and proceeded to speak.

"The reason we have everyone here is because we have identified four recent bodies as coming from the hand of the same person."

The room got a little quieter, and you could see some people sitting up and paying attention.

"We figure the more information and experience that is at hand might help us get pointed in the right direction. This guy is giving us very little to work on as far as evidence. We know he is wearing a condom because there is no trace of semen. We know he is killing the prostitutes and then taking them somewhere because when he disposes of them, they have been cleaned, washed, and posed."

Dr. Alonso looked over his bifocals at the group and saw all of them writing on pads. The two Homeland Security agents were not taking notes, however.

"He is violent obviously but is rough in having sex. The victims have had hair pulled out of their head. We feel he has had sex with the bodies after he has killed them. He has to have upper-body strength and strong hands based on the damage to the tracheas on the corpses.

"Other than that, folks, we do not have much in forensics. That is why we have asked everyone to pitch in, and maybe if we throw enough resources at this guy, we can narrow things down a bit. I will be passing out a white paper with locations where the bodies were found, age and name of victims, all known to be in the prostitution trade. Dr. Zane, your turn at bat."

Laura Zane was seated in the front row next to Nate. To say she had all the men looking at her as she made her way to the podium was an understatement. She was about five ten, long curly blonde hair, fair skin, and green eyes. She walked with a regal demeanor, like someone who had taken modeling lessons. She was not dressed flashy, but everything she was wearing was first class, matching perfectly.

"Thank you, Dr. Alonso. I must apologize for the little information we have, but this perp is very careful, and while I do not think we are dealing with a genius of any sort, he is very aware of evidence and how to cover his tracks. I will be meeting with the folks from the FBI to work on this profile, which needs a lot more information thrown at it than we currently have.

"I feel he is between twenty-five and thirty-five, a laborer, someone that works with his hands and is in the construction or handyman trade. Went to college but did not graduate. Is married and probably just became a father for the first time. He might have served in the military or had someone in his life that instilled a bit too much discipline on him like a father figure. Mother was either not home or emotionally vacant. His violence and the posing is coming from someone who wants to break the women first then molds them into what he wants them to be. He has become more confident as you can tell by the picture of the torso with the taunting written on it. " She closed her notebook and looked up at the group.

"I look forward to working with anyone who can help me shape this profile. In your packet, you have a rough sketch based on an eyewitness who saw him sitting in a car from twenty feet away. Thank you for your attention. In keeping with the baseball metaphors, Detective Devine, you are batting cleanup."

"Thank you, Ms. Zane." Nate stepped up to the podium, clapped his hands, and proceeded to address the group. "People, most of you have worked with me and my department in one way or another. You know how I operate, by the book and by the law of the land. What I am asking as a favor is that we have no interdepartmental jealousies or testosterone contests or hormonal catfights, pardon the stereotyping. We need to catch this guy sooner rather than later. I need your help, so please run everything through my assistant, Buck Taylor. Let's break into groups and get this bastard under wraps."

The two Homeland guys came over to Nate and said that if they could do anything to help, please contact them. The short agent gave Nate a card with just a phone number on it, nothing more.

Nate looked at the card like you would look at something that was curious. "Gentlemen, as a matter of fact, you can help me out with something unrelated to this case. If you can get me any information on the Vory—that's v-o-r-y—other than what is normally out there for the public. I have a friend working on a case that involves Sergei Volkov, and if I help him, it might get me some insight into some unsolved homicides."

Agent Smith took off his sunglasses and spoke, "Let me verify. You just said Vory and Volkov in the same sentence."

"Sho' 'nuff, Agent Smith, or is it Wesson?"

"Enough with the comedy, Detective. We need to talk, and we need to talk in private right now."

Nate shepherded the agents to his office and shut the door.

"Why the secrecy, gents? I work out in the open, and I share information. That is why there is a roomful of law enforcement types working together out there." Nate pointed to the other room.

"What do you know about Volkov or the Vory?" asked Agent Wesson.

"Obviously not much if I am asking you federales for help."

"Who is this friend?" asked Agent Smith. "Is he in law enforcement? Do tell us because we can find out who you talked to, when, where, how. We can pull e-mails and phone records, so save us the time and tell us, Detective. We are nicer when we have cooperation."

Nate had had about enough of these two. He went to his office door and opened it, made a waving motion, and said, "Gentlemen, I have been at this for a long time. I have dealt with hardcore criminals, mafiosos, serial killers, and corrupt politicos. I have been threatened by many, but I have never been threatened by agents working for the government I serve and pay taxes to. Get the fuck out of my office and come back when you want to act civilized and feel you do not need to push your weight around."

"Detective, are you sure?" Agent Smith asked while looking at his watch nonchalantly.

"I am sure as the color of my skin. Good day, gentlemen. I have a team to assemble and a killer to catch. Come back when you are ready to help."

CHAPTER 27

For dinner, I had ordered a steak milanese, which is breaded flank steak with a thin layer of red sauce and a sheet of melted cheese on top. Chris ordered eggplant parmesan, and Chini ordered the grilled vegetable platter since he is a vegetarian. We had two bottles of Argentinean Malbec wine from the Mendoza region, and I was getting ready to order a third.

"Here is the deal, guys. We need a Russian interpreter. The tape we have on Volkov has him speaking Russian, so we are stuck without an interpreter. We need to have someone we can trust because we do not know what he is saying. Any suggestions?"

Chris piped up first, "What about that gal you used to date before Kat?"

"You're a big help, pal. No, no, no, that would just screw up the works. We did not break up on the best of terms."

It was Chini's turn to pipe in, "Don't know if it's serendipity or not, but since we last saw each other, I have been dating a gal who is Russian. She works at the gym I work out at, and I trust her implicitly."

"If you say it, I believe you. I'll have Gafford download what we have so far to an audio file, and he will e-mail it to us. You can send it to your gal, and she can interpret and e-mail us her translation."

"Her name is Irina, by the way. She can do the translations in the morning. She doesn't go to work at the gym until three in the afternoon."

"Thanks, Chini, big help there. After dinner, you guys take the van, head out, and have a good time. I am going with Gafford to do our surveillance on the pharmacy father. One of you guys, please do me a favor and pick up Lesson after he gets out of work. I'll see you guys in the morning."

"Yessir. Cruising South Beach in a van with Jackie Chan riding shotgun, why didn't I leave Tinseltown earlier for this?" Chris was drumming on the table with his utensils.

"Bite my Chinese Cuban ass, you spaghetti-snorting goombah cocksucker."

"Fuck you, you black-bean-fried-rice-eating—"

"Girls, girls, please. Kindergarten is in recess," I yelled. "Stop your bellyaching. We will have plenty to do soon." Little did I know how prophetic that statement would become.

CHAPTER 28

The guys dropped me off at the shop and took off for South Beach. Gafford was already at the shop prepping Mother, so all I had to do was change into some comfortable clothes before we headed out.

Gafford asked me to drive so he could set up the controls. I saw a camera in the overhead compartment above me, and I counted eight minicameras around the roofline, and I asked him about them, "Those are new—what are they for?"

"That one right above is actually taping you. I need some footage for the holoportation program. Just forget it's there. I will let it run for a few hours. The others are part of the hologram projection. They are wireless, so I can set them up inside or outside. The outside range is about ten yards, and it works best at night."

I had received information from Ms. Pavarro that her father played dominos with his friends on Tuesdays, and he usually came home about midnight. If he was doing anything, it would be tonight.

We would follow him from his office and see what developed. I was not worried about being seen in Mother because Gafford had gone by Mr. Pavarro's office earlier in the day and tagged his car with an electronic bug, so we could track him from Mother.

We followed our mark to a nondescript house in Hialeah. We were parked in a strip shopping center about an eighth of a mile away. Gafford set up the camera and could see into the house. We could see that, indeed, there was a domino game going on.

Gafford started setting up the audio in case we needed it. I stayed in the comfortable driver's seat and lit up a Punch Churchill while he set up.

"Do you have to light up now? I just cleaned Mother and had her detailed and vacuumed earlier."

"Geezus, Gaff, you sound like a nagging wife. I thought I smelled a little ganja when I came into the van."

"There's a big difference between your smelly stogie and my medicinal herb."

"Medicinal herb? Is that what you call it?"

"JC, it's legal in California and Colorado. They have clinics you can pick up the stuff."

"California, the land of fruits and nuts, as well as things to eat. You've got to be kidding me."

"For real, man. California is way ahead of the curve in making weed accessible to those that need it for relief from chemo to MS to glaucoma to depression."

"So why don't you live out there?"

"Dude, I did live out there one time. After the first earthquake, I was out of there so fast it wasn't even funny." Jim was shaking his head.

"You really hated it that much?"

"Have you ever been in an earthquake?"

"Can't say as I have, Jimbo."

"When you are in a house and it's going sideways like a carnival fun house and you know if you stay in it, you will be found in the flattened rubble—it's a helpless feeling, my man."

"Is that how you wound up in Florida?" I kept looking at the monitor we had aimed at the domino house.

Gafford had taken pictures of Mr. Pavarro from the parking lot across his office earlier in the day and had put the face shot into the face-recognition software program he had in Mother's hard drive. If he had come out of the house, the monitor would beep to warn us. I still had to look at the screen every once in a while, old habits.

"Sure did. I wanted the flattest state without mountains and had to be near the ocean, so South Florida was it for me. JC, do me a favor and stand up and stretch then sit back down and continue to smoke that cigar. But don't talk to me, just sit there. I need that footage to add to what I have already."

I had forgotten about the camera. We had been here for an hour, and the domino game was going on. Typical Cuban domino sessions last a long time. On the weekends in the Castillo family, it would not be unusual to start on Saturday afternoon and play into the wee hours of Sunday morning. This was a weeknight; they might only go 'til midnight.

"Let's give it another hour, and if nothing happens, we can always track him with the tracer."

"Great, man. I will take the time to show you the holoportation program. Come on over."

I put my stogie out and went to the back of the van where the "toys" were.

Gafford loved the toys. He had to slow down when talking about any new ones because he would get excited about them.

"Okay, man, here we go. I have downloaded into this holo-gram projector footage of you that we took since we left the shop. I have also some footage on there from one of the corner cameras on Mother that I had pointed at you while you were working on the Cobra. There is also footage of me I took while I was working on Mother. Step over here and watch."

Gafford took a remote control and nudged me toward the front of Mother. He showed me which controls to press, and a screen came to life and hovered in the air. It was divided into four screens. One screen had me on it sitting in the driver's seat; the other, I was bent over, working on the Cobra. The other two had Gafford sitting in Mother's seat; and the other, he was working on the computer deck.

"Watch, watch, I hope it turns out okay. The only problem is that it does not work well in the daylight." Jim was almost hyperventilating.

He took the control from me and pointed at the screen that showed him at the deck, and the other screens disappeared. He clicked again, and he was able to move the screen toward the computer deck area. He clicked once more, and sure enough, the screen disappeared, and in its place was a hologram of Jim full size, leaning over the computer deck big as life.

"Okay, I'm impressed. What can we use it for?"

"Hell, man, I don't know. I just thought it would be cool."

"You don't know! I hope this didn't cost an arm and a leg."

"C'mon, man, you know I create surveillance programs for our friends in the covert agencies. They actually give me a lot of the latest stuff so I can incorporate it into my work. I'm like their independent research and development department."

"That is pretty cool. Hope you can use that toy someday." It was strange talking to Gafford and seeing his image four feet away, working on the computer deck.

"Let's pack it up, pal. We are almost on two hours here, and the only bone this guy is going to be handling tonight is those dominoes in front of him."

I was glad we were heading back. I was going to have a long day tomorrow; I needed to recharge my batteries.

CHAPTER 29

The next morning, sure as the humidity in Miami reaches 99 percent in the summer, there was the bell going off in the morning. Chini was on the second floor, looking down toward the front door. He was armed, of course.

I opened the door to see a man who could be described as short, fat, balding, and sweating. He was wearing a seersucker suit—which I thought was, number one, insane in this weather; number two, who wears a jacket to deliver cash? Number three, who has a lackey deliver money in a brown paper bag? And, number four, who buys a seersucker suit these days anyway?

"My name is Mr. Lorre, and would you please accept this package on Mr. Cash's behalf?"

So the Cash name had stuck. Interesting.

"You want me to sign the bag?" I couldn't resist.

"No, sir, a visual acceptance by me is enough." His voice was like a whinny baby, grating and annoying at the same time.

"Inside, you will find instructions on the surveillance location and a cell phone that Mr. Cash will call when he needs to talk to you."

No doubt the cell phone was a cash-card disposable one.

"Anything else you need, Mr. Castle?"

"No, Mr. Lorre. Thank you and have a great day." This smarmy guy reminded me of Renfield for some reason.

As soon as I closed the door, I signaled to Chini by pointing to my eyes and a motion to write, which he knew from our previous work in the field to look at the tag number and write down the numbers. He nodded and went downstairs out the side door.

I opened the package, and sure enough, there was ten thousand in cash in used one-hundred-dollar bills, no sequence in the numbers. Included in the package was a picture of a woman who would make a dead man rise from the grave and an address that I knew belonged to an upscale gym in Bayside.

There was also a typed note with the instructions to do the surveillance on a Tuesday or a Thursday from six to ten in the evening. My first thought was, *Who the hell owns a typewriter anymore?* My second thought was, *This is a setup. Interesting, today is Tuesday. What a coincidence.*

That evening, while Chris was taking Lesson to work and Chini had some business to take care of, I was on my own for the surveillance. I took Mother and parked one block away from the gym and pointed a camera at the front door.

On the computer, I hooked up to a live satellite feed from one of Jim's many covert agency clients, and I had an overhead visual for about two hours every time a satellite passed over. The initial feed was already one hour and a half in, so I had about thirty minutes left of live overhead.

On another computer, I had Google Earth live, so I was fully covered front, rear, and from overhead. I knew this was overkill for a flagrante delicto affair, but it would come in handy if we had a real ballbuster surveillance to do.

Mrs. Cash pulled in a few minutes after eight in a yellow Lamborghini. She was already wearing tights, a towel draped around her neck, and white sneakers. To say her body was taught and trim was an understatement. If Mr. Cash was tapping that, he was one lucky man.

Three hours later, she came out of the gym and headed out of the parking lot. I had already walked by the car while she was inside and tagged it with a tracker. I also had played poker on the computer, sent Kat an e-mail, and paid some bills online. Surveillance is not what is portrayed in the movies; it is tedious, boring, and mostly uneventful.

I tracked her on my monitor, and she appeared to be heading toward the Julia Tuttle Causeway, which meant she was headed to South Beach. Don't think she was going to play footsie tonight. I shut down everything but the tracker and headed home.

Little did I know the next surveillance would not be as uneventful.

CHAPTER 30

Pablo Lopez had been delivering newspapers for over a year since he lost his job at the manufacturing plant in Hialeah. He was doing what he could to make ends meet. His wife, Maria, had gone back to work in a day care because what he made delivering papers was not enough to keep up with their monthly budget.

They had cut back as much as they could, and Pablo felt bad his wife had to go back to work after retiring just three years ago. What little they saved with her 401(k) had lost over half its value because their son had suggested that they invest the retirement account in tech and bank stocks, two things that had not done well in the last ten years.

Now he was sitting in a room deep inside the Miami-Dade Police Headquarters, waiting to be interviewed about something he was not even sure he saw.

In walked a tall black man followed by a blond white man with a crew cut, who was fastidiously dressed, and a lady who did not appear to be in the police department (in fact, Pablo thought she looked like a doctor). They all took seats at the table he was at.

Pablo knew the police wanted some information from him, but he did not know exactly what they wanted, just that it had to do with that dead girl they found on Mr. Sinclair's lawn. He knew he had not done anything wrong, but he was a little nervous. In his native

Mexico, when people went in to the police department, sometimes they did not come out, or they disappeared.

He knew this was the United States, but still he had that old hometown police fear in his veins.

The black man was the first to talk.

"Mr. Lopez, thank you for coming in to talk to us. I am Detective Nate Devine. To your right is my assistant, Mr. Taylor, whom you have talked on the phone with. He will be taking notes even though we are taping everything."

"To your left is Tracey Rodriguez. She is one of our staff therapists, and she is also a psychiatric nurse." Tracey had a Spanish surname, but she was as all-American as apple pie: blonde hair, blue eyes, freckles, and a body that would make a dog break its chain.

Pablo was nervously shifting in his seat. "A psychiatric nurse? You need her for what?" Pablo had a worried look on his face.

"Not to worry, Mr. Lopez. I assure you she is just here to help you with your memory." Nate was his usual smooth self, calming yet authoritative.

"What we need, Mr. Lopez, is for you to try to remember that early morning of the murder, what you saw at the curb in front of Mr. Sinclair's house."

"But...but, Officer, I already gave your assistant a statement, and I cannot remember much more than what I told him. I threw the paper on Señor Sinclair's lawn, saw a couple at the curb in a parked car, and they appeared to be kissing, so I looks away and mind my own business. I do not remember anything more than that, Officer. Please believe me."

Nate got up from his chair and put a hand on Tracey's shoulder. "Mr. Lopez, that is why we have Tracey here. She can help you remember things you cannot or might have missed and are in your subconscious."

Tracey had a disarming smile, and she used it at this time to build some trust between her and Lopez.

"May I call you Pablo?"

"Si, señorita, como no."

She had that smile working already.

"Gracias, Pablo. What I am going to do is help your memory by using hypnosis, and it will only take a few minutes. You won't even notice."

Nate stepped back into the breach. "Mr. Lopez, we have someone out there who we believe has killed at least four, maybe more, and we do not have a clue. We need your help. You could be a hero, and there could be a reward from Crimestoppers if your information helps us catch that person."

"Reward? How much?"

Nate knew he had him. "For starters, one thousand, but I know for a fact that the mayor has upped the reward to ten thousand."

"Okay, let's do it. It won't take long, will it?"

"Not long at all. We'll leave you with Tracey. She will handle it from here. Thank you, Mr. Lopez. You are a good citizen."

As Nate and Buck left the room, Buck said, "We do not have a right to do that, and it won't hold up in court."

"All I need is a morsel of information for a lead, a break, anything that will open this case up. The description of a car, a license plate, anything. Right now, we have nothing. In your report, put in he came and volunteered whatever information Tracey gets out of him. He won't remember anything he says when she puts him under anyway. Let's go get a cup of coffee and give Tracey a little time to work her magic."

Nate and Buck went downstairs and across the street to a typical Cuban grocery store with the usual coffee counter. These are as prevalent in Miami like McDonalds are everywhere else. It's usually a walk-up counter where you get fresh Cuban coffee or a *cortadito*, which is a Cuban version of a cappuccino or the Cuban national breakfast drink: *café con leche*, which is warm milk with a shot of Cuban coffee with a heaping teaspoon of sugar.

There are fresh pastries like meat pies, guava-and-cream-cheese-filled *pastelito*, coconut-filled, and they also have cheap Cuban cigars for sale. There is also a counter on the inside for those who want to sit down and eat a Cuban sandwich or a full meal.

Nate ordered a Cuban coffee with a couple of ham croquettes. Buck ordered a *cortadito* and a *medianoche* sandwich, which is lighter than a Cuban sandwich. It has roast pork, ham, mustard, dill pickles, and swiss cheese. It is on soft, sweet egg-dough bread.

"Hey, Buck, you come up with anything else besides this guy? We are getting nowhere even with the ten-thousand-dollar reward."

"Damn, boss, I am coming up drier than a straight guy in Key West."

"Just because I tolerate your flaming lifestyle, do not start with the gay or penis references. I am eating croquettes, after all."

Buck burst out laughing. "Geez, Nate, on one hand, you are tolerant of my lifestyle. On the other, you are penis phobic."

"Sho' 'nuf, Buck, most highly testosteroned males are penis phobic, FYI. Let's wrap this up and see what Tracey has for us. Take care of the bill. I'll catch the next one."

"Okay, that makes three times this week, Nate. I'm keeping track." Buck thought, *Does this guy ever pay for a check?*

CHAPTER 31

Nate was walking into Tracey's office just as she was shaking hands with Lopez.

"Muchas gracias, Señor Lopez. I appreciate your cooperation."

"Gracias, señorita, un placer."

"Thank you, sir, much appreciated," Nate said as he walked up to Lopez and shook his hand.

"You will let me know about the reward, right, Officer?" Human nature never ceased to amaze Nate. He has seen every side of mankind working Homicide all through the years.

"Of course. I will have Mr. Taylor contact you. Have a great day." Nate ushered Lopez out the door. He turned to Tracey. "Okay, missy, give me the lowdown."

"I have taken the liberty of making copies of my notes."

"Good girl. You must be taking lessons from Buck."

"Well, he is anal-retentive, no pun intended." Tracey actually chuckled at her pun.

Nate smiled but suddenly grew serious. "C'mon, girl, give me something to work with. Tell me you turned him inside out."

"Here, read this," said Tracey as she handed Nate a copy of her notes.

Nate put his hand on his goatee and looked like a man deep in concentration. "Girl, if it wasn't against the department's sexual harassment policy, I would kiss you. Thank you. I can work with this."

Nate read the notes, and he felt a little jump in his blood pressure. It had a partial license plate number, a description of a light-colored, four-door sedan with a child seat on the backseat. He bounded up the stairs, bypassing the elevator to the IT department.

In that department, there was Woody Johnson, who reminded Nate of Woody Allen. Short, bespectacled, a dry sense of humor, but one of the wisest computer programmers on the East Coast. He was used to the wood and Johnson jokes after being in the department for twenty years.

"Woody, baby, I do not know what you are working on, but I need you on this ASAP."

"Imagine that, Detective, and I thought you were inviting me out to dinner, which I think you promised me the last time you had something special for me to do."

"Damn straight, son. You are right. I do owe you a dinner, my apologies. How about I make it two dinners? I need this bad. I have to catch a killer."

Woody tapped on his keyboard and cleared his screen. "Show me what you have, and I want to be at the press conference and get some credit when you catch this serial killer."

"Oh, so you know what this is about then," said Nate, admiring how up-to-date Woody was.

"C'mon, Nate, everyone around here is wound up tighter than a junkie on an eight ball. Of course, I figured it had to do with that case."

"Here it is, my man, the first two of a license plate. It's a sedan, light-colored, and it's all we have. You have my cell phone. Call me any hour of the day or night if you get a hit."

"That's it? That is all you have? What state is the plate from?"

"Don't know. That's it, better than nothing."

"Guess so, Nate. Give me a few days, I'll see what I can do. Two dinners, remember that."

"Anywhere, you got it. Just come through for me. This guy is getting more brazen as he goes along. You know how it is with these serials. The more they get away with it, the more bulletproof they think they are. Later. Work OT if you have to. I'll approve it."

Nate took off down the stairs all the way to the parking garage. He wanted to catch up with JC before taking a break for one day.

CHAPTER 32

The Miami Tribune offices were in Downtown Miami set inside a huge building that was built to process and print the old *Miami News* newspaper inside of it back in the 1960s. Due to the modernization of today's printing process, half the building was not being used anymore. Rumor had it that the old girl was being sold to an international gambling concern, which was planning to demolish the building and make a giant resort with a casino. The funny part was Miami-Dade County had tried to pass a law allowing casinos, but it had failed twice by referendum. Maybe this company knew something about the future that we did not.

More of old Miami was going by the wayside, replaced by monolithic structures that looked like they were created by a mad architect on LSD who was trying to outdo the latest modernistic tower across the street. A lot of the art deco buildings have been restored, but anything built in the seventies or eighties is not "chic" enough or sexy enough to be appreciated yet, so they are being demolished at a rapid rate.

In the conference room of the city desk floor was Elliot Goldenfarb, the editor of the newspaper; Henry Ramirez, city desk editor; Herman Horowitz, attorney for *The Tribune*; and Lola Sanchez, investigative reporter. They had been discussing Lola's latest idea, and they were at an impasse. The editor and the attorney were dead set against it, and Lola and the city desk editor were all for it.

Lola wanted to dress as a prostitute and work as a decoy to see if she could help flush out the Tamiami Trail killer. Henry was for it all the way.

"Lola, the newspaper will not approve of this crazy idea of yours. The liability, the bad press, no pun intended. It would not be seen in a good light by our stockholders." Herman was about seventy years old. His silver hair was slicked back, a thin carriage and nervous hands. He always had to motion with his hands while talking, probably from being in front of so many juries.

Elliot was an old-school reporter who was one year away from retirement. He had been a war correspondent for *Stars and Stripes*, which is how he would end up in the newspaper business. That was pretty far from what he wanted to be, an air force pilot. By looking at his Coke-bottle-lensed, horn-rimmed glasses, you could tell they could not possibly have considered him for flight school.

Elliot was a few pounds overweight but was still a commanding presence due to his six-foot-four frame. He was calm and had his hands crossed in front of him on the desk when he started to speak. "Lola, you know I have gone to the wall for you many times. I think you are a gutsy, pushy, hardheaded broad…err, gal…err…excuse me, woman, sorry. I still have a hard time trying to be politically correct. My apologies, but I cannot let this happen."

Lola squirmed in her seat a little. "Ay, chico, I've been called worse. Besides, you know what I will do for a story. I didn't hear you worrying about me when I was playing a drug dealer and got us both a Pulitzer. I see yours is prominently featured behind your desk."

"That was a controlled situation, Lola," the lawyer chimed in. "This situation, even if we have you under surveillance, is different. You are going to have to be alone with this guy to see if he is the killer. It's not like we are trying to bust johns. We are trying to catch someone who is methodically eliminating hookers and who is obviously twisted because of the positions he is leaving the corpses in."

"We have a team ready to do this, which consists of myself, Lola obviously, and Jeff Bloom, who is our current intern," Henry said.

"An intern! Are you out of your mind, Henry?" Elliot said as he stood up out of his chair, which for him was as violent a reaction as you would ever see.

"Henry, an intern, really? I cannot condone this. It is wrong in so many ways." Herman had his hands out, pleading.

"Look, guys, we need this kid. It's a two-man job at best. We will have Lola wired, tagged, and under surveillance, so not much can go wrong." Now it was Henry's turn to plead.

"Okay, chicos, here's the deal," Lola said as she got up and reached for a folder that was next to her. "Here are three undated resignations from us. If this deal goes south, date them the day before it hits the fan. Otherwise, I will sign it with today's date, and I will be working across town as soon as my noncompete clause is over. Take it or leave it, chicos."

"The intern is on board with this?" asked Elliot.

"He is like you in the old days, Elliot. He's hungry, and he wants a front-page byline. And I want another Pulitzer, and I do not care what I have to do to get it." Lola's nostrils were flaring, and her nipples were perked up.

"If you even think of going through with this deal, Elliot, I will be no part of it and leave the room," said Herman.

"You best leave the room then, Herm," Elliot said as he nodded toward the door.

As Herman gathered his notes and walked toward the door, he said, "My notes will be destroyed, and this meeting was not logged or reminded to me in any of my electronic friends. I did not get this far to be caught in an amateur play such as this. Best of luck."

"Okay, kids, here is the deal. I need to be in the loop 24-7. Just the three of us and the intern will know about this. I want a detailed plan in writing only, no e-mails or texts." Elliott looked sternly at both and pointed at Lola. "You be careful, young lady. Do not take any crazy chances, okay?"

"Jefe, do not worry. I will be careful, promise. Just keep this building from being sold until I'm done. I want the picture of my next Pulitzer with the water in the background."

"It's already sold young lady, but it will be a while until we move into that antiseptic band box across the way. Progress is unstoppable you know."

CHAPTER 33

As I pulled Mother into the driveway of my garage/condo complex, I saw Nate's Dade County–issue plain-black Dodge cruiser parked in a guest spot and figured the boys had let him in. I hit the remote on my garage door and slipped Mother in to her docking area. I plugged in the battery charger into the side of Mother, and I immediately smelled garlic and tomato sauce in the air.

I took the stairs to the second floor and saw Chris, Chini, and Nate sitting at the dining room table with two bottles of Chianti between them and what appeared to be remnants of an antipasto salad.

"Well, thanks for waiting for me, guys. Anything left for a hard-working man?" I could see a pot boiling on the stove and the oven light on, so I knew there was more coming. Just wanted to bust some balls.

"You know, paisan, I cook for an army, so you know there is more coming," Chris said while pouring me a glass of wine.

"Hardworking man, my ass. Air-conditioned truck, computers to watch porn or play poker on, radar, satellite feeds, five hundred cable channels—yeah, real hardworking man." Nate chuckled as he took a wrapper off a cigar. "Shit, bro, when I used to do surveillance, I would sweat my nuts off in this Miami heat listening to a ballgame on the radio while studying for my degree."

Chini piped in, "They had cars when you did surveillance, Nate? I thought you'd be on a horse or a dinosaur or some Pterodactyl back then."

We all cracked up at that, even Nate. "You black bean-eatin' motherfucker. I ain't that old."

"Just because I come from Cuban ancestry does not mean I love that type of food. Why, I believe you are stereotyping me there, Officer Devine," Chini said that in a perfect Southern drawl. "Ah believe if I said you liked chicken and watermelon, I would be accused of being insensitive and even a racist, even though I am of color. Mind you, a lighter color than you."

I had to put in my two cents worth. "You know, the only group that can call themselves real natives are American Indians. All of us come from different descendants, all of us have DNA that originated somewhere other than North America, yet we rag on each other like brothers because circumstances have put us together, and we each have had each other's back at some point."

"Oh, shit, I think I am going to cry." Nate pulled out a hand-kerchief from his back pocket and acted like he was drying tears.

"I was right about you being a dinosaur. Who the hell carries a handkerchief anymore?"

"A gentleman always carries one, Chini. Comes in handy wiping tears from a damsel in distress, blowing your nose, picking up a weapon so as not to get fingerprints on it." Nate was folding his handkerchief as he said this.

"Damsel in distress? In this day and age, there is no such thing. Women are earning more, can kick serious ass, and while there are issues with glass ceilings, you see more independent women every day. I rest my dinosaur case, gents. Let's eat." Chini bowed.

CHAPTER 34

The next morning at the breakfast table, there was Chini, Chris, Gafford, and me wolfing down some Cuban pastries also known as pastelitos, which Gafford had picked up from the Cuban bakery down the block. I made some Cuban coffee and heated some milk in order to make café con leche. I had also put on a pot of coffee in case anyone was crazy enough to pass on the café con leche.

We started to plan our days and nights so we could cover Lesson's comings and goings to and from work, the surveillance on Volkov, the investigation into the apartment explosion, and the transcripts from Chini's girl if there was ever anything interesting said in Volkov's office when he returned. We were going to be busy.

"Are you sure we have enough bodies to do all of this?' Chris asked while looking over the pastelitos and trying to decide which one to have.

"We are going to be stretched out, no doubt. To add to all of this, there are two days a week of surveillance on a lady that was prepaid by her strange husband. I might have Gaff do the Mrs. Cash surveillance since it is just amounting to nothing at this time."

"Gee, thanks, keemosabe, for giving me the primo surveillance job while you guys are chasing bad guys, or I'm doing research for you, which, by the way, did not give us any leads on the rental car Mr. Cash had showed up in. The rental was paid by a company credit card from a company in Honduras." I knew Gafford would want a meatier job, but I did not want to get him in harm's way. Little did I know I was putting him right in the line of fire.

"Thanks for the info, Jim. Why don't you get going? And when you have some spare time, look into that company and see who owns it. Back to your question, Chris, we probably don't have enough bodies, but I do not trust anyone else. I have a feeling things are a little more complicated than they appear. What do you guys think about the explosion at the apartment?"

Chini raised his hand and asked, "What is so important that Lesson might have overheard that they blew up his apartment?"

"The only thing that preceded this was that Lesson thinks he overheard his boss making plans about bringing in something that sounds like *seesum.*

Chris started laughing. "You don't think Lesson misheard them bringing in a load of semen, do you?"

"You are a real comedian, Chris. It is not illegal as far as I know, so no need to smuggle semen in. I couldn't see any reason or money in bringing that in."

I looked at Chini, and his brow was furrowed, and he was concentrating on something.

"Talk to me, Chini. What's going on in that mind of yours?"

"Seesum? Are you sure? Let me use your computer. I need to look something up.

I continued, "Okay, so Jim is to handle two days of surveillance on the Cash case. I had a voice mail on the cell phone Mr. Cash gave me, and he reminded me about the job he hired me to do. So Chini and Chris, please take Lesson to and from work, and you can do a bit of spying from the office we set up across from Volkov's. Have we received the translations from your girlfriend, Chini?"

"Not yet. She is putting it all on an audio file and sending what she has translated." Chris piped in, "By the way, JC. What are you going to be doing?"

"Ah, ever inquisitive, aren't you, Chris?"

"I am following up on the Pavarro case, a couple of days of surveillance, which I do not think will amount to anything. I will be looking into a couple of things for Nate, but for now, I would like to put my hands on that sweet Cobra downstairs. I am getting jumpy and need to finish her restoration fast."

"Good thing Kat is out of town. You sound like you would not have any time for her."

"You are probably right, Chris, but I sure do miss her. Jim, you can take Mother to the Cash stakeout. I will do the surveillance in the rental van I got for the boys. They can take the DeSoto."

"Wow, you are letting us drive the old gal? I am honored."

"Well, the DeSoto would stick out like a sore thumb on the surveillance, so just drive her easy and be gentle."

"Don't worry, JC. I'll be as gentle with the DeSoto as I am with a virgin."

"Yeah, okay. Find me a virgin over twenty-five years old in Miami, and I'll show you the next Mother Teresa. Virgins are like politicians. Finding an untainted one is like, well, finding a virgin at a Hells Angels convention."

"Too funny, JC, and you say I'm the comedian."

At this time, we heard Chini call us from downstairs, where I kept my computer in the shop's office.

"Hey, guys, you had better get down here and see this. We could be in a world of shit."

We gathered downstairs around the computer monitor in the office.

"Here is the deal—we are looking at a perfect way to cause chaos and harm. I remember from my days of explosives training that cesium was a very volatile product to use. It is the most reactive element nature has given us, and there is an abundance of it. It is not illegal to buy it, but its purchases are monitored. In a protective environment, it will last forever. It ignites spontaneously when it comes in contact with air, and when it comes in contact with water, it explodes and turns into cesium hydroxide, which corrodes glass, so you can imagine what it can do to skin and bones."

I noticed we were all quiet and paying rapt attention to Chini.

"So if I understand what you just said, you don't need a trigger or a detonator. You can throw it encased in a glass jar, and it would do much harm." I was starting to get a bad feeling about this.

"That's right, JC. I would imagine that if you had a big target or wanted to do major damage to something large, you would have to have a delivery vehicle to detonate whatever you placed the cesium in."

I was a little less worried, and I said what I was thinking, "In order to blow up a building, you would need a large amount of cesium, say a couple of hundred pounds of it, so it's not like you could smuggle a bottle in, say, a thermos would be my guess."

"Right, JC, but here's the catch. Cesium 137 is a by-product of nuclear fission and is, of course, radioactive and can be used to make a…"

"Dirty bomb…," all of us said it at the same time.

"So I hate to sound redundant, but we have an element that ignites with air, explodes when coming in contact with water, can rapidly corrode glass and who knows what else, is not radioactive until it is produced in nuclear fission. It is available for purchase in its elemental form, and if properly stored, it can practically last forever. Like you said, JC, you don't need a detonator or a trigger to set it off, sacrée fucking vache, man." Chini was frowning at the thought.

"Say what, dude? Was that French?" said Gafford.

"He said holy fucking cow. Now let's think this out. We need to find out exactly what Volkov is bringing in, and if it is cesium, there are no laws being broken, but if it's 137, that's a different story. We need to get those translations, and I think we need twenty-four-hour surveillance shifts at the office across from Volkov's. Let's meet tonight, and we'll put a plan together. Good job, Chini. Glad I brought you along."

"I don't know, Jefe. Last time you brought me along, I almost got my ass shot off."

"Don't worry. From the sounds of it, we are either going to get blown up or die of radiation poisoning, so don't sweat it." I gave him my best smirk.

"Thanks for the heads-up, boss. I'll check my will." This from Chris.

"All righty, dude, righteous to know that," Gafford said.

"Thanks, asshole. I feel much better now. See you tonight," Chini added.

"No respect, muchachos, no respeto. See you tonight."

CHAPTER 35

It was Lola's first night out on the Trail, and she had taken up strolling on the corner of Fifty-Seventh Avenue. It was commercial on the north side and residential on the south side. Jeff, the intern, was in a nondescript sedan parked behind a pharmacy on the northwest corner, and Henry was in a van with tinted windows parked in the northeast corner by a restaurant.

Lola was wired for sound but also had a MO-B803 fiber-optic minicamera that had been weaved into her necklace. She was wearing sandals with heels, a tank top with an open blouse, and shorts that she grabbed from her own wardrobe, so they were tight and very short, of course. Lola had her spies and informants in law enforcement, so she had received some information from the big powwow that Nate had put together.

She had an idea what to look for but, more importantly, what not to look for. If the "john" did not appear to fit the little information that they had given at the task force meeting, she would not even consider them, which made a few of them mad, and she was cussed out more than a few times. One guy was so incensed that he yelled at her, "Hey, you are a whore. You can't be so choosy." To which, she replied, "I can, and I will. Come back when you have more than two teeth and take a shower." When the guy tried to get out of his car, she pulled a switchblade from her pocket. "I'll cut what little dick you have if you get out of your car, so just move along."

After a few hours, she was tired of not getting the type of john she had in mind for the suspect. She decided to take a break and headed for the restaurant. The plan was she'd sit at the counter and have Henry and Jeff sit by her and carry on a very quiet or a coded conversation, depending on how many people were at the counter. Before she reached the restaurant, she saw a two ladies walking toward her. She figured they were working girls based on their clothes and their walk, that loosey-goosey, hip-swaying "here are my wares" type of walk mimicked by street girls everywhere.

Lola moved at a different angle, and the two girls moved to keep the same angle in her direction. *Well, well,* Lola thought, *at least customers will see us together, and that will help me blend in.*

"Hey, girl, you new to the area? What's your name? Mine is Lisa," said the little blonde. "I am Sharday," said the tall black one who Lola knew was a man as soon as he got to within five feet of her.

When they got up close, Lisa and Sharday looked her up and down, looked at each other, and shook their heads.

"Hi, I'm Stormy." Lola was worried she could fool the johns but not the real working girls.

Sharday had his index finger on his nose and was still shaking his head when he said to Lisa, "Honeychile, this girlfriend is so out of place it's smells rotten in the hood."

"What the fuck you mean by that, homey?" Lola tried her best New Yorkrican accent, trying to sound tough.

Lisa jumped in, "Sweetie, I don't know what game you is playing, trying to look like a hooker, but you have to get rid of the hundred-dollar pedicure, the two-hundred-dollar sandals, the salon-applied makeup, and Stormy? Really? Hookers don't wear makeup, honey. It gets on the john. It's all over when they get home to the little woman who ain't givin' it to 'em in the first place. Maybe a little eye shadow, that's all."

"Shit, that obvious, huh?" Lola was deflated. "Guess I need to rework the look. Thanks for the heads-up."

"Anytime, sister, but you are not a cop, so what are you doing here?"

"I'm trying to get a lead on this crazy fuck that is killing these girls out here."

"Nice to know someone gives a shit about us…hey, wait, I know who you are. You're that reporter from the newspaper. That's ballsy, sister."

"I'm Sharday, nice to meet you," Luis said as he put his hand out.

"I'm Lola, and I'm calling it a night since I need to rework the look. Can I buy you two some dinner?"

Luis and Lisa looked at each other and said at the same time, "Sure thing."

As they walked toward the restaurant, Lola talked into the mic in her necklace, "Henry, Jeff, I am calling it a night. I am taking my coworkers to dinner, if you would care to join us." She pressed her hand to her ear. "Okay, Henry, hasta luego. See you inside, Jeff."

Lola turned to Lisa and Luis. "Hope you don't mind one more, just a harmless intern."

"Three's company, four's an orgy," said Luis while stifling giggles.

During dinner, Lola found out that Lisa was from Tennessee and had moved to Miami to work in the cruise-ship trade. After being away for a few weeks, she came home from a trip to find her husband had gone back to Tennessee and had shacked up with his ex, who was more than willing to support him. She found out he hadn't paid the last months' rent, and the landlord had sold what he could of hers and had thrown the rest out. Naturally, she was fired when she asked for time off to get a place to live, buy clothes, get some type of assistance, which of course, required that she apply at county and help agencies. It is a Catch-22 when you are down and out. To get help, you have to go to many different agencies, which are scattered all over the city; and if you do not own a car, forget about public transit. Miami isn't New York or London, which have subways and buses that work in unison.

"Here I am, a nice country girl from Nashville turning tricks until I save some money. Who'd a thunk that, eh, Lola? Me, former homecoming queen and all." Lisa looked beaten down by the mean streets of Miami. She was thirty-five but looked much older. Her blonde hair, blue eyes, and freckles had long ago lost their luster.

Luis was twenty-eight and from Santo Domingo. He met a lover on a beach resort that he worked at and had moved to Miami following him there, thinking there was more to their relationship than cheap sex by the beach. But that was all it turned out to be. After getting beaten and robbed on South Beach on the way home from his waiter's job, he became homeless when the restaurant he worked at fired him because his face was swollen from the beating he took. They did not want to upset their chichi clientele.

"Ay, chica, at least I am getting paid to suck cock. It's like a dream job if it wasn't for the hours, the drugs, the rip-offs, the beatings, the muggings, and the ones who don't pay. Yeah, a dream job."

Lola didn't know if Luis was sarcastic or serious, but by his sigh and the haunted look in his eyes, she felt he was older on the inside than he looked on the outside. He was tall, lanky, with that coffee-with-cream-colored mestizo look that is prevalent in some natives from the Caribbean.

Lola thought about all the strange twists and turns that get us to where we are in life. Sometimes that fork in the road takes you where you never expected: a dead end, a wrong relationship, no money, an empty life, lost and all alone. For a wrong turn here or there, she could easily have been in Lisa's shoes. She thought about how happy she was to have a loving family and great friends. No significant other, but her career was first, and it would take a strong and secure man to put up with her, and she knew it.

Jeff had been pretty quiet taking it all in. He was twenty-two and fresh out of college. He had graduated from the University of Iowa and apparently had not seen much sun in his life. He was as white as a ghost, had red hair and freckles. He was six feet five and was gangly but had that small-town innocence you rarely see these days. Miami had not hardened him yet.

Lisa looked at Jeff and said, "What's your game there, Opie? Got a girlfriend? A boyfriend?"

"No, no, no, not yet. I have been in town for just a few months." Jeff was blushing

"Oye, Lisa, leave my homeboy alone. I am looking out for my Jeffy, making sure he doesn't get in trouble. Besides, he knows if he wants trouble, he can find it with me," Lola said as she cupped her breasts.

Jeff was really blushing now. "Hey, Ms. Lola, I am going to get crackin'. I am working on a masters program at the U, and it's an early class."

"Well, I'll be damned. I went to the University of Miami too, Jeffy. Good boy, go home. I'll have my new friends walk me to my car. I parked it about five blocks off the Trail. Won't be long."

"Okay, Ms. Lola, as long as you think you'll be safe."

"Don't worry, sugah. I'll be just fine. Now run along, youngster. See you tomorrow."

"Good night, folks. Nice to meet you." Jeff was as sincere as he sounded.

Luis chuckled and said, "He's as white as a glass of milk. That boy needs some sun."

"He's come to the right state for that. I'll get him out to South Beach once he gets acclimated to our weather." Lola waved to the waitress for the check.

"I'll be back tomorrow, hopefully with some cheap clothes on and no makeup. Maybe I'll meet you here, and you can check me out and give me your opinion."

"How about it, Luis? You game? I am," said Lisa

"Sure, honey. She's a star. We are dealing with someone special here. Count me in, and maybe we'll make the newspaper as Lola's eyes on the street."

"Luis, you are such a dreamer. Let's just keep this girl here out of trouble." Lisa patted Lola's hand that was resting on the table.

"Oye, puta, everybody has fifteen minutes of fame, why not us?"

"I don't think our fifteen minutes of fame will be for any good deeds unless they give out awards for blow jobs and hand jobs. C'mon, Luis, let's get this girl back to her car so she can rest for tomorrow."

CHAPTER 36

Ankara, Turkey

Officer Mehmet Bay of the Ankara provincial police department wanted to get out of the cold weather and sit next to a fire with a hot tea and a bowl of Guli soup. He could almost taste the green cabbage and stewed lamb. He was chilled to the bone and wanted to get this surveillance over and done with. Officer Bay was on loan to the provincial command's antismuggling unit because they were working in an area that he patrolled regularly, and they needed an extra body.

He had been assigned to watch a house at the end of a block with only one way in and one way out. Unfortunately, the only way to watch the front of the house without being seen required him to be on a rooftop half a block away. The wind was howling, and it was thirty-seven degrees. He figured with the windchill factor, it was more like twenty degrees. He was dressed like a bum, so he was not able to wear his best coat or his police-issued one either.

Mehmet had been on watch for five hours, and the contact time had come and gone two hours ago. The field commander had checked on him an hour ago, and he said they would shut down the operation in an hour or so if nothing happened soon. He was shuffling back and forth on his feet because he was starting to lose feeling in them due to the weather conditions. His radio's incoming dial lit, and he raised the volume knob to hear: "Officer Bay, you are relieved of duties. Report back here tomorrow at the same time." He was glad to be leaving the cold rooftop. He hurried downstairs for the ten-block walk back to his patrol car, looking forward to a warm car, hot tea, and hot soup.

It was a bit past midnight when Mehmet passed an alley and overheard someone say, "Be careful with that. I don't know what it will do if exposed." It came from the vicinity of three men who were standing by a pair of cars in the alley.

Mehmet backed up and turned into the alley, heading in the vicinity of the voices. The men were huddled over one of the cars' trunk, handling some glass containers that looked like Mason jars. Mehmet had his badge out, and he made a coughing sound. The men were so focused on the jars that they had not heard him sneak up on them.

"Back away from the car. What do you have there, drugs?"

One of the men started laughing. "Officer, would we be dealing out in public? It's just some powders and chemicals that we use in our construction jobs. We are trying to figure out if there is any market value. We are trying to feed our families, you must understand. My name is Hasan."

"Can you prove ownership of whatever these are? I am sure it is illegal to sell it, so back off so I can call this in."

"Officer, look, it is harmless. Let me show you." The man had a metal cylinder in his hand. He unscrewed the cap and smelled it and pointed it at Mehmet. It was a yellow powder; it smelled acidy.

"Put the lid on that container and step away. What is in the other silver container?" Mehmet noticed a shift in the men, and they started to look nervous.

"Oh, that one is a little sensitive. That is why it's in the metal container. Like nitroglycerin."

"Like?" Mehmet was starting to get a little nervous himself. He had his badge out since he approached the men, and he did not want to reach for his radio with his other hand. He took a step back and ordered the men on the ground.

The man in the middle who did all the talking put his hands up in a pleading fashion. "Look, Officer, I will tell you the truth. We will make a lot of money with these things, enough to keep our families in good standing for a while, and there is enough to share with you. These things are sold on the black market and, what the infidels do with them is away from here and for a good cause."

"A good cause, what do you mean? Keep talking. What do you have there?" Mehmet had no intention of taking part of this deal. He just wanted to know what they had. He put the badge in his pocket.

"Look, my friend, this is sold near the border to the highest bidder and away to do harm to the great Satan—the infidels you know?"

"I try to do my job, feed my family just like you, but I try to do what I can to keep the faith to my God and keep a clean conscience. Last time I ask you, what is in there?" Mehmet was getting ready to use his radio.

"My friend, one moment. I offer you many liras to let us go. When we come back from the border, we will find you and split what we get four ways, eh, my friend?" Hasan attempted to reach out to Mehmet as if to pat him on the shoulder.

Mehmet moved sideways and pulled the radio out of its holster. "What is in there, for the love of Allah?"

"Okay, okay, my friend. Look, there is a fortune in those containers. That's what is in there, a fortune. The yellow powder is yellowcake uranium. The silver container has cesium 137 in it, which is priceless on the black market, and the large sealed package has cesium ore. We have a buyer waiting at Batumi, Georgia, who will pay good money. Let us go. We will come back and pay two years of your salary with your cut. I will give you a down payment if you don't believe me."

Mehmet clicked the talk button on his radio as he was reaching for his gun. The man on his right grabbed the hand that had the radio, and the man on his left tried grabbing his gun. Mehmet was too fast and shot the man on his left. Hasan had reached in the trunk, where he had hidden a tire iron. He swung it at Mehmet, and a glancing blow dazed Mehmet enough to cause him to drop his gun and stagger for a few moments. That gave the other two men a chance to jump in the car and take off.

The other man said to Hasan, "Why didn't you kill him?"

"My soon-to-be rich friend, I may be a smuggler, but I am not a murderer. By the time they find him and he gets over his headache, we will be halfway to Batumi."

"But you told him where we were going. What do we do now?"

"Batumi is a big place. We will stay in the shadows until we meet the broker. I will get my cousin Rafat to trade cars with us. We will be fine."

CHAPTER 37

Gafford parked Mother a block from the gym. He had a picture of Mrs. Cash on the computer along with a description of the car and the plate number, so all he had to do was wait and see what happened. He had a camera locked in at the gym parking lot, so he would get a notification when Mrs. Cash pulled into the lot. He had the other external cameras on auto; they would pick up any motion or light within fifty yards of Mother. He wondered why Mr. Cash wanted his wife watched while she was working out. It's not like she was going to do whoever she was banging in the parking lot. He guessed the plan was to follow her after to see where she went or to verify that she was at the gym when she said she was.

About thirty minutes passed, and there was a beep on one of the computer screens. Gafford saw the Cash mobile pull into the lot, so he knew he had at least an hour and a half before Mrs. Cash would be finished and heading home. He went to the rear of Mother where he started to work on the holoportation system. He had been sent a software update from a Department of Defense contractor that was supposed to improve the quality of the image. Gafford down-loaded the program and was going through the instructions when he decided to turn on the hologram and project a picture onto the front of the vehicle. He chose the one of JC sitting in the driver's seat, smoking a cigar.

The quality of the projection had improved since the last time, and he was hoping the daytime projection had improved too. That was the weak link in the program, and he couldn't wait to try it in the daylight. He turned on the air ionizer in Mother, which he purchased to help with JC's cigar smoke, coming in handy now since he was lighting up some medicinal herb his friend sent him from Colorado.

While he was waiting for Mrs. Cash, he started to work on an algorithm program for a DOD contractor who, in turn, had sub-contracted Gafford because he was one of the best code crunchers on the planet. Gafford heard what sounded like a double clink from the front of the van. He looked toward the front and realized the program was still on, showing JC in the driver's seat. Gafford turned off the hologram and headed to the front of the van.

He noticed a small hole on the driver's side window. When he touched it, he knew what it was: a bullet hole. He looked at the window on the passenger door and saw a hole through the glass just a bit larger. There was nothing but a field to the left of the van, which, based on the indentation of the glass, suggested the shot came from the left. This was not a random shot, Gafford surmised, nor was it an accident. The shot was planned by someone who knew what they were doing.

Gafford called JC and got his voice mail. "Hey, Jose, keep your wits about you...someone just tried to shoot you while you were sitting in your van."

Dmitri had practiced the getaway enough that his best times in taking the shot, removing the scope and bipod, and placing the high-powered rifle in its carrying case was right at fifteen seconds. As soon as he fired the shot from the Dragunov SVD rifle, he did the breakdown, which he had practiced in the dark many times. He was walking away in fifteen seconds from the area he had set up, which was about fifty yards from where the van was parked.

He would contact Volkov so that payment would be made by direct deposit to his account in Barbados. He was glad to not have to deal with Castillo anymore. He was a smart-ass, and it really bothered him to be called Mr. Cash. He thought it was childish and immature at best.

CHAPTER 38

Gafford was freaking out. He shut down everything inside but kept the outside corner cams on and switched the incoming footage to his i-Pad, which he had put on his lap as he sat down in the back under the computer desk. There was no movement on the outside. After a few minutes, he slowly got up and inched his way to the front of the vehicle. He grabbed the ATN MARS 4×4 night vision scope that JC kept in Mother's gun safe and scanned out the windshield then quickly looked out both front windows.

Seeing no movement or an infrared silhouette anywhere, he jumped in the driver's seat, started Mother, and took off. On the drive back to the shop, he kept looking at the display coming from the rear corner cams for anything, but what was he thinking? If someone was careful enough to shoot at Mother from a safe and hidden area, they were not going to come at him with guns blazing in the streets of Miami. In Miami, it wouldn't be shocking after the cocaine cowboy shoot-outs in the seventies and eighties, the Mariel refugees' crime wave of the eighties and early nineties, and the gangbangers who are fighting turf wars currently.

Gafford slowed down not only his speed but his breathing too as he reached in his guayabera's pocket for the ever-present rolled medicinal herb. He lit it and took a huge drag, feeling surreal. Even though he wasn't being shot at, he was still wired. He considered all his complaining about getting this dull surveillance job and didn't think that bullet was meant for him, especially since JC's hologram was projected on the front seat and he was unnoticeable in the rear. Just being in the same vehicle that was being shot at had him unnerved. He tried JC again and got an answer.

"Hey, man, head to the shop. I am headed there. Someone took a shot at you."

"What the hell are you smoking, Jim? No one's taken a shot at me."

"I...I was playing with the hologram, and I had you in the driver's seat when a bullet came through. It was not an accident, dude. See you at the shop. I am replaying the outside cameras and see if I can spot anything. Call you back shortly."

"Okay, heading back to the shop. I am not far. Be careful."

As Jim pulled into JC's bay, he took a sigh of relief, hoping there was no more gunfire headed his way. He did notice the nondescript rental car that had pulled into the parking lot across the street. It looked familiar.

Dmitri had followed the black van. By the time he reached the car, threw the gun case in the trunk, took off his fingerless Browning mesh shooting gloves, and lit a Nat Sherman Classic Blue, he saw the black van getting on the ramp to I-95. He dropped the cigarette from his mouth as it fell on to his lap. He had to do the old pants-on-fire shuffle to keep the ash from burning a hole through his eight-hundred-dollar Lanvin trousers.

He didn't know if he was more pissed about his trousers almost getting burned or that he somehow had missed Castillo. He sped up to the ramp and followed the van, and as soon as he saw it taking the southwest Eighth Street exit, he knew something had gone terribly wrong. He knew from his reconnaissance of Castillo that the hospital exit was the next one north. Since the van was not heading in that direction, no one must be hurt. He followed the van that appeared to be headed in the direction of Castillo's place. Sure enough, that's where it pulled into. Dmitry went around the back and parked in the movie theater's parking lot, which was behind the complex.

He was gripping the steering wheel so hard that he heard his knuckles crack. He had never missed a target so stationary, so close, so easy. Dmitri saw a tall, thin long-haired man get out of the van after it had pulled into the bay. He recognized him to be one of Castillo's friends, and he appeared to be in a hurry. He waited five minutes to see if someone came out to offer assistance or bring a first aid kit out, but to no avail.

Dmitri reached into his briefcase for the phone tracking device and turned it on. He wanted to see the whereabouts of Castillo. The phone he was given was dialed in to his tracker—brilliant, he thought. As long as Castillo had the phone on him, even if it was off, Dmitri could track him.

It took a few seconds to get the unit up and running, so Dmitri lit up another smoke. There was something wrong with the unit, so he started to fiddle with the dials, searching for the proper coordinates. The blinking tracer was not moving from the center of the dial, and it was like it was right on top of him. *This is not possible.* He was getting ready to take the battery out and reinsert it when he came to a bad realization. He started to reach for the Sig Sauer under the car's seat when there was a simultaneous metallic tap on the passenger-door glass and a red dot hovering on his chest.

He put his hands up and saw a gun being pointed at him from the passenger window. He saw another man pointing a laser sight at him from the front of the car. His car door opened, and Castillo waved his arm like a matador.

"Come out, come out, Mr. Cash. We have a nice welcoming committee for you. We are going to show you some real Miami hospitality." The traditional Castillo smirk followed.

Dmitri could not believe he had been trapped by these idiots. He was kicking himself for letting his pride get the best of him. He should have known something was not right when the van did not go to the hospital and the police were not called. "My name is Dmitri. Don't call me Cash again."

"Dmitri, I am not going to cuff you out of professional courtesy. You are obviously outnumbered, so just walk with us and we'll have a nice chat at my place over some espresso. Chini, bring his car around and bring everything in it upstairs."

"Chris, let's escort this shooter over to Casa Castillo. It's going to be a bumpy night." Chris turned off his laser sight and pointed it at Dmitri then toward the shop with the barrel of his gun.

"How could you figure this out so fast?" Dmitri said as he started to walk, spitting his words out in disgust.

"You thought you were so smart, hiring me for this fake surveillance job, creating a sitting duck so you could just pick me off. Smart, but you did not have a backup plan in case of changes. I knew something smelled funny. When Gafford called me from the van, I put two and two together and figured whoever did it would be curious why the van wasn't being driven to the hospital. So we waited at the only place you could park and have a view of my place. All of us are ex-military, as I am sure you are. We know about vantage points and using shadows for cover."

"Are you going to turn me in, you smug prick?"

"Now, now, it's too early to tell. Let's have a cup of coffee, some ouzo, and see if we can mutually exchange information first. Smug prick? You have your American colloquialisms down pat. Good job at the Kremlin in training you."

"Not the Kremlin. Don't be fooled by my accent. I was trained in by the Stasi." Dmitry figured he would give out some information to seem cooperative.

Chris chuckled. "Our friends from the East German secret state police trained you? They disbanded in 1990, didn't they?"

"Long enough for me to be trained since I was twenty years old. That's all I am saying at the moment." Dmitri spit at the floor.

"Wrong there, cowboy. After we get to talking, your choices are going to be limited in what you will be able to do." JC was starting to feel his Cuban temper rising.

"I am not afraid of the police. Bring it on as you say in this country."

"Muchacho, the last people I will turn you into is the police. That would be doing you a favor. Come, mi casa es su casa. Let's make a deal."

CHAPTER 39

The boys were sitting at the dining-room table with Dmitri sitting between Chris and Chini. Jose was leaning against the kitchen counter with the open rifle case behind him. The espresso machine was steaming, and the smell of strong coffee was in the air.

Jose was the first to speak. "So here we have someone with a sniper rifle in the trunk of their car. Smells like it's been used recently. Bet there is a shell within fifty yards of where the van was parked. I am sure our friends at Homeland Security would be very interested in talking to you."

"So why haven't you called them?" Dmitri snarled in Jose's direction.

"Why? Because if I call them, they can hold you indefinitely, no charges have to be filed, tough to see a lawyer. You'd either be in a maximum security prison or in Guantanamo, never to be heard from again, or you'd be in a federal supermax prison with an indefinite pass from Uncle Sam."

"For what? I am not a threat to national security."

"True, but you don't have to be a national threat, just a threat, and the Department of Justice will take its sweet time getting around to you if a certain Miami homicide detective suspects you are guilty of certain murders. Besides, I am sure a man with your résumé has some folks who are mighty ticked off at you. Say, Volkov, for example. He doesn't want to be tied to you."

"You can't tie me to Volkov. There is no record of electronic communication with him. All our communications were in person with no one around. Nice try, Castillo."

"Ah, amigo, but I can. I have an employee that works for Volkov that can not only put you at his office but at his club too. And I have his office under surveillance, so I have all the cards. Don't play poker with me. Like Volkov says, I'll crush you like a bug."

Castillo was gambling that Lesson had seen Dmitri around Volkov at some point; Castillo could bluff with the best of them. Dmitri did not know what employee Castillo had under his control.

Dmitri sipped his espresso, looked at Jose, and said, "Speaking of American colloquialisms, let's make a deal then."

"Be right back with you while I discuss this with my associates. Better have something good to trade with." Castillo headed toward the balcony and pointed at Chini to follow him. Then he pointed to his eyes and back at Chris then at Dmitri, which was the signal for Chris to watch Dmitri.

Chini was scratching his head. "Listen, JC, how do we play this? This guy won't roll over on Volkov. We don't care who else he's offed. There is no leverage there."

"Fuck, I know. We turn him over to Homeland, we get nothing out of him. He won't roll over on Volkov. We can't double whatever he is getting paid, which I am sure is a mil or more. Homicide won't take him because he didn't kill me, so he would be out in the morning once he gets an attorney."

Jose looked at the downtown Miami skyline with the art deco hues, the palms swaying in the breeze, and took a moment to appreciate the view. He missed sitting out in the balcony with Kat, enjoying a good smoke and some fine wine.

"Well, Chini, my mind is fried. All I can think of is taking our Eurotrash friend out to the alligator farm."

"I know it's hard to have an asset you cannot cash in. You are right about turning him in to the police. There's no evidence to charge him. He'll be out in the morning." Chini was as frustrated as JC was.

Castillo took a deep breath. "Chini, try to talk me out of this wild idea. I am thinking of taking a picture of Dmitri and posting it on the Internet and seeing who bites. I know it's crazy, but I am at a loss as of what to do with this guy."

"You must be fried. What are you going to do, post his picture on match.com? Really? *Soldier of Fortune* magazine no longer takes gun-for-hire ads. Lost and found? Geezus, man, snap out of it! Next you'll say you'll run his picture on Facebook for fuck's sake."

JC's eyes lit up. He snapped his fingers. "Great idea. Let's go."

Chini chased after him. "No, no, I was just kidding, man."

By the time JC had reached the kitchen, he had his i-Phone out and was pointing it at Dmitri. "Say *fromage*, asshole," JC said as he snapped a picture of Dmitri.

Dmitri figured out was just happened, and he was furious. "How dare you? I have rights," he said as he slammed his fists on the table.

"You gave up your rights when you aimed that rifle in the direction of my van. I am going to decide what happens to you unless you have something to trade for. Here is what I am going to do. I will post your picture on every mercenary website I can find with a reward for whoever can identify you. Of course, I will send your picture to Interpol just to be thorough. So that's door number one and two. Door three is just a trip to the alligator farm in the Everglades, where you will be the main course du jour."

"That's barbaric. Just turn me in to the authorities."

"Barbaric? Really? This coming from a contract killer. Shit, you are ticking me off, man. You know the authorities won't be able to hold you. Tell me what Volkov is up to and why he wants me out of the picture."

"Will I have assurances there will be no harm to me?" Dmitri seemed to relax in his chair.

JC read Dmitri's body language, and he knew it was time to play ball. "You have my word. I will not cause you any bodily harm." JC placed his hands on the table as a gesture of openness. He not only knew how to read body language but knew how to use his own as a tool.

"Does the same go for your associates?" Dmitri was testing the waters.

"Yes, none of us will cause you any injuries, and I will make sure you are safe and out of harm's way. Again, my word on it." JC clasped his hands together.

Dmitri fidgeted in his chair like a racehorse in the starting gate. "Volkov wants you out of the way because he thinks you know about his plans in Bimini. He thinks one of his employees overheard him talking about it…but what would that have to do with you? Unless… oh, I get it now. That is your in with Volkov. That employee and you are connected…interesting." Dmitri was nodding to himself as if had just finished figuring out a puzzle.

"So what is he doing in Bimini, pray tell?

"He is meeting with some folks who are coming from far away and selling something he wants very badly. I do not know what it is, I swear."

"When is this happening?" JC sat at the table next to Dmitri.

"Very soon from what I can figure out."

JC looked at Chris and Chini and nodded. "Get Dmitri another espresso, and me too, guys. Hey, Chris, don't forget to reserve that basketball court for tomorrow."

"Okay, let's wait a little and see if my source inside Volkov's world can corroborate. Hey, thanks for the coffee. Hope you added some ouzo." JC grabbed the cups and handed one to Dmitri and clinked cups. "Nostrovia"

"Ah, spasiba. You are versed in Russian, eh?" Dmitri felt very comfortable all of a sudden.

"Yenimnoga, just enough to get in trouble."

"So you play basketball?" Dmitri was looking a little sleepy.

"Oh, sure, all the time, as long as my knees can take it."

Chris came back into the room. "Court is reserved, boss."

"Great, man, thanks. Let's wrap this up."

Dmitry slowly lowered his head on the table and muttered, "You bastard," just before he started snoring.

The mention of the basketball-court reservation was code to call Nate to come over.

CHAPTER 40

"What in the flying fuck have you done now, JC, kidnapping and drugging? I'll be damned. You just don't know where to draw the line, dammit! I don't know whether to shit or go blind, mother-fucker!" Nate was pacing up and down in JC's kitchen while nursing a glass of Chivas.

Dmitri was out like a light and would be for a while after what Chini had put in his coffee.

JC was leaning against the kitchen door with his hand on his mouth, trying to stifle a laugh. Chini and Chris were at the table, looking down, trying to do the same. All were waiting for Nate to calm down.

"Let's see. You failed to report a shooting, you are holding a man against his will, you drugged him, tied him up, and he is sleeping in the other room, knocked out. When did you go batshit crazy, JC?"

Chris couldn't take it anymore, and he just guffawed. "Oh shit, this is better than a night at the improv."

That, caused Chini to burst out laughing too. The two were laughing so hard their eyes were watering.

"Funny? You think this is funny? You two could be held as accomplices." This made Chris and Chini laugh harder.

'What are you looking at, JC? I don't see you laughing."

"I'm just amazed that with all your pacing, yelling, and screaming, not a drop of that scotch has fallen out of that glass."

Chris and Chini started with the laughing again. Nate smiled and started laughing too.

"You Cuban cockroach, I can't get too mad at you. Please tell me what you were thinking."

"Nate, my brother from another mother, see it this way. We have no witnesses that saw him shoot at my van, By the time all evidence is gathered, he will be out on bail and gone. I can't turn him over to Volkov because he wants him gone as he is the only connection back to him. I am not turning him into alligator chum because he just doesn't fit my protocol for that at this time."

"At this time...at this time...I like it how you keep a flexible option with what you will or won't do with someone who merits your type of karmic punishment." Nate was suddenly serious. "So if he merits the alligator farm, it would be depending on your code of honor or something like that? Do you have a list of dos and don'ts? Is it based on a scale? C'mon, JC, how long have I known you? I still can't figure out what makes you do what you do sometimes. You have a contract killer on your hands, and while I cannot break the law, I have seen you break it many times in order to right a wrong or balance out your karmic scales of justice. I am surprised you already didn't turn him into chum, but he is alive, and it appears you are leaving him that way. You belong in the seventeenth century with the Yakuza and their code of honor."

JC noticed his arms were crossed and uncrossed them. He looked at Nate and was thinking of how much to show. He rarely showed what made him go. "Yes, Nate, I did study and lived in the Far East, but I am a product of my path. Everyone's path takes them to a different place in time, and these experiences make us what we are and, more importantly, what we evolve into. Being sent to Miami when I was five, being raised in those mean streets, not having my parents around in my formative years, college, the war, my relation-ships, the time in the Far East, all these things made me what I am today. I do not have any preconceived notion of what I will or won't do to right a wrong. I don't have a list, rules, or follow any dogma. I just do what I think is right and hope for the best. It's not easy sometimes."

"Good Lord, are the violins coming soon? Please carry on, my brother. I have always looked away when you've bent the rules. I am curious at what makes you tick." Nate took out a Black & Mild cigar, stuck it in his mouth, and started chewing on the wood tip.

"That's all there is, what I just said. Look, Nate, if we let him go and Volkov finds out I am alive, Dmitri is a dead man. So what? Well, he was just doing a job that he failed at. I got the information I needed out of him. I promised no physical harm would come to him. Yes, he tried to kill me, but it was a contract. He did not hate me. He was just doing a job, his job, his path. I respect that."

Nate looked at Chris and Chini and shook his head. "Boys, I am afraid he's had too many mojitos or something. This crazy Cuban is, well…fucking crazy. What do you guys think?"

Chini spoke first, "In my case, you know I am going to agree with JC because I do get hired to do occasional cleanup work, but luckily, I have only been hired to clean up bad guys. I would never do a cleanup on a good guy."

"And who determines whether he is a good guy or not?" Nate was on point.

Chini pointed at himself. "I do. I read their dossier, and if I do not think it merits it, I will refuse the job. Sure, they can hire some-one else, but as JC says, my conscience is clean at night, as strange as that sounds."

Nate pointed his cigar at Chris. "And you, my brother? More of the same?"

"Mostly more of the same, but, Nate, you are tied by your badge and your oath. How many times have you been sickened to your stomach to see a killer or an abuser get away scot-free?"

"More than I have gray hairs, my friend."

Chris pointed back at Nate. "Not that we are vigilantes or anything, but we only have our consciences or moral compass to guide us."

"In Chris's case, his compass is always pointing south of his belt." JC wanted to lighten the mood and change the subject. "More ouzo, anyone?"

"JC, ever the jokester. Thanks, goombah." Chris got up and grabbed Nate's almost empty glass. "Fill-up coming up, bro."

"I am going to start calling you misguided fucks, knights of the noble table. What a bunch of Don Quixotes windmill tilters. Geezus, if my Mama heard all this sappy right-and-wrong shit, she would whip each and every one of your asses. However, this does not solve the problem of the tied-up gentleman in the other room. What do you propose we do?"

"You know anyone in Homeland? I figured they need suspects to keep the machine going. After about six months of interrogations, I figure they will find nothing about him tying him to terrorism, and they'll probably try to turn him or keep him on the short list of specialists that have no ties to any government agency. What do you think, Nate?'

"I think you've been reading too many spy novels, JC. Let me make a call. I think I know a couple of Homeland knuckle draggers that might be able to take Dmitri for an extended vacation."

CHAPTER 41

The next morning, while waiting for Gafford to show up, I was with Chini and Chris at the breakfast table.

"Okay, kids, this is what we have so far according to Irina's translations." Chini was reading an e-mail he had received from his girlfriend. "There is something coming in soon that Volkov is buying. The exchange will not take place here."

"Great, all we need is a date and time....sheesh." Chris was his usual doom-and-gloom self.

"Chris, don't be so negative. We know what is coming in is the cesium, so it has to come from abroad. If we keep surveillance on Volkov, we should be able to stay within arm's reach." I was trying to be the voice of reason.

"Brother, how the hell are the four of us going to keep surveillance on Volkov, protect Lesson, and track and trace a shipment?" Chris always saw the glass half empty with bugs in the water and poison in it too.

"Through the wonders of technology, my negative friend. We will soon have Volkov's limo tagged, thanks to Gafford's friends at spookville. I have asked Nate to have Metro-Dade keep tabs on any request for a shipping manifest from any of his companies. Nate has pulled a favor from Homeland. He is in good graces with them since he turned Dmitri over. If Volkov applies for anything with Customs, we'll know about it, and of course, we have the electronic wizard himself, Gafford."

"C'mon, Chris, we have been against all odds before, and we made it. Stop with the Chicken Little 'the sky is falling' shit." Chini was always the one to bring Chris back to earth.

"Thanks for being positive, Chini. We will be all right. Any idea on the rest of Irina's translations?"

"There is a bit of confusion there, JC. It appears there is either a communication issue with whomever Volkov is dealing with. It might be a few days to a week when this is supposed to take place. There is a comment about dealing with ignorant foreigners from Volkov on the tape."

"Wow, Volkov complaining about ignorant foreigners? That's funny with his accent and all." I helped myself to some of the scrambled eggs I made for the boys.

Gafford came in and had that look that meant he had just fired up some herbs or was truly excited about something. "Hey, guys, I have the list of phones that Volkov's company pays for. Based on the minutes logged on one of the phones, I have determined which one might belong to Volkov."

"What does that do for us all, great and powerful Oz?" Chris with his doubting-Thomas attitude.

"What it does is that it allows me to track all those phones by tower pings, and I have downloaded an app to my phone, which I will forward to your phones, so we can all track the phone that I choose. Just like the same service Jose, Lesson, and I have on our phones. We keep track of each other that way. It's like we are part of Volkov's phone plan. He just does not know we are tracking him."

"What happens if Volkov goes out of the country?" Chris again. Sometimes a negative attitude helps cover all bases.

Gafford was rubbing his goatee. "That is going to be a bit tougher, amigos, so I thought we would give Lesson a tracking device.

I can put a GPS chip in his watch and track him through any of the online map direction sites."

I decided to set the course for the next few days. "Here is what we have. Obviously, the Cash surveillance is over. The Pavarro surveillance has not amounted to much and does not look like it will. Lesson is being ferried to and from work, Volkov has not incriminated himself about the firebombing or the cesium, and we have to wait to try to intercept the cesium purchase at a date and time we do not know, at a place we do not know. And when we do know, we will have very little time to act."

"Other than that, we are in real good shape, eh, paisan?"

"I can always count on you to think positive, Chris."

"We will have to be flexible. Jim, get the watch hooked up for Lesson. Chris and Chini, keep your schedules with Lesson but have your go bags ready. I'll have Kat's boat out of dry dock fueled and ready to go. If we have to fly, I have an account with Private Jets, so we can leave out of any airport in South Florida on short notice, or we can use Pinder's Island Service if need be. Chini, check on the surveillance mic across from Volkov's office every six hours instead of twelve. Explain the sense of urgency to your girlfriend and ask her to please stand by, translate, and send back the transcripts as soon as she gets them. I am guessing in about five to seven days, this thing is going to happen."

"That will work out great. I have about seven days left before I have to head back to Hollywood."

"Ready to get back to Tinseltown, eh?

"I do miss it a bit. I might be a small fish in a big town, but I swim in nice circles."

My cell phone rang, and it was Nate calling. "Hey, brother, what's the good word?" I tried to sound chipper. A call from Nate was usually not filled with good news.

"Nothing good, JC. Homeland has informed me they will only be keeping Dmitri for another day or two. He might be a bad guy, but they have nothing on him, and he has no information on anything they are working on."

"Great, thank Heckle and Jeckle for me at Homeland." I was mad. I knew Volkov would know that I was alive, and I wondered what he would try next.

CHAPTER 42

The visit from Homeland boys was unexpected, but what do you do when a dog is chasing its tail? I had just put the finishing touches on the Cobra and was getting ready to call Bobby, my auto detailer, to start the buffing and waxing process when the front doorbell rang. I cleaned my hands and stepped to the office to look at the surveillance camera on my computer. I saw a couple of guys in black suits, ties, and sunglasses at the front door. They reminded me of *Men in Black*. I figured they must be the Homeland grunts Nate had warned me about.

Anyone wearing a suit in Miami in the summertime is either from out of town or a masochist. I opened the door just a bit and decided to mess with them.

"Sorry, gentlemen, I am not interested in a Jehovah's Witness brochure today. I am an agnostic anyway."

The short agent whipped out a badge and ID card. "I am Agent Smith, Homeland Security. This is my partner, Agent Wesson. May we come in?"

I didn't open the door any farther to let them bask in that hot sun. "I am kind of busy in the middle of a project, and I don't have much time to spare."

"We will only take a few minutes of your time, Mr. Castillo." The tall one was sweating like a pig.

"I will give you five minutes on one condition: take off your sunglasses. I like to look into someone's eyes when I talk to them."

"Okay, deal," Shorty said, nodding to the taller one as he started walking toward the door.

"Take the glasses off first, gents, or no entry." What was another minute in the sun?

The tall one was starting to fidget. "Now, look here, Castillo, stop being such a prick and let us in. It's brutal out here."

"My, my, first it's Mr. Castillo, now it's Castillo, and a prick to boot." Another minute out there, and they would be melting. "Take off the sunglasses or no entry."

"Okay, okay, there you go." They both took off their shades.

I opened the door wide and motioned them to the office. I know it was a petty thing about the sunglasses, but it established they were on my property, my time, and my rules. I enjoyed using psychological warfare.

"Help yourselves to the soda machine, and the bottom slot has Amstel Light in it." I had the soda machine rigged so that no coins were needed.

"No, thank you. No alcohol while on duty," said Agent Wesson.

"There is cold pop, water, even that goofy sparkling water all the chichi restaurants are serving on South Beach. I have eclectic clientele."

"Is Victor Volkov a client?" Smith just let it out.

"I like that, just get right to it, waste no time." I wanted to get these guys out of here as quick as possible. "No, he is not. A very good friend of mine works for him. There was a strange situation with my friend, so I am looking out for him."

"The strange situation must have been the explosion, right?" Wesson was smiling.

"Okay, boys, so you are up to speed. You know I am not working for Volkov. You know Lesson works for him. Let's get down to brass tacks and let me get back to work."

"Just keep us informed if there is anything that might be of interest to Homeland."

"Of course, I am a patriotic American. I would never think of cutting you guys out of a situation." I put my hand on my chest for effect.

"Look, Castillo, your history dictates otherwise. You are a loose cannon with no regard for authority, regulations, or protocol, and if it wasn't for Detective Devine, your ass would have been grass a long time ago." It was Smith's turn to be bad cop.

"Agreed with your assessment of me, but I can get into places you can't. I can speak more languages than you can, and I don't have to follow rules, procedures, or jurisdictional borders. So what that means, I can get a lot more done without red tape, and I don't have to wait for orders from above. Keep that in mind. If I need your help, and I probably will in the near future, believe me, I will be in touch."

Smith was fidgeting in his chair. "Why do you think you'll need us?"

"As soon as I get all my facts together, I will call you. This might be even over my head." That elicited a relaxation on Smith's shoulders. His brain accepted my comment, and his body showed the result.

"Can you give us a hint?" Wesson was pressing again. These guys made a good team.

"Again, gents, you'll be the first to know after I do. Now I have to get back to work." I stood and headed for the office door.

Wesson stood up and pointed at me with his index finger. "Please do inform us as soon as you know anything. I would hate to have the weight of Homeland pressing down on you, Castillo."

I brought out my most sarcastic tone. "If you had actually done your homework on me like you say you did, you would know I don't take kindly to threats. Now get the fuck out of my shop before I call your boss, General Thompson, and tell him you are annoying me."

This made them stop in their tracks. "You know our boss? How?" Smith was staring at me while Wesson was slack-jawed.

"Small world. He was my CO when I was in Ranger School. By the way, guys, I know you probably got handed those suits and sunglasses after graduation from spook school, but you are in Miami for fuck's sake. You stick out like sore thumbs, and the chafing between your thighs is gruesome to think about, talcum powder or not. Get with the program. You are in the tropics, not the Midwest. There should be a sign at the airport and the borders to ditch the suits and go to the nearest Jimmy Buffett's Margaritaville store and buy cargo shorts, Hawaiian shirts, and flip-flops upon arrival, only way to survive down here."

I had steered them toward the front door by now. "I will be in touch, gentlemen. I did get your number from Nate, so rest easy. Good day." I closed the door on them, grabbed an Amstel, and went back to work on the Cobra.

CHAPTER 43

Nate heard a far-off ringing, and it was bothering him. He tried to ignore the sound, but it would stop after six rings and then start again. Damn that alarm. Nate was in a haze. He was tired, and he did not feel like getting up from his well-deserved slumber. These eighteen-hour days were wearing his ass out. He slowly realized it wasn't his alarm but his cell phone that was ringing.

He reached for it, and of course, it was on the sixth ring, so it went to voice mail. He looked at the clock, and it was about 6:30 a.m., thirty minutes before his alarm was set to go off. He noticed the missed call was from his assistant, Buck, so he knew Buck would call back shortly.

He sat on his bed and knew he was not going back for that last half hour of sleep. He shuffled to the kitchen and turned on the coffeemaker and was glad he had set it up the night before. He had his phone with him and picked up on the first ring. "Hello, Buck, this is probably not good news. I am sure."

"Sorry, boss, but I wouldn't have called unless I had to. You need to get over to the Valencia street entrance to Coral Gables. Our boy, the strangler, has struck again."

"It's not going to be a good day when it starts like this. Any other good news?"

"Actually, boss, it's worse. The victim appears to be that reporter from the paper, Lola Sanchez. We are waiting for confirmation, but it's a sure thing it's her."

"Motherfucker, the press is going to be all over this. Cordon off the area two blocks in either direction. Anyone crosses the barrier, have them detained immediately. Call Miami International and tell them I want a no-fly zone over the area. I want a lockdown of the perimeter immediately and call for whatever backup you need. Get as many of the task force that is available on site. Canvass the entire area within a five-block radius. Anything unusual happens, I want to know about it no matter how trivial, comprende? I will be over shortly."

"On it, boss. See you soon."

"Thanks Buck," Nate poured himself a cup of coffee and speed-dialed Jose.

"Hey, amigo, I hate to shit on your morning, but you need to go the Valencia entrance to the Gables. Buck will be there if you get there before me. Your friend Lola appears to be the latest victim of the strangler. I know you know her family, so I need your help with them."

"Geezus, Nate, I know you wouldn't kid about this. Thanks for the heads-up. See you there."

JC was numb. He thought he and Lola were good friends, not great friends. They rarely socialized together, but they used each other in certain cases when it was convenient and would help each other out when possible. They had gone on one unofficial date a long time ago, but he came to the conclusion that two strong type A personalities like them would not be a good mix. He knew that she felt it too because she backed off after that, just the usual flirting that she did with all men she met or needed something from.

He had met her family two or three times and liked them very much. They reminded him of his close-knit family. He wondered how her mother would handle this. It was not going to be easy. He put on black slacks, a white dress shirt, and grabbed a black Henri Grethel sport coat from his closet and headed to the Gables.

On the way out of the elevator, he ran into Gafford, who had just arrived.

"Hey, JC, I have some good news. I might be able to tap into Volkov's phones. It might take a little work and some help from my friends at Industrial Magic and Video, but it looks promising."

"Is that what you call your friends at braniac university? Okay, work on it and let me know how it turns out. I have to get going."

"Where are you going, a funeral? You are dressed in black."

"The funeral is not yet but soon. You'll see it all over the news. Lola is dead. All indications it's the Tamiami strangler. News at eleven o'clock—if it bleeds, it leads. Tell the boys I will probably be home late."

Gafford just stood by the elevator. JC fired up the DeSoto and backed out of the garage bay.

Nate dressed in a hurry and headed out. He noticed an envelope on his windshield. He opened it, and all it said in block letter was: SOMETHING BEING SMUGGLED IN, KEEP YOU POSTED AS INFO APPEARS.

Interesting, Nate thought. He would send the envelope and letter to his forensics team for analysis, hoping to get some tips or details where it came from. He also thought, *That's all I need, another person fucking with me.*

CHAPTER 44

Lola wanted to get a leg up on tonight's street walk. She wanted to follow up on a story about the Miami Tunnel, which was being built under Biscayne Bay to service traffic in and out of the Port of Miami. It was a marvel of engineering and had taken three years of drilling under the bay. It was a boring story that only engineers would appreciate, but it would probably sell a few more Sunday newspapers once she put a human angle on it.

She called Jeff, the intern, to meet at seven o'clock instead of eight and also notified her boss, Henry, about the earlier hour. She left a voice message on his office number and cell phone. Lola knew Luis and Lisa would be around since it was a Friday, and that meant payday for the johns.

Sure enough, as soon as she walked from behind the restaurant where she parked, she saw Luis and Lisa sharing a soft drink. "Hey, kids, how's tricks?"

"Very funny, Lola. One week out here, and you are so comfortable. Are you supplementing your income from the paper with our help?" Lisa had her hands on her hips in an exaggerated manner.

"Oye, putica, where are your watchdogs? They usually don't let you out of their sight for a minute." Luis was preening like a peacock.

"You two, you are busting my balls if I had any. I can give it out as well as take it."

"Lola, you're the bomb, baby girl. You have cojones to be out here chasing a crazy fucker. I wouldn't do what you are doing for all the tea in China Chiquita," Lisa said as she hugged Lola.

"Hey, let's get started. My boys will be here soon. Besides, I have you two looking out for me."

"Hey, chica, did you leave the phone in your car like I suggested? Most hookers don't own Blackberries."

"Sure, Luisito. I have my mic on. All Jeff has to do when he gets here is turn on the receiver he has, and we are good to go. Speaking of going, let's go and catch us some clues."

"Better clues than crabs!" Lisa said with a laugh.

Jeff Bloom was caught in a traffic jam. The Florida Marlins had a night game starting at seven o'clock. This screwed up traffic in Little Havana, the 836 east-west expressway, US 1 southbound, and basically any artery heading east or west. He tried reaching Henry, but the phone had gone to voice mail. He tried to keep his cool, but Miami traffic was bad enough without all the extra crap going on right now. Lola's phone went to voice mail too. He pounded the steering wheel with his palms and cursed under his breath.

Henry Ramirez, the city editor, had a simple cavity to fill at the dentist. He had a four-o'clock appointment and figured in the worst scenario, he would be out in two hours. Because Henry was afraid of needles, he found a dentist who would give him laughing gas to put him under during any dental work. He was a grown man, a former marine, had fathered five kids, but he would absolutely turn white at the sight of a needle or the sound of a drill.

His last dental visit with a cavity had gone smoothly, so he figured he would be okay to meet Jeff and Lola at eight o'clock and set up for the two-hour walk. That was his last thought as he put his phone on silent.

Dr. Fernandez had started working on the tooth with the cavity but noticed a problem with the molar next to it. He probed and saw that it needed a root canal. Since Henry was out, it would only add about another hour to what he was doing. He was sure Henry would be happy to knock off two birds with one stone.

He asked his assistant, Mandy, to prep for a root canal.

"But, Doctor, the last time we did a root canal on Mr. Ramirez, it took us three hours due to his condition."

"Don't worry, dear. I am right here. Shouldn't take long. Worse scenario, we'll be done by seven o'clock. Hand me the pick, and let's get started."

After some issues with sealing the tooth properly, Dr. Fernandez started bringing Henry out of his sleep.

"Mandy, stay with Henry while I clean up." He looked at his Rolex. "Look, it's only seven o'clock. We did it in record time. How long does he usually take to come around?"

"About ten minutes to fully walk, talk, and drive."

"Okay, let me know when he is ready so I can release him."

CHAPTER 45

It had been a busy half hour. Lisa and Luis had racked up two blow jobs and a hand job in that time. It certainly was payday. Lola had turned down three offers because she did not feel they met the profile. She used a copy of the profile from a contact she had at the task force. She studied the report, and the details were fresh in her mind as she began her night's work.

The first offer was a good ole boy in a Peterbilt truck. The second was an elderly man in a Cadillac, and the third was a woman wanting some girl-on-girl action.

Lisa and Luis were pulling their johns behind the restaurant parking lot if it was a hand job, or in an alley on the Gables side of the Trail if it was a blow job or backseat quickie. If anyone wanted a motel stay, they would send them ten blocks to the girls at Sixty-Seventh Avenue. That way, they could keep an eye on Lola.

Luis had a customer ready for a blow job, so he gave Lola the signal, which was to point to his lips. So she knew he would be at the alley.

Lisa had a customer, and she nodded no at him about five times. She finally nodded up and down, so Lola knew it was either a money or location issue that was solved. Lisa motioned up and down with a closed fist, so Lola knew it was a hand job.

About this time, a sedan pulled up to Lola. The man behind the wheel looked about thirty and was wearing sunglasses and a baseball cap.

"How much, mamacita?" He did not have much of an accent, if any.

"Depends what you want," Lola said as she walked up to the passenger door.

"Honey, what are you doing out here? You are so fine. Did you get thrown out of your old man's house? Did he find a younger muchacha?"

She noticed his hands looked strong. He was twirling a small piece of rope in one hand, making knots and loosing the knots with ease. She peeked in the backseat and saw nothing but a child's seat.

"Is this your car, papito?"

"No, mami, it is not. It's my brother's. He lends it to me from time to time so I can get things done."

"I noticed a navy sticker on the window. Are you a vet?"

"No, ma'am, that would be my brother."

"Is your brother a recent father?"

"Oye, puta, you want my brother or my money? What the fuck is this, twenty questions? Are you a cop?"

"No, I am not a cop. I am a reporter after a story. If your brother is a vet, a recent father, works with his hands and owns this car, I need to talk to him before the cops get to him. I can get him some help."

"What has he done, sister? Is he in trouble? I know he has a temper, and he has had trouble with women."

"He could be. If I can talk to him and see what he is all about, maybe things will go easier for him."

"I usually drop him off at the bar around the corner while I do my business with the girls here. He has a drink or two. If I take too long, he walks home since it's only a few blocks from here."

"How long ago did you drop him off?"

"About ten minutes, he should be on his second drink since you and I have been talking for five. Better hurry if you want to catch him."

"Take me to him." Lola looked for Luis and Lisa and didn't see them. She hoped Jeff and Henry were by the restaurant and would pick up on her microphone. "What's the name of the bar?"

"Eight Ball, like behind the eight ball you know. Hop in, sister. Even though it is only a couple of blocks, you have to buckle up. I would hate to get a ticket for a seat-belt infraction."

Lola got in and buckled up. Her pulse was racing. "What's your name?"

"Julio Lopez, nice to meet you."

"Thanks. I want to get to your brother before the cops and the media. Hey, buddy, your seat belt is not buckled. You just have the shoulder harness draped over."

"Yes, it's broken. My brother keeps promising to fix it." Julio pulled up behind the bar and went to the far corner of the parking lot and pulled in.

"Julio, you said your brother had a temper and trouble with women. What type of trouble?"

As soon as Julio braked, he elbowed Lola in the stomach, which took all the wind out of her. The blow was so intense that she could not even scream. Jose moved over on the bench seat and straddled her. He had one knee on her left hand and held her right hand in a vicelike grip. She was gasping and trying to catch her breath when he grabbed her by the throat and started to squeeze. She made one last violent effort to break free and just managed to butt heads with him. She was helpless, buckled in by the seat belt, straddled, and held down. Lola felt terrified.

"I can't believe you fell for the brother story, you bitch. I won't be able to enjoy you while you are alive, but I sure am going to have fun with you when you are dead."

Lola's last thought was of her mother before she took her last breath.

CHAPTER 46

I arrived at the crime scene, which was like a circus, to say the least. Television vans were nearby. The police had done a good job of cordoning off and securing the area. When I got to the barrier, a cop held up his hand to keep me from going in.

I heard Buck Taylor's voice from behind the cop. "Hey, Officer, he is cool. He's with me."

The cop waved me through.

"Geezus, I hope he doesn't think I am really with you. All I need is my manly reputation to take a hit. Next thing is, I will be decorating in fuchsia."

"Castillo, you are such a caveman. Lighten up, my friend. We are everywhere. Besides, you could use a little decorating help. It if wasn't for Kat's help with your place, all you would have would be milk crates for storage and bricks and lumber boards for an entertainment center."

"Great, I come to a crime scene and get a lesson in *Better Homes* and decorating."

"I know you really love me. You just won't let your feminine side come out."

"My feminine side is buried deeper than Jimmy Hoffa, amigo. But you are a good friend to Nate, so that puts you on my good side. You need help, I am there. Just don't ask me for help with your zipper."

"You should be so lucky. Many have wanted to help with my zipper."

"Okay, okay, enough already. I'm getting nauseous."

I always found it interesting in a serious situation how people turn to humor to try to lighten the mood. It's morbid, but it's human nature at its best.

"Come on, follow me. This guy is getting more ballsy."

There was a city park a block away. As we walked into it, there was a crowd of technicians about twenty-five yards into the park around a tree.

Sure enough, there was Lola, blindfolded and tied to the tree in a stand-up position. Her feet were bound together at the ankles; her left hand was positioned upright like the Statue of Liberty. Her right hand was by her side and molded as if she were gripping something. There was a *B* and *J* written on her forehead with a magic marker. I could smell the disinfectant on her body from five feet away.

"He sure does clean them up, doesn't he, Buck?"

"Yes, he does. This guy has time. He must have a place he can do this. Go take a closer look at her right hand. Let me know what you think."

I got a little closer and turned my head sideways so I could see her right hand. The fingernails were missing. Based on the skin hanging from the tips of her fingers, they had been ripped off. Interesting.

"Well, here goes. It appears, based on the missing fingernails, that he must have wanted them as a trophy. Based on the initials on her forehead and her posture and the blindfold, it reminds me of the blind justice statue in front of the courthouse."

"Very good, Castillo. You would make a good detective. Those are the same conclusions I came to. Come work for Homicide anytime you are ready."

"No, thanks. The hours suck, the pay stinks, and I can't be tied down with rules and regulations."

"Unfortunately, even with all these clues, we are no closer to finding him. I am hoping when Nate gets here, he has some ideas or directions. It's going to take days for these analysts to process all of it."

"Speak of the devil. Here comes my brother from another mother."

There was Nate in his tan chinos, white shirt, and Eddie Bauer boots. He took one look at Lola and shook his head. "Motherfucker, this guy is going to get caught, even if it costs me my badge. I will bend every rule if I have to."

I could tell this was weighing heavily on Nate.

A foot patrol officer came over to our group. "Detectives, I have someone who saw something suspicious at the park early this morning, and he wants to only talk to whoever is in charge."

"Bring him over. Let's see what he has and hope it's not a red herring." Nate stretched his neck, trying to wake up.

The officer brought over a man dressed in a jogging outfit. He looked about thirty-five, well-groomed, probably a professional. He had that wiry frame that most runners have.

"This is Joel Shapiro. He was jogging by this morning and didn't think of anything strange until he heard on the morning news what was going on."

"Thank you, Officer. We'll take it from here," said Buck.

Shapiro immediately turned to Nate; he knew who was in charge.

"If this has anything to do with the strangler case, I know there is a reward, and I want in on it."

"Nice to meet you too, Mr. Shapiro. Glad to see your priorities are straight. I am Nate Devine, Homicide." Nate was in no mood for this.

"Hey, Officer, I am just looking out for myself, if you don't mind." Shapiro was getting testy.

"It's detective, not officer, and your cooperation will be greatly appreciated." Nate was becoming testier.

Buck jumped in to cool down the situation. "Mr. Shapiro, you have our word that any information you supply will be credited to you and any reward will be coming your way."

"I read online that the reward is up to fifty thousand dollars. I want it. And I want more than your word, and I want assurances that I'll get my money." Shapiro was a pain in the ass, and this was not going to go well.

"Tell us what you saw, and let's see what we have." Nate was steaming.

"On my jog, I saw a sedan in the parking lot. I also saw a city truck, but I thought that was for the grass cutting over by the baseball diamond. I didn't think anything of it. In retrospect, I thought that it was too early for anyone to be at the park."

"We'll know as soon as you give us a description, won't we?" Nate was just under the boiling point.

"I want assurances about the reward first." Shapiro was going the wrong way on this.

Nate was breathing slowly, which meant he was trying to cool down. "Mr. Shapiro, if you refuse to cooperate, I can take you in as a material witness and hold you until the cows come home, so play ball here please." Nate never said please; I knew he was at the end of his rope.

"I want my lawyer right now." Shapiro was holding fast.

I saw Nate clench his fists and steady himself. I figured I would act before he went nuclear.

"Hey, Shapiro, I am an independent observer and not with law enforcement, so why don't you take me where you saw the sedan and let these gentlemen sort out your reward issue?"

"Who the hell are you, and why should I tell you anything?" This guy was annoying as hell.

"The victim was a friend of mine, just trying to help out."

"Okay, I'll show you, but I am not divulging much."

"Thanks, just give the lawmen a chance to cool off. I am sure they will work with you on your reward." I was starting to really loathe this guy.

We walked to the parking lot. It was now filled with police cruisers, medical examiner vehicles, CSI vans, and Nate's Charger.

Shapiro showed me where the sedan was parked this morning. He pointed to the other side of the parking lot and said that's where the city truck was parked.

We were standing between two CSI vans, so no one could see us from the park.

I bitch-slapped Shapiro with my right hand and grabbed his neck with my left and slammed him into the side of the van while lifting him off the ground.

His eyes were the size of half dollars from the shock. I had his throat tight, so all he could get out was a squeak.

"Here is the way it's going to happen, you little prick. Tell me the description of the sedan. I will give it to the hardworking detectives, and I will make sure if there is any reward, you will get it. It's the only option you have, or I will break your leg and say you tripped. Got that?"

He nodded. From the fear in his eyes, I could tell it was something he never experienced before.

"I am going to let go of your throat slightly. The only sound I want to hear is year, make, and model. Nod if you agree."

He nodded. I let go slightly.

He croaked, "Four-door, tan-colored, Florida plates, Navy sticker on windshield, probably a ten-year-old Mitsubishi or Nissan."

I let him go. He was rubbing his neck. "You are a fucking barbarian man. I was just looking out for myself. Fuck you."

"I was looking out for me, my dead friend, and my friends over there. Go to hell and stick your reward up your skinny ass, you parasite."

I went back and gave Nate and Buck the info. "If I remember correctly, we have the first two of a license plate already, which should speed it up."

"I hope we don't have to call Shapiro to testify. I see him rubbing his neck over there."

"I know, I know, Nate, obtained in a way that won't hold up in court. But if we find the car, we'll have our man, and he will be breakable."

"Thanks, JC. I'll see what we can do with this." Nate started to head to the command center.

"Anytime. I will take it to Gafford. We were working on it already, so I might get the info sooner. You know no bureaucracy or red tape for me. Hey, you might send an EMT over to Shapiro. He might have choked on something while we were talking."

Nate chuckled. "Yeah, bet he did. I figured you might cross the line that I can't. Thanks. See you, bro."

Another day, another right wronged. Don Quixote marches on.

CHAPTER 47

Buck had passed on the car's description to Woody and his database folks. They proceeded, to sort by vehicle size, color, and make. Just to be safe, they added Camrys too. It would take longer but would be more thorough. "You get back to me or Nate as soon as you get a hit."

Buck was headed over to Nate when he was called by an officer manning the barricades. There were four people around him. The officer started walking toward him. "Sir, I have four people who want to talk to Nate about the deceased. Two are obviously street people, but they said they have been working this area the last week with her. The other gentlemen worked with her at the newspaper. They seem to be beside themselves."

"Send the two street people over first." Buck walked over to Nate, who was talking to one of the forensic technicians. "Hey, boss, I have some folks who want to talk to you about Lola. I think you'll find the first two interesting."

"Yes, I recognize those two. I talked to them a few days ago. Send them over."

Lisa and Luis walked up. They looked upset, and Lisa was crying. She said between sobs, "We are so sorry. We were supposed to look out for her. The two men from the newspaper were late. We thought they had her covered."

"Are those the two men over there?" Buck nodded in the men's direction.

"Yes, that is them." Luis was sniffling a bit too.

Nate took a deep breath. "Tell me everything that has transpired the last few days, leave no detail out. Buck, go check those men's story, and we'll compare notes after."

After Lisa and Luis were done, Nate gave them a business card with his cell phone on it. "Look, you two are going to be hounded by the media, especially the gossip sites and probably get offered some money to give your side of the story. First, you are going to put yourselves in danger if this guy is not caught. Two, if you can wait a week, I can get you some reward money from my discretionary funds, so get off the streets and come see me in about five days. In the meanwhile, go to the Salvation Army on Brickell and tell them I sent you. They will give you shelter and food until you come see me. I will have one of the cruisers drop you off at the shelter."

"Thank you, Detective. Hope you catch this guy," Lisa said as she hugged Nate.

Nate waved at Buck, who was with the two newspapermen. Buck arrived and introduced them. "Boss, this is Henry Ramirez, editor, and Jeff Bloom, an intern."

"Gentlemen, sorry to meet you under these circumstances. I am Nate Devine, Metro-Dade Homicide. I have to take a moment to confer with my assistant, so I will be with you in a moment." Nate stepped away out of earshot.

Buck proceeded to tell their story to Nate; it jived with the others' story. "Okay, so other than being in over their heads and being idiots, they have not broken any laws." Nate had his arms crossed and was looking in the men's direction and shaking his head. "Let's go make them feel worse than they already do."

The two men shuffled nervously as Nate walked up to them. "To say that you two amateurs screwed the pooch is an understatement. A young lady is dead because of this fiasco. Lucky for you, there are no laws against stupidity. If there were, I would be locking you up right about now. Any information or notes from Ms. Sanchez, I want in my office by tomorrow morning. My assistant will be taking your statements. We might call you in for additional interviews in the future. Let my office know if you are going out of town. That is all, gentlemen. Good day."

Henry raised his hand. "Detective, you cannot feel worse than we do. If there is anything we can do or the newspaper, please let us know. We are at your disposal. Thank you for listening."

"I might need use of your newspaper in the future if I want to plant a story. I will definitely take you up on your offer." Nate always kept as many chits or favors as he could, every tool possible at his disposal and then some. "You are welcome. Good day again, gentlemen." Nate could be dismissive without even trying.

CHAPTER 48

I dreaded going to the Sanchez home to give them the news about their daughter. I knew that Nate would do it, but I had a relationship with the family, and I felt it would be better coming from a friend. When I arrived at the Sanchez home in Hialeah, there were a lot of cars there, and I was relieved. They already knew, and I felt the visit would be longer than anticipated.

When I walked in the open front door, Mrs. Sanchez was sitting in a La-Z-Boy with a rosary, and one of her sons was fanning her with an old-fashioned church fan and another of her sons putting a wet towel on her forehead.

The mood was somber. Novena candles were lit, and the sniffling and whimpering coming from various parts of the house made the situation very sad. As soon as Mrs. Sanchez saw me, she raised both her arms to me.

"Ay, Jose, que animal le hiso esto a mi hija?"

"Yes, it was an animal that did this to your daughter. I am so sorry, Mama." I reached down to hug her, and I was not going to release her until she let go.

After what seemed like five minutes, she still had me in a hug and whispered in my ear. "Jose, has lo que tengas que hacer para captar a ese animal. Yo te pago lo que quieras."

"Yes, I will do whatever it takes to capture that animal, and no, you will not pay me a thing." I released her, and she leaned back in her chair with a pained expression.

Her three sons gave me a hug. Pepe, who was the oldest, said, "Whatever you need, you can count on the three of us, Jose, okay. Twenty-four-seven, okay? Surveillance, follow-up on leads, lean on someone—you use us. No questions asked."

"Gracias, Pepe, I plan on it. I do not have the manpower the cops have, so do not be surprised if I use you guys. Count on it. I will be in touch. Let me know when the service is going to be."

"Oye, Jose, whatever you need, brother. No stone left unturned, anytime, anyplace, we will be there." This from Jorgito, the youngest of the brothers.

"Muchachos, you can count on it. Be ready at a moment's notice. Here is my cell phone. Call me with yours now so I can save them. I know you are well armed, so no problem there. But if I need you, it will be for lookouts, surveillance, or to babysit someone. I have cleanup hitters if we need firepower, although I don't think we will need them. You guys get ready. We are going to use you to patrol the Trail."

"Why can't we start now?" This was from Sergio, the middle brother.

"I will call you later with the type of car we are looking for. We have some information, but we are trying to narrow it down. Ten pacensia, Sergio." I knew Sergio was the hothead, and that is why I wanted to slow the Sanchez boys down a bit until their Latino tempers cooled.

"Patience, my ass, JC. I want the monster that did this." Sergio was jumpy like a bull in a rodeo chute.

"We all do. I will call you soon, so be ready to roll. But there is one catch: hold on to this one, boys, until we get proof. Remember that. Hasta luego."

They say bad things come in threes. How true. If I only knew about the five-hundred-pound shit hammer heading my way, I would have ducked.

CHAPTER 49

I met the boys for dinner at Versailles Restaurant on the Trail. While it was not a trendy place in South Beach, it was a place to get good Cuban food with desserts to die for, and of course, a cup or two of Cuban coffee, or rocket fuel as some of us call it. It is on Tamiami Trail or Calle Ocho, as it is better known. It's in the outskirts of Little Havana before it turns into Coral Gables. Douglas Road is the border between Little Havana and the Gables—hardworking blue-collar Latinos on the Havana side; Addison Mizner–type architecture, glass-office towers, the University of Miami, mansions nestled throughout very old banyan trees on the Gables side.

Versailles started in the early seventies as a little two-window walk-up where you could get Cuban coffee, a Cuban sandwich, and cigars. It grew as fast as the Cuban community did. The bigger the neighborhood grew around it, the bigger the restaurant grew. It was in the same location but had absorbed the buildings it was attached to and could now easily sit over 150 patrons. It still has the original café counter. You can see the mayor of Miami, and even a president or two has stopped off for a photo op when courting the Cuban/Latino vote. It became the unofficial cultural and political center for Miami's Cubans, where they could congregate, have dinner, or stop for a shot of coffee and a cigar and have like-minded brethren around to discuss—or, more than likely, argue—about politics. The talk would eventually gravitate toward Cuba, Castro, and his gang of communist cowards and when Cuba would be "free" again.

It was a typical summer evening with a light breeze coming from the east off Biscayne Bay, just enough to make the heat and humidity tolerable and the palm tree fronds sway a little. Most of the men were wearing guayaberas, which are traditional summer-fare shirts worn in Cuba, a tradition that continues in the United States. I was still in my black slacks and white button-down long-sleeve Paul Fredrick Oxford shirt. I rolled up my sleeves not only because of the heat but to look more relaxed and to get the "funeral" look off me.

As I walked to their table, I saw Chris, Lesson, Chini, and Gafford sitting there chatting. I could not help but think of the *Last Supper* by da Vinci. I had that gut feeling that the tides were changing. You know that feeling. You know it's coming. You can't help it, but you just hang on, go with the tide, and hope your ship is upright after the storm. That is what I felt as I walked up to the gang. I knew the strangler case was getting close to the finish, and I felt something was going to break with Volkov. I just didn't know when and where, and I hoped that it would not all happen at the same time.

Gafford was the first to speak to me, "JC, I need to talk to you later. I have some reports on the license plate search that I did. I haven't shared it with Nate or his team yet."

Lesson was next. "Boss, lots of activity at work, but they are keeping me away from it. I was told I might get a week off with pay since the boss is going out of town."

I asked Chini if he had any new translations from his girlfriend. "Irina says nothing important, JC. The chatter from Volkov's office has quieted a bit in the last few days. Most of the talk from Volkov's has been about a trip to the farm, wherever that is." Chini did not seem like himself; I asked him if he was okay. "All good. It's just one of those weeks." I did not believe him; he wasn't his usual self.

"What is up with you, Chris? I know you need to get back to So Cal soon. Just give me a heads-up a few days before you have to leave."

"No problem, JC. My client just checked herself into rehab again, so I probably have a couple of weeks before I head back."

Dinner was served. Gafford had ordered paella, which is saffron rice with shrimp, chicken, lobster, scallops, octopus, and mussels. Chini had ordered Caldo Gallego which is a Spanish version of navy bean soup. Chris had liver Italiano, which had onions and peppers in a light tomato sauce. Lesson had roast pork chunks. All came with white rice, black beans, and fried plantains, except for the paella. I ordered a Basque omelet, which had ham, chorizo, shrimp, and marinated pimento.

I hated to talk shop at dinner, but with everything going on, it was rare that all of us were at the same table, let alone the same room. "Here is the plan, boys, subject to developments, clusterfucks, and the karma wheel roll."

"Oh, damn, don't start with the karma wheel horseshit."

"Don't worry, Chris. No diatribe about the wheel, not yet anyway."

"Thank gawd. All we need is the monk in you to start sprouting that Eastern philosophy crap."

"I'll wait for this all to pass before I put that spin on it."

"I hope I'll be on a plane back home when you start. You can send me the short version in an e-mail."

Gafford joined in, "Chris, the difference between us and the animals is that we can think, reason, and hopefully learn from what happens around us. Self-analysis is what makes us adapt and change as needed depending on the situation."

"Oh boy, JC. It's started already, and you have Gafford drinking the Kool-Aid. Please no more psycho karmic babble at the dinner table."

"What say you, Chini?" I asked.

"No comment, men, just chillin'. Leave the analysis to you guys."

I knew Chini was quiet, but he at least would give his two cents' worth on a subject if you asked. I figured he was bored, being the adrenaline junkie he was.

"Well, then let's do some planning. Gafford, check for any farms owned by Volkov's companies so we can get a lead on that. Chini and Chris, put the go bags in Mother. Once we get the list from Gafford, we can use Lola's brothers to track down the plates we have that might match. That will give us six of us looking."

"Are you going to give Nate the perp when we find him?" asked Gafford.

"I don't know. Situation will be dictated by what we find."

"Hey, JC, I don't need to be charged with obstruction of justice or kidnapping or whatever this turns out to be. I need my licenses clean."

"Don't worry, Chris. I will keep you clean and clear of anything that is not aboveboard."

"What about me, boss?" Lesson looked hurt he was not included.

"Lesson, you will be at my place protecting it, and if Kat comes back from her shoot in the islands, I want you there to pick her up at the airport in case we are tied up."

"Okay, boss, thanks. I will take care of the shop and Kat."

"Let's get some dessert, boys, and we'll head back to the Castillo castle."

"Very funny, JC. Your name translated to the queen's English is 'castle.' Good play on words."

"Chris, you always get my sarcasm."

I ordered four desserts: tres leches, which is sponge cake made with condensed milk, evaporated milk, and heavy cream (hence the name *three milks*); flan de leche, also known as crème custard; coco rallado, shaved coconut meat smothered in heavy syrup and served with cream cheese slices; and last, buñuelos, a Cuban version of a doughnut made with dough and flavored with anise, served with a clear syrup, either bathed in it or served on the side.

All of us took a bite of each. There was tie for favorite between the flan and the tres leches. Thank goodness none of us were worried about calories.

After turning in, I checked my e-mails, and Kat wrote that she would be done soon and would be flying home in a couple of days. I wrote back for her to call the house first since we would probably be on stakeouts and, if she didn't get any of us, to text Lesson then. A few minutes after I sent that text, my phone started to ring. It was Kat.

"I'm afraid to ask what you boys are up to, but I probably wouldn't sleep if I didn't call you. Text Lesson if I couldn't reach you? Sounds ominous there, big guy."

"Hey, darling, glad to hear your sweet voice. Looking forward to seeing your beautiful face soon."

"Don't flatter me and try to change the subject. What mischief are you and the boys up to?"

"Long story, baby, hard to explain, and you know sometimes uncle has big ears." My signal to her that my phone might be tapped.

"Oh, I see, so I'll just have to wait for the news to see what's going on, huh?"

"Don't get your Okie temper up there, Miss. Part of what we are involved in won't make the news, the other will. Just know the boys are with me, and I have the backup of the Sanchez brothers."

"Lola's brothers? How is that slut doing? She still after my man?"

"She's dead, baby, part of what we are working on. Details when you get in."

"Oh, Daddy, I am so sorry. I'll let you go. You must have your hands full. Love you, my big gorilla."

"Love you too, baby. See you soon."

Little did I know I would have to go on an island rescue trip if I ever wanted to see her again.

CHAPTER 50

Nate had assembled his team with the new information about the license plate.

"Glad to see all department heads here. Please pass on this info to your street teams. We have 148 possible matches to the two license plate numbers we know of. Coordinate your efforts so we do not duplicate our search. Any subjects even matching a close description, bring in. We'll worry about the legal mumbo jumbo later."

Susan Schliff, executive director of the Florida Department of Law Enforcement raised her hand.

"Yes, Dr. Schliff?" Nate was not surprised Schliff was raising her hand. She was tough as nails, a former prosecutor with the US attorney office who had a doctorate in clinical psychology and who had also served in the Israeli army in her teens. And rumor had it she had a third-degree black belt in tae kwon do.

"Detective Devine, imagining that I didn't hear your legal mumbo-jumbo comment, what would you like FDLE to help you with? And if we catch him, do you want him first? We suspect he might have been in North Florida where we have a few cases with similarities. And please call me Susan or Schliff, no formalities needed."

"Okay, Susan, if you catch him, let me have him first. Afterward, he is all yours. I want to make an ironclad case against him. Help-wise, I just need all your agencies to have the car info. If you spot him, detain and hold for us. And please call me Nate."

"Will do, Nate. If we get to him first, we will make sure the 'legal mumbo jumbo' is covered. That way, there is no technicality he can get off on, no pun intended."

So she does have a sense of humor, Nate thought. Twisted, as it sounded. "No disrespect for the law, Susan, just making sure we cover every lead, and anyone remotely suspicious or matching any of the characteristics, I want to put my eyes on them. Besides having a high-profile victim the last time, the press is having a bigger field day than usual because she was one of their own. From our perspective, he has been taunting us, so now it is getting a bit personal."

"Agreed. We'll work together on this. I do want to talk to you privately after on another subject."

"Sure, Susan. Let me wrap up here. Okay, teams, pass on the information, get your eyes and boots on the street, and start canvassing." Nate waved to Susan. "Come in to my office. Can I get you anything?" Nate was curious as to why she wanted a private audience. "Please have a seat."

"No, thanks for the drink. I am okay, and this won't take very long." Susan sat and removed some imaginary lint from the sleeve of her suit. It was a smart outfit: gray skirt, knee-high with matching jacket, and a light-blue low-collar blouse. She would fit in any corporate boardroom with that outfit. She was petite. Nate figured about five foot one, but she had the economy of motion in her walk and looked fit. She had short blonde hair and light-blue eyes.

"Nate, you know how rumors go in our business. No matter how crazy it sounds, you can't discount it because if it comes through, then your conscience or career suffer or both. Could I have prevented it curse? You know how it goes."

"Sure do, but please get to the point. You and I have a heavy load to shoulder, so let's get to it."

"I don't like beating around the bush either. I have on a good source that there is some stolen radioactive material that could be making its way to Miami, so keep your teams hypersensitive and follow anything that comes your way and share with me what you have, and I will do the same."

"Good Lord, all we need. Do you know the size? How? When? Where?"

"It's bigger than a breadbox, probably the size of a large suitcase or large trunk. How? Probably through the Caribbean first. Where? Possibly within the next few days." Sue patted her jacket sleeve.

Nate was curious. "By any chance, have you run across Agents Smith and Wesson from Homeland Security?"

"I am not allowed to say that, Detective, but if I had to, I would have to say they remind me of Mutt and Jeff."

Nate smiled; that was her way of saying she had met them.

"Thanks. I wonder why they would not tell me the same thing. After all, I have jurisdiction on all airports and ports in South Florida. Interesting."

"Maybe it's a pissing contest. It's the testosterone thing with you men. Maybe they think I am harmless because I don't look the part."

"Sister, I've heard you can chew nails and spit them out faster than a nail gun."

Susan chuckled. "Nate, you are a barrel of fun. I don't spit them out as much as I used to, but in a pinch, you will want me watching your back."

"Hope I don't need to, but glad to know I can. Thanks."

Susan stood up and stuck her hand out. "Glad to be on the same team, Nate. Stay in touch." She had a grip of steel.

"Will do. Take care." Nate wondered why the Homeland soldiers did not confide in him about the smuggling.

CHAPTER 51

Back at the shop, espresso was made and passed out with some ouzo, Hennessey, and Grand Marnier for after-dinner drinks. Chris made a big production of a pouch he took from his travel bag.

"Boys, I have a special surprise for you from the Beverly Hills Cigar Club. You are about to enjoy a Louixs, one of the most expensive cigars on the planet. You have to have connections to get these babies."

"Thanks, Chris. I know they are expensive, much appreciated," Chini finally said something other than yes or no.

Gafford had set up his Rock Xtreme SL8 laptop on the kitchen table since we were already sitting around it. Gafford had on what I called his *uniform*: Hawaiian shirt, jeans, and sandals. The design on the shirt changes; the sandals never do. He gets them from Kino's in Key West. It's the only thing he puts on his feet. All that went well with his ponytail and granny glasses; he reminds me of John Lennon.

"Gentlemen, what I have is a list of possible hits on the license plate numbers. The difference between my list and what we will probably get from the IT geeks at Metro-Dade is that my list has more in-depth information like cross-referencing car owners to insurance policies to finance companies. A different algorithm program than Metro has."

"What does that mean to mere mortals like us, Jim?" Chris, ever the smart-ass.

"What this means is that my list is going to be shorter. I just downloaded Metro's list right now. It's a three pager with approximately 150 names. Mine has 48, so I will cross-reference both lists, and whatever names are on both will be our master list. I will have it ready in about five minutes."

Brilliant, thought JC. "Hey, Jim, can you break that down and tell us which cars would be most likely and which cars would be least likely to be our man?"

"JC, I would have to write a code for that program. It would take days, and unfortunately, we don't have that luxury."

"You are right. I just want to give the least-likely list to the Sanchez brothers. They are hot to trot after their sister's killer. Those boys are your typical hotheads. I am going to suggest that we give the Sanchez boys the list of addresses farthest from the Trail. I remember reading somewhere that the perps usually strike within a three- to five-mile radius of where they live."

"You are right, JC. I had already put that equation into my program. Our suspect should live between two to five miles from the epicenter of the crime scenes."

"Let's hope so. Okay, teams are going to be me and Gaff, Chris and Chini, and the Sanchez brothers. If we run across any officers doing their search, our story is that we were hired by the Sanchez family to investigate Lola's death. It's partially true. I haven't actually been hired, but her mother did ask me to look into it. You know I said yes, and I always keep my promises."

"Another pro bono case. How do you stay in business?" I was glad Chini was starting to be his old self.

"You know, Chini, thank goodness for my car-restoration company. One or two jobs a year gets me by with the occasional reward from a skip tracer or bondsman."

"What, no reward for dog kidnappers?" Chris could not resist his own joke and laughed like a loon.

"Very funny, although there was one time a rich bitch from Palm Beach was offering a ten-thousand-dollar reward for her lost poodle. You should have seen the island being run over by private investigators. It looked like a PI convention was in town. The finder of the dog, after some inquiries were made, turned out to be a cousin of one of her gardeners. It was an inside job all along."

"Did you get that one?" Chris, as always, pushing the envelope.

"No, I turned the job down after interviewing the owner, just one of those gut-feeling things. A few years later, her husband turned up drowned in his hot tub. How do you drown in a hot tub?"

Gafford looked up from his laptop. "I remember that one. The toxicology report on the husband showed antidepressants, muscle relaxers, codeine, Xanax. He was just a medicine cabinet full of shit. The ME was surprised the guy could walk."

"Of course, the missus inherited a tidy fortune and married the lifeguard at the Breakers, imagine that. A few months later, I was doing surveillance on a socialite when I saw the lifeguard coming out of Taboo's with a young lady on his arm, so I knew that marriage was doomed then."

"Geez, JC, you have these cushy jobs—Palm Beach this, Key West that, Brickell Avenue stakeouts, tough life."

"Chris, you're one to talk, Mr. Hollywood."

"Listen, JC, getting puked on by a starlet, having to strong-arm some low-level coke dealer, rousting obsessive fans from hotel lobbies is not exactly Hollywood glamour." Chris used his fingers as an air quote when he ended that sentence.

"Well, my friend, as cushy as those jobs sound, it is disheartening to have to testify in court at a divorce or custody hearing. People use their money, their children, and even their pets as battering rams to get back at the other spouse. It's a perpetual war, and it doesn't matter what side of the tracks you come from, whether you are rich or poor. A pound of skin or a quart of blood taken is the only satisfaction some people get. I wish people would just move on. If someone doesn't want you, move on and let go of it. That simple. But the divorce attorneys would go broke."

I couldn't agree more with him and told him so.

"Human nature is what it is. In Hollywood, some people would run over their own grandmothers to get a part. And when there is a divorce in Hollywood, it's like chumming the waters in a shark tank. The attorneys would sell their soul to get a piece of the action. I've been in an attorney's office in Hollywood when he got a call from a client that wanted a divorce. The first thing he did after making an appointment for her is he called the local Mercedes-Benz dealership and ordered the top-of-the-line sedan. The first words out of his mouth after hanging up with the dealership were, 'That's paid for already with my first bill to that actress.' Sorry, JC, but we are both in a nasty business, and the splash back sometimes gets on you, and you can't get it off no matter what you do."

Gafford brought us back to the real world. "Dudes, I am done. Here are the four pages with twelve possible perps on each page. Give these two pages to the Sanchez boys, which is the group farthest away."

"Okay, guys, let's break it up and go hunting. Lesson, you man the fort. Anything happens, you call, okay?'

"What fort, boss?"

Sometimes I forget how to phrase things to him. "That means just take care of things here. Kat may call for a ride from the airport, so please pick her up and remember you are like the big guard. Okay?"

"Okay, boss, got it." Lesson puffed out his chest and felt like part of the team. We all feel the need to be needed, some more than others.

CHAPTER 52

A lot of detective work is mundane, boring, and tedious, but sometimes, perseverance and just plain blind luck makes you trip over a clue or a lead. On the way to follow up on our perp list, I received a frantic call from Mrs. Pavarro. She was hysterical about her husband's whereabouts. I calmed her down and told her to start from the beginning, slowly and without the drama.

"I went to his office when he told me he had to work late and was meeting some clients for dinner. You know, it's one of those gut feelings, Mr. Castillo. I just knew something was up."

Many a marriage or relationships have ended because someone had a gut feeling; I can vouch for that personally.

"Go on. Where is he at?'

"He went to a tapas bar in the Gables. I can't go there because it could be a business dinner, and I would look like the typical jealous Latina. Can you follow him and see what he is up to?'

"Mrs. Pavarro, I am currently on a case, and it is a priority. Which bar is it?"

"You must at least go in and look. I have a feeling. It's the Spanish bar on Ponce Boulevard. You must go, please."

"I know where it is. I promise to go look in on him, but again, I have a priority case. If I get a hit on that, I must go. Call you in a few." I hung up as she was starting to sound shrill. "Never a dull moment, Gaff. Small detour, you are going into a restaurant to see who Mr. Pavarro is drinking and dining with. Remember what he looks like?" I was already pulling into the restaurant's parking lot.

"Sure do. Be right back."

Gafford was back in three minutes. "Lord, have mercy. That girl who is with him would bring a man back from the dead, goodness gracious! They looked like they were settling the check. Just two drinks on the table, no food."

"Well, hell, let's see what develops." I reached for my bag and pulled out the camera with the long lens. So much for camera phones; you still need a good old-fashioned telephoto lens for a long shot.

A few minutes later, Pavarro and what looked like a girl half his age came out of the restaurant. She was short, probably five feet tall, blonde hair, and was wearing a skirt that looked like it had less material than a handkerchief—and a tank top that had even less.

I whistled. "Geezus, they keep making them, don't they?"

"Makes you want to pound your head against a wall, doesn't it?" Gafford chuckled.

"Makes you want to pound something, all right. Wow!"

I called Mrs. Pavarro. "We have him under watch, so I will keep you posted. Please stay away and let us do our job."

"I want to catch the hijo de puta." She was already hyperventilating.

"That son of a whore will be paying you a better settlement if we have proof. Let it play out." I hung up on her again.

"She wants to bust him in person, doesn't she? The hotheaded response is to instill humiliation, hurt them back as much as they are hurting."

"Gaff, you are on point, not bad for someone who's never been married."

"Precisely the reason why I've never married. I can't expend that type of negative energy. I agree with your premise that if someone doesn't want you, don't walk but run as far as and as fast as you can. If they don't love and want you in their life, there is nothing you can do. It's not defeatist. It's just common sense. Some people don't take rejection well. They try harder. Why do they try? More love, more gifts, more attention? If they don't want or love you, something has died in them toward you. Move on, soldier. Move on, give your attention and love to someone that appreciates it, needs it, and wants it. Plenty of folks out there."

"You are smarter than I, my friend. It's taken me three nuptials to find the right one. Lots of rubble left behind but worth it. I don't think I would appreciate Kat as much as I do unless I had been kicked to the curb like I have been."

"Ironically, here we are on a pussy chase, and someone here will be hurt." Gafford had a pained expression.

"Speaking of irony, the current Mrs. Pavarro is twenty years younger than him. She used to be his secretary, and she stole him from the original Mrs. Pavarro. Some kind of payback, eh?"

"Oh, wow, dude, in spades. Holy karma wheel."

Pavarro got into the girl's car, very smart to leave his car at the restaurant, especially with a license plate that read Pavarro-1. I had a feeling they weren't going to church.

We followed the car as they turned onto the Trail and headed toward the heart of Little Havana. They did not go too far when the car turned into a motel that was famous for its room themes. They had a room, which was a jungle room; room B, which was like a baby's room; room C, which had a giant champagne glass that was a hot tub; room D, which was a dungeon; and of course they had a room that was mirrored from floor to ceiling. I had busted many a Lothario and adulteresses there over the years. We could not pull in with Mother because that would have drawn too much attention to us. I pulled around the block and parked behind a used-car lot that was adjacent to the motel.

Gafford was already at the back of Mother, working the outside cameras. Since Mother's rooftop was so tall, the corner cameras might give us a shot over the carefully planted eight-foot hedges that were around the motel parking lot. Each room had a parking spot that was planted with hedges on the sides so when you drove to the front door and got out of your car, you would not see your neighbor and vice versa.

"I have the back of the girl's car on camera three. Engine is running, interior light is on. She must be putting on makeup. Mr. Pavarro has gone to the desk to pay. Of course, I am taping it all."

"Gaff, after all this time, I knew you would be."

I sat next to the console and watched the monitors. We had a view of the front door of the love nest. We had a partial of the driveway next to theirs, and our front camera was pointed toward the entrance of the motel.

"JC, why do you think they picked such a sleazy place? Pavarro can afford any hotel on South Beach."

"Besides proximity to where they met, probably the rush of the forbidden. The knowledge you are doing something bad gives some people a rush. This place is a twenty-four-hour fuckathon. They should have courtesy parking for private dicks, no pun intended. Last time I staked this place out, I had to share a space with Tracy Lewinski, who was trying to get the goods on a politician who liked young men."

"Tracy Lewinski of the At Your Service commercials? That's one that advertises on late-night television, right? What's her slogan? 'Let Tracy trace your skip tracer'?"

"One and the same. She also does process serving, PI work, bounty hunts, federal fugitives. Says that pays the best. Tough broad. If I was in a bar fight, I would like her watching my back."

We were chatting, passing the time, waiting for them to come back out. Gafford would have everything taped and cataloged for any mediation between the Pavarros. Florida being a state where everything is equally divided that is accrued while the couple is together does not keep many a wife from trying to squeeze a little bit more out of the husband if he is rich, famous, a politician, or all three.

I noticed out of the corner of my eye that a car had backed up to the driveway next to the lovebirds' room. I could only see the right side of the car since it was being filmed by our right rear camera. I looked out of boredom, waiting to see who was going into the room next door and why they were backing in. The man went to the trunk of the car. I wondered what he could possibly have in the trunk that he was going to take to the room. I did notice it was a tan Camry sedan. My radar started to twitch.

As he came around the front door to lock his car, he had a mop, a bucket with some bottles in it, and a roll of paper towels tucked under his arm. No woman or man came around the other side of the car. Oh well, time for housekeeping to show. Guess a place like this had twenty-four-hour cleanup. I couldn't shake a weird feeling, though. I had the inner radar going off, but what was not right?

When I get that feeling, I have to move, do something, or my thoughts consume me. I told Gafford I was going to go talk to the clerk at the front desk and to keep an eye on the room next door to the lovebirds' den. If anything strange happened, he was to call me ASAP.

I knocked on the plexiglass window. In a minute, a bored-looking college-aged kid shuffled up to the window, took off his headphones, and languidly asked what room I was interested in.

I had a one-hundred-dollar bill in my pocket and showed it to him. He did not look impressed; in fact, he yawned.

"Whadaya want, mister?"

"Just some information, kid." I held up the C-note.

"Mister, do you know how many times I have been offered money for information? Really? A C-note? You are going to have to do better than that."

I got a whiff of the air coming through the partition. "I will be right back." I went to Mother. "Hey, Gaff, I need some of your medicine."

"My Sour Diesel? No way, dude. I get this straight from Colorado."

"Come on, man. I know you have a big stash, and you carry at least ten joints in that metal cigarette case. I need it to get some info from the desk clerk, and money won't motivate him."

"You got to make this up to me, man. I don't like parting with my medicine."

"I will. Now let me have three of them."

Gafford reached in his cargo shorts and pulled out the metal cigarette case and extracted three perfectly rolled joints. He looked wistfully at them like he was saying good-bye to a friend and stuck out his hand to hand them to me.

"That's good, my amigo. They are going for a good cause."

"What better cause than my well-being and karmic balance, dude?"

"You will be fine. We both know there's many more than this in your stash."

"Okay, okay, go before I regret this."

"Do me favor and call Mrs. Pavarro and tell her we will have all the evidence she needs and it will be on tape."

I went back to the window and knocked. Lazy boy shuffled up and looked as disinterested as before.

"I have something for you, but you have to let me in."

"Sorry, sir, I can't let you in. It's after hours."

I slipped one joint through the partition. The kid's eyes lit up like a Christmas tree. He picked it up and smelled it and looked at me and blinked. "Holy fuck, what is this? I have never smelled shit like this before."

"They call it Sour Diesel, and it comes from Colorado. I have two more, but you have to let me in."

The kid could really move fast when he wanted to. He opened the door and let me in before putting the lock on.

"I don't want any trouble. I am just trying to keep my nose clean, pay my tuition."

"What's your name, kid?" He was about six foot three, wiry, had a mop of red hair and freckles.

"Robbie, sir. What do you want to know about the couple in the champagne room?"

"How do you know I want to ask you about them?"

"Come on, mister. I have been working here for a year. I can see an affair a mile away, and of course, what follows an affair but a private detective. Do you know how many times I get offered a bribe to get a copy of a credit card slip from those stupid enough to pay for the room that way or to leave a master key outside so they can bust in the room and take pictures or evidence?"

"I guess you are right, so I will get to the point. The gentleman paid cash, right?"

"Yes, sir."

"Does he tip you well enough for you to forget what he looks like should you be deposed?"

"As a matter of fact, he does every time he uses us, not because he wants me to have amnesia but because he leaves a real mess. The room smells like piss. We had to steam the carpet the last time. He is not like the gentleman in room D, the dungeon. He doesn't tip, but he leaves the room cleaner than we do."

"I am surprised he leaves it cleaner than your people do. I have never seen housekeeping work so late."

"We don't have housekeeping late. Are you kidding? Our rush hour is from 10:00 p.m. to 5:00 a.m. The management would never stop to clean a room during those hours. It's one quickie after another. We have plastic sheets on all the beds, and after checkout, one of us goes in and changes the sheets and towels for the next go-round. In the morning, we get the cleaning ladies in here. They do all the heavy lifting."

My radar was going off, almost like a dull ache.

"Okay, kid, please explain to me why I saw a guy go into the room next to the lovebirds with a mop and bucket at this time of the night."

"Oh, that's got to be Mr. Julio. He is a regular, stays with us for a couple of days. He is the one who leaves the room spotless, and management loves him."

"What does he sound like?"

"I don't know. He makes arrangements with the late shift, pays in advance, and in cash, from what I heard."

"You've never talked to him?"

"No, sir. I work the morning shift. Tonight I'm filling in as a favor. From what I heard, he stays two to three days, no more."

"Kid, listen to me. Stay inside. If anything happens, don't go outside, don't be curious. Cops will be here soon."

"No shit. For an affair, really? For sure, man."

"No, kid, not an affair, something a lot worse if my instincts are correct."

I called Gafford. "Hey, just do as I say and get Nate on the phone and tell him to get down here. Just say we have a solid lead on the strangler he needs to see. I am going around the back of the car to see what the license plate number is and see if we have a match. Stand by."

Gafford called Nate's office and cell number. Both went to voice mail, so he left the same message on both. He was watching the rear camera and saw Jose's shadow coming along the parking lot toward the car in driveway D. The resolution was great with the night-vision program. He looked down at his controls and made sure he was recording.

Jose had to walk up the driveway to get to the back of the car since the hedge would not let you go around to the rear. Gafford could not take his eyes off the screen. The car was backed up almost to the door, so Jose had to bend down to see the number. Gafford saw a sliver of light behind Jose coming from the door before he was blinded by the light coming from the suddenly opened door. Less than a minute later, he heard a horrific crash. It took him a few moments to get his eyes adjusted. When he looked at the monitor, all he saw was the empty parking spot and Jose slumped on the ground.

CHAPTER 53

Jose was trying to figure out how to get to the back of the car to see the license plate without being seen. With the hedge down the sides of the parking space, the only way was to just go straight back and read it. There was no way to hide or sneak or use shadows to keep from being noticed. All he was hoping for was that no one would look out from the room. He checked his holster and took the strap off for easy access. When he reached the back of the car, he heard some glass crunching under his feet and was glad he was wearing his Frye boots. He saw a sliver of light coming from behind him and felt stupid because he knew the glass had given him away. As he started reaching for his gun and turn toward the door, he heard a crackle and felt a sharp pain in his arm before he blacked out.

Gafford grabbed his cell phone and jumped out of the side door while hitting the key fob to arm Mother's security system. He was running toward the motel around the block because of the damn hedge when his phone rang. It was Nate.

"This better be good. I was on a date with a Miami Heat dancer, my friend."

Gafford was not in the best shape of his life. He was breathing heavy and had to slow down to talk. "Get down to the Trail Motel. I think we spooked the strangler. Jose is in trouble, hurry!"

"Motherfucker, what are you two amateurs doing following the strangler? You were supposed to call me first. If Castillo has screwed the pooch on this, the both of you are going to be spending a nice long time in Raiford."

"It was pure luck, Nate. It happened so fast. I did call you, so lay off me, dude." Gafford stopped, took three deep breaths, and hung up on Nate. He'd never talked to Nate like that before.

He walked around the corner and saw that two cars were involved in a head-on collision at the entrance of the motel. One of the cars was on fire, and people were trying to put it out with rags and towels, but to no avail. Gafford heard the sirens from far away and wondered if they could get there in time. It looked like an SUV had barreled into the motel as the Camry was trying to exit. The SUV went over the hood of the Camry and had caved the windshield into the cab. The driver of the Camry was surely crushed, seeing as how the SUV's front bumper was up against the front seats. If he wasn't dead already, the fire would surely kill him.

To Gafford, it looked surreal, and he wondered if he was tripping. The SUV was also on fire, and soon the people trying to put out the fire just stood back and gawked. He walked around the back of the SUV to get through the entrance to Jose when he saw the vanity plate on the SUV. It read Pavarro-2. He had to be hallucinating. What was Mrs. Pavarro doing here? He talked to her a short time ago and told her all was good and she would have her proof. He thought he was in a Kafkaesque dream.

Gafford was walking toward Jose when he saw him stir and sit up while holding his head. Jose was shaking his head like trying to loosen the cobwebs. Gafford was so relieved that his black humor came out. "Glad I don't have to plan your funeral. I wouldn't know the proper protocol for seating your ex-wives. Oldest to newest or meanest to sweetest. I'd have to consult Ms. Manners."

"Oh, goody. I wake up with a headache like I've never had, and you have turned into a comedian."

"Shocking, isn't it?" Gafford couldn't believe he said that.

"No, no, no you didn't go there, did you? No shocking, electricity, or zapping jokes, amigo, or you are going to be sent to the comedy corner in the Grove. Help me up. I don't know whether to shit or go blind."

"Glad you are okay, Jose. Our friends didn't turn out so good. The suspect is probably dead, and Mrs. Pavarro is toast, literally." Gafford could not believe what was coming out of his mouth; he needed a smoke.

"Mrs. Pavarro? What the fuck is she doing here? I asked you to call her, not to tell her where we were. Was she following us?"

"I don't know. I called her, and I guess she knew the gig was up, so she probably came to cause a scene and embarrass him. Based on the speed she was coming into the entrance, she was one hot Latina lady. Unfortunately for our suspect, he was in such a hurry to get away from you that he was hauling ass too."

"My friend, you are either naïve or not cynical enough to know how the female mind works, especially a hot-blooded Latina. They are normally jealous when they exit the womb."

"Wow, JC. After hearing that, I am glad I am not cynical enough."

"So you told her where we were, huh? Never thinking she would show up."

"I didn't tell her. She knew what restaurant. She must have followed us. Sorry, JC. Hope it does not fuck up my karma."

"It won't. You didn't drive her here. She did it of her own volition."

"Thanks, dude. I feel better about it, as sick as that sounds."

"Have you seen our lovebirds?"

"They peeked out of the window. Guess they are preparing their stories. We'll see them shortly, no doubt."

"Well, let's get ready for an all-nighter of Q and A with every department Metro-Dade brings out to this clusterfuck. Any Cuban coffee around?"

"I'll go get some. Go take a breather and get recharged." As soon as that came out of his mouth, Gafford knew he had to spike one up. He was losing it.

"Recharged? Really? Get the hell out of here and go light one up."

"Oh, for sure. I need to calm down, or I am going to keep babbling nonsense. See you in a few minutes. I am not looking forward to the circus that is coming."

"Yeah, see if you can find some peanuts and Cracker Jacks. It will fit right in with the circus."

Gafford was glad Jose's sarcasm was showing; it was a sign he was coming back around.

CHAPTER 54

I checked my phone for e-mails, texts, or voice mails since I knew the crime scene was going to be a long ordeal. Gafford and I were probably going to be held until the wee hours of the morning. There was an e-mail from Kat with her flight information. I forwarded the info to Lesson's phone while making a mental note to call him and walk him through the process. I called Chris and Chini to tell them to call off the search from their end. They wrote back that they were going to the Magic City Casino and try their luck at the poker tables. I did the same with the Sanchez brothers. They wanted details, so I told them to wait for details.

I called Lesson and told him what to do: call the limo service to pick him up and go get Kat at the airport and get her to her boat safely. I told him that I did not want her taking a taxi. Kat's home was a fifty-four-foot Beneteau Oceanis sailboat that was docked at Dinner Key Marina in Coconut Grove. It was her home when she wasn't at my place. This boat was a monohull cruiser with only eight feet of draft, small for such a big boy. Equipped with a diesel engine for backup, it had more amenities than the Ritz in Paris. We had taken it out many times to the Keys, Naples, and most of the islands in the Caribbean. Besides being a luxury yacht it was also nice to use the sails to keep the carbon footprint down. There's nothing like the only sounds you hear while you are moving is that of the sails flapping and the rustling of the wake you leave behind. It's peaceful being on that boat, to say the least—a stress reliever for sure.

Gafford was walking up carrying a tray with some Styrofoam cups, which I was hoping had Cuban coffee in them. I saw some cigars sticking out of his shirt pocket. Nate was walking next to him with a scowl on his face.

"Hey, amigo, nice to see you. You brought Cuban coffee, cigars, and a churlish detective. Let the fun begin."

"I am in no mood for your sarcasm, Castillo. You and your Dr. Watson here would fuck up a one-car funeral procession. I'll take one of those coladas and a cigar if you don't mind."

Gafford had Cuban coffee, much like a cappuccino. The Romeo and Julieta cigars were a nice touch. It was going to be a long night.

"No need to jump all over our ass, Nate. We were following a husband for a client when the guy in the Camry showed up. If it wasn't for us, you would have nothing, and this guy would have sterilized the room and be on his way. I am sure Gafford filled you in on what happened. Was the tag number the correct one?"

"Churlish? Don't be using them fifty-dollar words on me, Jose. I am just a grinder of a detective with a little bit of college."

"Cranky, cantankerous, pissy—what do you want me to use on you?"

"Whatever. The first two of the tag matched what we had. The car matched the sedan and color, baby seat in the back—it all fits. And unfortunately, the suspect is deep-fried. We had no DNA anyway, and we have no one to identify him, so it's a good guess it was him. I have Buck checking the times he rented here versus the times the girls were killed. I am sure the times will match."

"I think you owe me and Gaff an apology, and let's talk about the reward money."

"I'll think about the apology. I'll probably have a press conference with you two amateurs as the heroes. The mayor will love it, and the press will eat it up like Kobayashi at a hot-dog-eating contest."

"Holy cow, Nate. That's an obscure cultural reference, and you say you are just a grinder with a little bit of college. I think not. You are deeper than you appear to be."

"Keep it to yourself, JC. Now you will be in for a long night. Buck will take your statements, and we'll talk reward later. FDLE will be here for the same. I will leave shortly. I am meeting the Homeland grunts."

"What do you have to meet them for?" I was curious.

"Nothing at all. There's rumors that some radioactive material is going to be smuggled into Miami from some island. Don't know which island, when, or where, but soon, and it could be in a suitcase or trunk, nothing bigger. And you didn't hear it from me."

Gafford looked at me with arched eyebrows. I shook him off, glad Nate didn't catch that.

"Okay, Nate. We will cooperate, be nice, answer all the questions. Let me know when the forensics come in on this one. Meanwhile, good luck with the husband and adulteress in that room over there. He is the husband of the crispy-fried lady in the SUV."

"Motherfucker, what a clusterfuck. Well, I guess if you weren't following them, you never would have seen our subject. Thanks. See you later, boys."

CHAPTER 55

Lesson had called a limo service to pick him up first and take him to the airport to pick up Kat. It was his first ride in a limo not work related. He liked it, and he was looking at the bar to see what it had for drinks. He heard a crackle over a speaker, and the driver's voice came through. "Please feel free to drink anything. It's complimentary and part of our service."

"Oh gosh, thanks, mister. I think I will pass." Lesson was nervous enough already he did not want to appear clumsy or make a fool of himself.

"No problem, sir. When we get to the international terminal, I will drop you off. I will be in the limo area. When you bring your friend out, call my cell phone, and I will come around and pick you up."

"Sure thing, mister. I will call right away." Lesson was getting ready to step out as the limo was pulling up to the curb.

The intercom buzzed again. "I can come around and get your door."

"No need to, mister. I am okay. See you in a little bit." Lesson stepped out of the car. He saw people looking at him and got a little self-conscious. He didn't want to disappoint anyone hoping to get a glimpse of a movie star or a famous athlete. It was just him. He picked up his gait a little.

He stood at the gate with the limo drivers who were waiting for their fares. He didn't need a card with Kat's name on it. He was happy about that.

Lesson saw Kat trudging down the concourse and got as close to the exit ropes as he could. He saw she was pulling two suitcases on wheels and had a duffle bag draped over her shoulder.

Kat saw Lesson and smiled. She didn't wave because she had her hands full. She was wearing jeans, cowboy boots, and a T-shirt that had the University of Miami logo on it. All of this topped off with a straw cowboy hat.

"Lesson, you are a sight for sore eyes. Thanks for picking me up."

"Anything for you and the boss, Ms. Kat." Lesson grabbed both suitcases. "Oh, wait, I have to call the limo man." He dialed and said they were coming out.

"A limo for lil' ol' me? I feel important."

"Ms. Kat, the boss he says you are very important, and I need to be his eyes when he is not around."

"Well, thank you, Lesson, much appreciated."

They stepped out to the curb. The hot air bouncing off the asphalt and the humidity was palpable.

"Goodness, I keep forgetting how humid it is here. At least in the islands, you have a breeze coming off the Atlantic." Kat took her hat off and ran her hand over her forehead, which was damp already. Her hair was tied up in a bun on top of her head. She fanned herself with the hat.

A limo pulled up to the curb, and the trunk opened automatically. Lesson went to the trunk to put the suitcases in while Kat stepped into the limo. Lesson closed the trunk and stepped into the limo, where he saw a look of fear in Kat's face. He saw two men who looked familiar sitting in the opposite seats. Both had guns with silencers on their lap. There was a third man who was sitting up front next to the driver.

"Come in, come in, Lesson. We are taking a little ride to the beach. Now I need both your cell phones and your laptop, Miss. My name is Sergei, and I have been asked to escort you to Mr. Volkov's office."

Lesson was thinking where he had seen this man. It took him a minute to figure it out. "I seen you around the club."

"Correct, my slow friend. I do special projects all over the world for Mr. Volkov. You and the young lady happen to be the current special project."

Kat was sitting straight up with her hands clasped on her lap. It was hard to tell whether she was meditating or getting ready to pounce.

Kat looked at Lesson. He looked back at her and was cracking his knuckles. He was starting to breathe a little heavier. She looked straight at him and shook her head and motioned her palms down. Lesson immediately relaxed and sat back in the seat.

Kat turned to Sergei. "I am sure you want to deliver us in one piece. You have us outnumbered and outgunned, so let's make it a nice ride. No more comments about anyone being slow, no need to be insulting. I am sure your IQ is not in the top 50 percent, seeing as what you do for a living takes more brawn than brains."

"So no insulting comments, Miss, but you are commenting on my intelligence."

"We have a saying here in America, Boris. Can't stand the heat, get out of the kitchen."

"It's Sergei, not Boris."

"See, you get it. It's not nice being condescending. Now be a nice chap and pour me some champagne."

"You American women are so bossy. No wonder your men order brides from Mother Russia," he said that with so much disdain that he practically spat out the words.

"The men from America that order brides from Russia or any-where for that matter couldn't get laid in a whorehouse with a fistful of hundred-dollar bills."

"Bah, Ivan, pour some champagne for this bitch. I won't give her the satisfaction of serving her."

Lesson twitched in his seat. Kat looked at him and shook her head slightly. "All in good time, my friend."

The limo was coming off the 112 Expressway heading east. Kat could see the curtains of glass, steel, and cement that made Miami Beach. Giant towers stretching from the south to the north on a sliver of sand and limestone so delicate that she wondered if the ris-ing sea level would swallow it in her lifetime or in her young nieces' and nephews' lifetime.

She took a deep breath, swallowed the last of her champagne, and wondered where Jose was and what all of this had to do with him. Lesson was looking a bit nervous. She reached and squeezed his hand. "It will turn out okay, my friend. Not to worry."

"Ah, Ms. Kat, boss trusted me to get you home safe. I failed. I sorry."

"It's not your fault, Lesson. There is no way you could have prevented this. It is what it is, and I am still safe, aren't I?"

"Safe for the moment, bitch." It seemed like Sergei was smiling and snarling at the same time.

CHAPTER 56

Lesson and Kat were ushered into Volkov's office and told to sit on the sofa. They were told Volkov would be with them shortly. Kat couldn't help but notice the view. It was spectacular. You could see all of Downtown Miami, the Port of Miami, the bay, the coast guard base, the cruise ships, and of course, tower after tower of condos and hotels stretching toward the north on the beach.

A moment later, Volkov made a grand entrance through double doors. He was dressed in an all gray suit with a vest and a pocket watch. Very dapper, Kat thought. It had to be a Savile Row suit.

"My dear Katrina and Lesson, I am so sorry for this intrusion." He was walking toward them with his hands stretched out like pleading for mercy.

"Listen, pal, I have never met you, so stop acting like a long lost friend. What you seem to have done is to kidnap us."

Volkov laughed like a man who is used to getting his way. "My dear, I am not kidnapping you. I am treating you and Lesson to a short vacation down to my compound in Roatán."

"Roatán, the island off Honduras? Are you kidding?" Kat stood up and put her hands on her hips.

"I don't need no vacation. I am just fine." Lesson stood up, looking confused.

"Lesson, we are going on this trip, whether we want to or not. Right, *dear*?" Kat dragged out the *dear* part while staring at Volkov.

"Ah, a woman with…how do you say it here? Spunk?"

"Yeah, sure. We don't roll over here, pal."

"Here is the situation. I have a deal that I am doing. Your fiancé, Mr. Castillo—Castle or whatever he calls himself—has been snooping around my business due to his misguided loyalty to this gentle giant. However, I believe that Lesson might have mistakenly overheard my plans, and to make matters worse, your fiancé thinks I mean to harm this man. So I have to take precautions because even though I do not know what Lesson and Castillo know, I cannot or will not take any chances with my operation. So you and Lesson are my chits while my operation is in progress."

"It must not be legal if you are taking extreme measures to protect your so-called operation." Kat was pacing to the glass windows and back.

"My dear, what is illegal here might not be in other parts of the world. Your country is so paranoid since 9/11. I could be bringing in the cure for cancer, and they would probably shoot me at the border."

" I seriously doubt you are being so benevolent, especially if you don't want Jose in your business. You have no idea who you are messing with."

"Oh, famous last words, my dear. If I had a Euro for every time I've heard that, I'd be a millionaire. But wait, I am a millionaire many times over." Volkov laughed maniacally. "I have inquired into Castillo. I have been told he is like a pit bull. He is honest and incorruptible but will bend the rules according to some bizarre code of honor that he and only he knows the coda for. Like Galahad, he is so antiquated he should be in a museum somewhere."

"You don't think he will come at you with everything he has at his disposal?"

"I know of his military background. I even know things you don't know, my dear. I know about his lost years when he was off the grid and either in a monastery or being a gun for hire. I know he will come for you and after me. That's part of my plan. Keep your enemies closer. I want to know where he will be. That way, my operation won't be compromised. He is so predictable. He will come."

"In a monastery, really, gun for hire, Jose?" Kat was stunned.

"Ah, see what money gets you, knowledge and secrets. Knowledge is power, and power is everything, my dear—everything. You and Castillo can catch up when you are sharing a bungalow in my jungle compound. Let's head downstairs. Time to take flight."

CHAPTER 57

Buck had just finished organizing his notes from the witnesses when he walked over to Nate, who was leaning on the trunk of his police-issue Dodge Charger. He was smoking a Black & Mild wood-tip wine-flavored cigar. He was looking at the wisps of smoke that he was exhaling as they floated up into the sky. He had an envelope in his hand.

"Okay, boss, I've got everything wrapped up, and everyone has been sent away with notices to be at our beck and call. Anything interesting in that letter, boss?"

"Not a damn thing, son. I want to run the contents by the Homeland team. Meanwhile, just enjoying the calm after the storm, the dance of the smoke as it floats and dissipates. Like souls leaving the body and this earth, if you believe in that shit."

"Geez, boss, just when I think you're not so gruff and tough. Thought there was a light at the end of the tunnel there."

"Only light at the end of the tunnel is a freight train coming without brakes, and the train engineer is dead from a heart attack."

"That's the Nate I know, glass half full, and it's full of poison."

Nate chuckled. "Guess I am a bit jaded after twenty years of this horseshit. What do you have for me?"

"Pretty open and shut. The perp caught Jose snooping, zapped him, panicked, tried to hightail it out of the driveway when the lady whose husband was in the room next door was rushing in herself and thus the crash, the fire, the charred bodies and cars."

"How is the husband doing?"

"He shed some alligator tears, appears to be remorseful, but, I hate to say, looks relieved."

"How's the hottie?" Nate lit another cigar.

"Not too well. Looks like the weight of the world is on her shoulders."

"What is she, about twenty-five?"

"Twenty-eight. She works as a pharmaceutical rep, so hence the connection with Pavarro Pharmacy."

"I am not in the mood to smooth it over and try to make her feel better. She can hire a shrink for that. Let's wrap it up, make sure all agencies that have been working with us on this get an update."

"I will do two updates: one on the current situation and one after forensics are in. CSI is going over the room for DNA. After that, they will go through the trunk of his car. The fire was put out before it reached the trunk, where all the cleaning supplies were stored. Should be a treasure trove of evidence. Apparently, our boy was going in there to sterilize the room. Seems he did that every time he rented here, one reason the management liked him so much, literally letting him get away with murder. He didn't get to clean up this time, thanks to JC and Gafford. Interesting coincidence he was doing surveillance here at the same time.

"Yeah, Buck, timing is everything, right place, right time. I was hard on those two. I should thank them when I get a chance. Call me if you need me. I am heading to the office to meet the Homeland guys then home to get some rest."

"Okay, boss. Will let you know when the reports are in."

Nate felt his phone chime in with a text. It was from JC. All the text showed was: "Call me 911." JC rarely used that unless it was important.

CHAPTER 58

Jose and Gafford had stopped at the Latin American cafeteria on Coral Way for breakfast after hours of tedious interrogation by the Metro-Dade teams. Jose ordered toasted Cuban bread, ham croquettes, and an empanada. Jose had chosen ham today. Gafford had a Spanish omelet but asked that the chorizo be left out. Both had ordered orange juice, which—in most Cuban cafeterias, bakeries, and coffee shops—is freshly squeezed.

"Have you heard from Kat?"

"You know, Gaff, I was so rattled by the stun gun and then the hours of redundant questioning by the cops that I totally forgot. When I did remember an hour or so ago, I figured she was fast asleep from her trip, so I didn't want to wake her. Strange, I haven't heard from Lesson. He is pretty good about checking in. We'll be there in ten minutes anyway, so not to worry."

JC and Gafford pulled up to the shop and noticed all was quiet when they went in. They had to turn off the alarm, which told them there was no one there. He called both Lesson's and Kat's cells with both calls going directly to voice mail. He texted both with no answer coming after five minutes. He called Chris and Chini, and they had not heard from them either. JC called the limo company, and they said their driver had not checked back in, and they could not raise him on the radio or cell.

"Gafford, go fire up the computer in Mother. Check to see if any of Volkov's companies filed any flight plans in the last twenty-four hours. Also, turn on the GPS that you put in Lesson's watch. You had looked into Volkov's holdings. Anything like a mansion or ranch within flight distance, say, in the Caribbean or Mexico?"

"I have some notes from earlier. Will get back to you in ten minutes—make that fifteen. I will ping Kat's and Lesson's cells and see if I get something."

"Good idea. Glad you are thinking. I am so tense I can't think straight."

"Hang in there, JC. There has to be a logical explanation."

"Gaff, you know I am not gloom and doom, but the only logical conclusion is that Volkov has them."

"Let's hope not, let's hope not. See you in a few."

Nate was calling; JC picked up right away.

"Nate, I need your help, and I have some information for you that I probably should have run by you earlier, but I didn't have proof, just speculation."

"Fuck me and the horse I rode in on, Jose. You need my help, and you have information you should have told me about sooner. Great, let me sit down for this one. I can't wait."

"Look, Nate, I did not have any proof, and I still don't, but things have escalated, and it's going to get out of hand."

"What do you have first? Then I will see if I can help you."

"Okay, okay. You see, Lesson works for Volkov, and he thinks he overheard him mention something about *seesum*, but you know Lesson is not all there, so it could be cesium, which is volatile but not too bad unless it's cesium 137, which is radioactive—"

Nate cut him off, "Motherfucker, son of a bitch, Judas H. Priest, go on."

"I think that's why Lesson's efficiency was blown up, Volkov thinking Lesson might have overheard his plans."

"Motherfucker, I swear I am going to lock you up as long as I can."

"Nate, I don't have any proof, my brother, but Kat is gone, and so is Lesson, and that is all I can think of. He's got them so he can protect himself, or he will use them as hostages to keep me from sniffing around his operation. I don't fucking know, and I am going insane over this. What was I going to tell you? About some plan I thought Volkov had with no proof?"

"I will call you right back. I have to make a call. What favor do you need?"

"I might need you to stall on this info for one hour. I have to get the team ready to go. I don't know where we are headed to yet but will soon. If I corner Volkov and need to squeeze him, I will need your help on that too."

"That's two favors. I will do what I can, no promises. Remember, I have no jurisdiction outside of Miami-Dade. I suggest you get going because after I talk to FDLE and Homeland, they are going to want to have a chat with you, and they will not take kindly to your stalling or tap dancing. Best of luck, amigo. Go get your girl."

"That is exactly what I aim to do."

Nate thought about the second envelope he found at the door-step of his condo. It had the same block letters, and it had SOMETHING BIG TO BE SMUGGLED IN, WILL KEEP YOU POSTED. He was wondering who was trying to tip him off. Whoever it was appeared to have the info that Jose had. Nate wondered if the person was making sure he got the same information. But why?

CHAPTER 59

JC called Chini and Chris and told them to head to the shop and to get their go bags ready. Gafford came in with his i-Pad. "Jose, here it is. Volkov's company filed a flight plan to Honduras. According to corporate documents, one of Volkov's holding companies owns a fish farm in Roatán, which is an island off Honduras. As soon as I get the coordinates, I will have my friends from spookville let me piggyback on their surveillance satellite when it flies over those coordinates, and I will get us a 3-D map of the area. Next flyover is in an hour. No news on pinging Kat's and Lesson's phones. Last time they were on was at South Beach. They were turned off shortly after that, and the GPS chip on Lesson's watch died after being an hour out of Miami, so it's either been found, or it could be out of range."

"Damn, man, thanks for your efforts. When you get the 3-D map, send it to my phone and to Mother. We can print and download on the way to the seaport."

"You mean airport, right, Jose?" Gafford was confused

"No, Gaff, we are taking an amphibious plane to Roatán. I am familiar with the island. We can land on the water and make our way in that way. They will never expect us to come in from the ocean."

"So we'll be dragging John Pinder into this?'

"Yes, Pinder's seaplanes have seen more unauthorized flights and off-the-grid excursions than you want to know. Pinder is an old friend. I owe him a lot, and he has flown into some places the CIA wouldn't dream of going in and out of. His kids are following in his steps. His daughter Coral now runs the company. The old man doesn't fly anymore since he hurt himself trying to fly me out of Nicaragua a few years ago."

"Nicaragua? I haven't heard that story. When was that, Jose? How did Pinder hurt himself?"

"In another life. One day over a stiff drink, I'll tell you. He took some shrapnel on that flight, flew us back with one eye working, one shut."

Jose's mind was racing. So much to think about: planning to rush in on a compound in a foreign country with no legal authorization, no advanced scouting or intel, hoping not to cause any danger to Kat or Lesson and praying they were not walking into an ambush. He was thinking about how life repeats itself sometimes. Different people, same scenario, hopefully better results.

The front-door sensor went off, and Chris and Chini showed up, went to get their gear, and loaded into Mother. Gafford and JC were in the office, turning off computers and getting their gear together too.

"Where are we headed to, Chief?" This from the ever-inquisitive Chris.

"Roatán. It's an island off the coast of Honduras. Kat and Lesson are not here. Their phones have been turned off, and their last location was South Beach. Kat's boat is in Biscayne Bay, and Lesson wouldn't be anywhere but here."

"I guess Volkov must really think Lesson overheard him. Why else would he take both of them?"

"Well, Chris, I heard from Nate that most law agencies have heard rumors of a shipment of radioactive material, so it all adds up to Volkov. Chini, any word from your girl on translations in the last day or two?"

Chini was preoccupied with something; it took him a few seconds to acknowledge the question. "No, nothing of interest, just basic business talk. If it was important, she would have said something."

"Okay, boys, let's get cracking. We'll go over what we have on the plane. Any questions?"

Chris piped up, "So we are going into a foreign country, no law enforcement behind us, no proof of a crime? We're armed to the teeth, and we are going to break into the private compound of one of the richest men in the world who also happens to be in the Russian Mafia?"

"Yes, that about sums it up, Chris. You might want to add we'll be outnumbered. We don't know the terrain, and we have no intel."

"Just checking, Chief. Calculating the odds, I'd say the over-under on us making it without being arrested or shot is three to one."

"Hey, remember we do have guile, experience, and the element of surprise on our side."

"Well, hell, Chief, I feel better now. Those bastards don't stand a chance."

"That's more like the Chris I know and love. How about you, Chini? How do you feel?"

"Ready, Chief, just like old times, ready to roll."

As they pulled Mother into the Miami Seaport, Gafford saw three men by the office with duffel bags at their feet.

"Who are those guys?"

"Oh, that's the Sanchez brothers. I figured we could use the extra bodies. Don't know if we are running into a skeleton crew or a small platoon at Volkov's."

"Shit, Chief, amateurs? C'mon."

"They served in Desert Storm, so they are not greenhorns. Except for the short one who is a hothead, they will follow orders. Don't worry. They will be between Chris and me as we get close to the compound. We'll station Chini on a high mound where he can pick anyone off who comes out of the woodwork."

"So that is it? You and I go in flanked by the three stooges with Chini as our insurance and Gafford manning communications?"

"That's it, my brother. If you are not with the program, let me know. That's the best plan under the circustances."

"C'mon, JC, you know I am there. It is what it is. You mean circumstances, right?"

"No, *circustances* it is. It's a fucking *circus* with the cesium, kidnapping, a megalomaniac billionaire, and the Russians thugs. Not to mention the Homeland boys will be up on our ass soon. And we could, of course, all land in a Honduran jail or even the friendly confines of a nice, warm federal penitentiary. So yeah, it's a circustance."

"Let's send the clowns in then, Chief." Chris started laughing at his own joke.

Old man Pinder came out of the office, shuffling on a cane, an eye patch on his right eye. He was older and heavier than when Jose had seen him last. "Jose, how are you, amigo?" he said in his Bahamian accent. He gave JC a bear hug.

"Damn, old man, you are getting along just fine. That caviar and champagne is doing you some good." Jose patted him on the back.

"Some good it's doing me. My one eye is shot, it's a shame. I am afraid it's going to be Kalik beer and conch salad for me, Jose. Got to keep my cholesterol down, doctor's orders. Sorry to hear about Kat."

"Well, that is what we are doing here. Going to find her."

"Who would do such a thing to that sweet girl? Whatever you need, Jose, you just ask."

"Long story, but the less you know, the better you'll be. We will discuss this when we get back over some conch chowder and cold beers. If any federals show up, just say we chartered to the Bahamas, okay?"

"Sure, I'll call my cousin Cecil in Nassau, and he'll say you guys pulled up and went fishing, which will buy you some time."

About this time, Coral Pinder stepped out of the office. The Sanchez boys straightened up, and Chris cleared his throat. She was six foot, one inch tall with milk-chocolate skin, green eyes, and legs that were muscular. She was wearing riding boots, tight gray slacks, and a tank top that was full, to say the least.

She walked up to Jose, kissed him, and hugged him. "Jose, long time, my friend. That girlfriend of yours come to her senses and throw you out yet?"

"Not yet, still got her fooled. But we have to go get her, and we are running out of time."

"I know. Papa briefed me. I have my baby fueled and ready to go. Come on, boys, let's load." She gave her father a kiss. "See you soon, Papa."

"Be careful, Coral. Don't worry about Jose. He might seem crazy, but he is not insane."

"I know, Papa. You've told me some stories."

"Only what I could, child, only what I could. Godspeed."

Coral's "baby" is a Bombadier 415 amphibious plane. It is used for fighting forest fires, marine search and rescue, and of course, transport. It can land on water or on dry land. It can scoop up 1,600 gallons of water in about twelve seconds. Cruising speed is 207 miles per hour and has a range of about 1,500 miles. She had "The Spirit of Miami" painted on the fuselage with a pink flamingo wearing sunglasses painted under the cockpit windows.

"Well, they'll think it's a convention of interior decorators or drag queens coming to Roatán when they see that plane."

"Chris, that baby can turn on a dime. It got her father and me out of Cuba in a jiffy back in '95. Besides, no one will see that plane. We are coming in and landing on the ocean and taking a Zodiac in."

"What the hell were you doing in Cuba in '95, JC?"

"Long story. One of these days, amigo."

"Geez, you think you know someone. You are an enigma, paisan."

Coral had gone through her preflight checklist before the group had arrived, so all she had left to do was to prime the two Pratt & Whitney Turboprops. "Lock and load, boys. We are moving out in one minute. No in-flight meal or stewardess today," she said over the intercom.

Everyone was checking and rechecking equipment. Gafford was setting up a dual-screen setup on his laptop. Jose passed out the Gentex communication gear. "Our comm system will be tied in to Coral, so keep chatter to a minimum. She will land four miles away, glide in to two miles, and we'll raft it in from there. Gaff will have a 3-D screen set up shortly, and we will go over our positions when we are airborne."

The plane shifted when they heard over the intercom, "Belly up, gentlemen, belly up," as Coral slid her baby on the water and pointed the nose east on Government Cut.

CHAPTER 60

Meeting at Nate's office were Susan Schliff of the FDLE, her assistant Lazaro Gomez, and the two men from Homeland. Nate had called them together without divulging much. He was hoping they thought it had to do with the Tamiami strangler.

Nate looked at his watch; it was about an hour since Jose has asked him to stall. "Ladies and gentlemen, it has come to our attention through some street-level confidential informants that in the next few hours, we might have a lead on the smuggling of the cesium."

At this mention, the two Homeland guys stood up and tensed up. One reached for his cell phone and stepped into the hallway. Schliff shifted in her chair and was paying rapt attention.

"I need those informants in here as soon as possible," said the shorter of the Homeland guys; Nate remembered he was the one named Wesson.

Nate stood up. "You don't understand. These are unsubstantiated rumors. As soon as I have proof, we will act on it, not before."

"We can scan your communications and pick out who is contacting you and bring them in, Detective."

"You guys are still working out of room 641A?"

"Very good, Detective, but room641A is old-school compared to what we have now. Room641A was ahead of its time, but the technology is so advanced we are years ahead of that. We are working on Black Chamber II."

"Black Chamber II—damn, I remember reading about that. That was one of the original surveillance ops, wasn't it?"

"Yes, it was, Detective. A bit of nostalgia naming the latest surveillance program after one of the originals."

Schliff stood up and crossed to the window overlooking Downtown Miami. "When you gents get done talking about black ops and NSA surveillance projects, let me know."

Nate walked to the center of the room, "Here is the deal. As soon as I have evidence of anything, you will know. After all, I will need help from both of you once we know where the point of entry will be. Whoever contacted me left me the info in the form of a letter, so don't waste your time gleaming through my phone or e-mails. There is nothing written down on any electronic device or communication. Just plain paper and pencil, more on that in a minute, so be ready to move once I call you. I do not know at this time if it is coming in by air or sea."

Agent Smith had come in from the hallway and motioned Agent Wesson to him. They convened in the corner and were whispering to each other. Schliff walked up to Nate. "You have my cell. Call me when you need us. I have everyone on standby and ready to go, no furloughs. I will have birds at Opa-Locka airport, boats in the water from Key West to West Palm Beach. Highway Patrol is blanketing I-95 and US 1 for us. I like to plan ahead."

"Thanks, Susan, appreciate the backup. Go, I'll deal with Mutt and Jeff over there." Nate nodded toward the agents.

"Good luck with those arrogant pricks."

Nate walked over to Smith and Wesson and asked them to take a seat. "Look here, gents. Like I said, I do not have any evidence, just someone feeding me info on a rumor, and I need to emphasize that it's possible that something might break on this."

"Give us all the info you have. We'll decipher what is going on. Our forensic team can determine where and when it's coming from." Smith had a serious look on his face.

"Look here, my man. I get an envelope left on the windshield of my cruiser, one slipped under the office door and one at my condo. I had my forensic people go over them, and there are no prints or DNA evidence. Handwriting analysis did not come up with anything, and it appears the letter and envelope was put together in a secure, clean room."

"Nothing at all?" This from Wesson.

"Nothing, my Homeland friends. Here at Metro-Dade, we do have the latest equipment, so we are not far behind you guys as far as technology."

"Keep us informed. We have go teams on standby from Key West to Orlando. We have coordinated with FDLE, so we can cover any area within those locations in fifteen minutes." Wesson looked serious too.

"Do you guys ever relax and smile?" Nate couldn't help it. He also wanted to change the subject.

"Listen, Detective, we take our job seriously. There are a lot of dangers out there aimed at America," Smith said this as he crossed his arms.

"Not saying you don't, but you guys need to lighten up a bit. Any of you married?"

Smith and Wesson looked at each other. Smith spoke first, "No, just career-driven for me."

Wesson cleared his throat. "I am, but I am never home."

"Son, here is some advice. My first marriage was over because I was never home. Anytime you get a chance, go home and spend time with the wife and kids. No matter what you make or what pleasure you get defending your country, there is no replacement for familial love. I know both of you are young and want to climb up the ladder, but don't lose sight of family. Smith, you don't have a family, but don't be so blinded by devotion and ambition that you find yourself in twenty years in an ivory tower office with a great title but with no foundation of family or last-name legacy."

"What do you mean by last-name legacy?' Smith looked puzzled.

"Do you have any brothers?" Nate was glad he had broken through a little.

"No…ah, I see, no one to carry on the family name. Interesting, hadn't looked at it that way."

"Yes, whatever the last name might be." Nate chuckled.

Smith smiled too once he got it. "We are not allowed to say our real names. You know that."

"I know. Let's stay in touch, and I promise to keep you posted."

"We'll be around. Promise that too." Wesson smiled back.

Nate wondered how long it would take for them to try to tap his phone if they hadn't done it already.

CHAPTER 61

Coral switched on her intercom. "Gentlemen, we will be in our target area in ten minutes. I will land four miles away, float in two miles, and drop you off there. I will float back out to the other side of the island and wait to hear from you. I will turn on the green light by the cargo doors when it's time to get off."

"I'd like to get off on that gal." Chris chuckled.

"Turn off your mic next time, you horny bastard." Coral heard every bit of that.

Chris hit the top of his forehead with his palm. "Stupido."

Everyone laughed. It was an unintended tension reliever.

"Okay, everyone, last-minute equipment check, comm, weapons, magazines. You Sanchez boys handle the Zodiac, and we will jump in once you have it set up."

Jose looked at Gafford, who was as white as a ghost. "Hey, Jim, deep breath, pal. You just stay back and track our movements, see if you can get your buddies at spookville to hook up on their satellite feed. It's going to have to be the infrared scan since it will be dark by the time we get there."

"S-s-suuure, JC, will do, just never done anything like this. I will try to scan the place for any alarm or security system and see if I can override it. If I cannot get the satellite feed, I do have a drone in my package with infrared cameras that I brought as backup."

"Good, man, glad you thought of that." Jose patted Jim on the shoulder, hoping that would calm him down a bit.

"Okay, gents, we've gone over our positions. Jim on comm and surveillance, Chini will be on the hill and will be our safety valve. The Sanchez brothers will be next in line backing me and Chris who will try to penetrate first. Once we get in, if need be, the brothers will follow us for backup or fuckups, hopefully the former and not the latter."

"Guess we don't shoot unless they shoot first, right, JC?" Chris was just checking the orders.

"Let's try to sneak in first. If we take fire, we fire back. I don't know about law enforcement in the area. I am sure they will investigate a full-blown firefight. So in that case, let's use silencers, and we will adjust to the circumstances."

"You mean circustances, right?" Chris, ever the smart-ass.

"Touché, my brother, good point. You got me there. Okay, everyone, cell phones off, just the comm unit on. Get ready to roll."

Chini went to switch his phone off but noticed a message from his girl. He opened it up and was staring at a picture.

"Hey, Chini, I said cell phones off."

"Yeah, okay." Chini was staring out into space like he'd seen a ghost.

The red light on the cargo door started blinking faster, which meant in two minutes, the green light would go on. Everyone double-checked their packs, slings, batteries, and magazines. Night goggles were readied, and all they needed was to be switched on.

They felt the plane gently land on the water and glide slowly.

"Man, that gal can sure fly, can't she?" Gafford was looking a bit less nervous.

"Just like her daddy, smooth as silk." Jose nodded

"Bet her legs are smooth as silk." This from horny Chris.

"Guess you forgot about the com being on again," Coral's voice came over the headphones.

Chris's face was turning red. "Ay, que stupido."

Jose stood up. "All right, kids, get ready. It's showtime. Line up and fall out."

The red light stopped flashing, and the green light went on. The cargo doors opened, and the Sanchez brothers rolled out the Zodiac. Chini and Gafford rolled next with Jose and Chris last. All jockeyed for seating on the Zodiac and headed toward the shoreline.

It was a cloudless night with a large moon and plenty of humidity. The trolling motor was quiet but slow. It was good that there were no waves and the ocean was as smooth as a plate.

Jose wondered what he had gotten his friends into, but it was something that had to be done, and he was glad all went along with the plan. He hoped no one on his team would get hurt or killed out of this mess. It would be all on him. He did not mind killing others in a combat situation, but he did feel a bit of guilt dragging his friends into this.

They cut the trolling motor half a mile away and started paddling toward the shore. Gafford had picked an inlet about a quarter mile from the compound. He was guiding the Zodiac toward that location. All went smooth as they rolled with the surf, and in what seemed like one motion, everyone was out of the inflatable and it was being carried into the sea grapes to be hidden.

Gafford turned on his laptop and pointed out where everyone was to station themselves. Chini was first about one hundred yards away from the compound. There was a knoll there he could set up his rifle with a scope on it. One hundred yards was child's play for him; he had a perfect score from a thousand feet at marksman school. The night was calm, and there was very little breeze, which would help with his target acquisition and trajectory calculations. Gafford stayed at this location too.

Next was a sand dune just to the right of the entrance to the compound, which was about fifty yards away. They dropped off the Sanchez brothers, and they spread out in a semicircle around the dune. It had taken a few minutes to get the boys situated there as the sea grapes and vegetation was a bit thicker the nearer it got to the compound.

Jose and Chris started working their way toward the compound slowly since they had to work around the dunes, the sea grapes, and the mangroves. They had worked their way to thirty yards from the front gate when a swath of light came from the compound wall, sweeping across the entire front of the compound.

"They didn't say anything about a searchlight, did they?" Jose whispered to Chris as they crouched behind a big sea grape tree.

"Don't remember that being on the brochure, bro," Chris whispered back.

All of a sudden, they heard the sound of bullets hitting the ground near them. They flattened out and hoped they were not using infrared binoculars from the compound. Jose whispered into the headset, "We are taking fire, looks like from in front of the main gate, can anyone pick them out and take out that searchlight? Chini? Anyone?"

Gafford's voice came over the headset, "Dude, Chini is gone—gone, man!" He was breathing heavy.

"What the fuck do you mean gone?" Jose wanted to yell, but he did not want to give their location away.

"He explained it to me, but I couldn't understand. He showed me a picture on his phone of some girl with a gun to her head, and he said to tell you, and you would hopefully understand." Gafford was almost hyperventilating.

Some more bullets hit the mangroves to their right, so Jose was relieved the shooters did not know their exact location and were just taking wild shots.

"Explain later. Right now we are pinned down, and our only safety valve has vanished. Give me a moment to think. Anything from your spook friends and the next satellite flyby?"

"Sorry, Jose, next flyby is in six hours. Too late to help us."

"Gawdalmighty, okay, here is what we will do. Sergio, can you take out the searchlight?"

"Consider it done, sir."

Five seconds later, the searchlight was out.

Coral's voice came over the headset, "I have an idea, Jose. Hear me out."

"Fire away, honey."

"I am already airborne as soon as I heard about your situation. I will be scooping up a load of water, will be there shortly. I will cut the engines about a quarter mile out, glide in the back way, and drop sixteen hundred gallons of water on that entrance. That will buy you some time. Do with it what you can."

"That sounds crazy, but at this point and if it works, I'll marry you."

"Jose, do not threaten me like that. Besides, you know we are here for your honey. Let's do it. Then I'll have war stories to tell my papa for a change."

Chris piped in, "If he won't marry you, I will."

Coral chuckled. "Typical man. He is in a bind and is still thinking of pussy. Paisan, if your dick is as big as your mouth, maybe we should talk after."

"Could you two get a room after we get out of here in one piece, please?" Jose sounded semiserious. "Coral, give me about a two-minute head start. We have some growth to get through."

"Will do. Throw a flare at the front gate when I give you the two-minute warning."

"Roger, will do. Gafford, stay put and just ride it out. If we do not make it back in thirty minutes, get in the Zodiac and have Coral pick you up and destroy everything you have on this trip. Brothers, work your way toward the front gate. Two of you go fifteen degrees left of our position, one of you go twenty degrees right of our position, wait for the flare, and head for the main gate. Copy?"

"Copy." This from one of the brothers.

"Gafford, do you copy?"

"Yes, yes, I do."

"Okay, then tell me if there is a side entrance I can use."

"Yes, there is a service entrance by the side road."

"Thanks. Okay, keep the chatter to a minimum. Good luck, guys. I will try the side, hope to see you all inside. Gafford, switch to channel two please."

Gafford did. "What, Jose?"

"What did Chini show you?"

"It was a picture sent to his phone of his girlfriend with a gun to her head."

"That's what he was looking at on the plane. Geezus, she is Russian, isn't she? Irina or something. Volkov must have his hooks in her. Holy shit, hard to believe Chini bailed on us, but I don't know if I wouldn't have done the same. Okay, back to channel one, thanks."

All they had to do now was wait for Coral's special delivery.

CHAPTER 62

Inside the compound, Kat and Lesson had been served dinner by themselves in a huge dining room. The decor was Disneyesque, Kat thought, because it reminded her of Fort Wilderness at Disneyworld. It looked like a safari outpost, which was funny because this was an island in the Caribbean Sea.

There was a big tiger rug in front of a huge fireplace and animal heads mounted on the walls. She thought Sambo and Bwana Johnny were going to appear any minute. But instead, it was Sergei and one of the goons. Oh joy, she thought.

"You two must finish now. We have to take you to your rooms."

Kat wasted no time in trying to get under Sergei's skin. "You wait. We are almost done with dessert." She slowly raised the spoon to her mouth. The crème brûlée was delicious.

"You come now. It's for your own safety." Sergei went to grab Kat's elbow, but she moved it away.

He had not noticed, but she had bent her spoon into the shape of a U and was holding it between her knuckles like a prod.

The next time he went to grab her arm, she swung at his face and aimed for his eyes with the spoon. He was too quick for her, and he grabbed her wrist and twisted until she screamed in pain. He then slapped her hard across the face.

Lesson was trying to jump out of his chair, but the goon was holding a stun gun near his neck.

"You bastard, hitting a woman." Kat's lip was bleeding.

"Trying to take my eye out, you deserve it, bitch. If Volkov did not give orders to keep you alive, I would have slit your throat and thrown you in the sea already."

"Big tough guy, we'll see, we'll see. Take us to our 'rooms,' which sure look like cells to me."

Lesson's face was red, and his fists were clenched. He had a look of frustration and despair.

Kat patted his shoulder. "Don't worry, big fella. We will all be okay soon."

"Yes, Ms. Kat, I be okay, just don't know why all of this is happening. Why is Mr. Volkov mad at us?"

"We will explain when this is all over. You hang in there."

As Kat was led into her room, there was a big noise that came from outside. She didn't know if it sounded like a water-filled balloon when it splatters, or when you flip over a bucket full of water from a second story, or when you hit the target on the dunk tank at the state fair. But it was a big *woooosh*.

Sergei pushed her in the room, locked the door, and started running toward the front of the compound.

CHAPTER 63

Everyone was in position, waiting to get the okay from Coral. The firing had stopped. Whoever was firing from the compound did not know where they were and had just taken random shots to see if they could get lucky and spook the group.

Over the comm set was Coral's voice, "One minute to flushing, boys. Give me a target in thirty seconds."

"Ten-four, fly pants. I'll set the flare for you." Chris, being the smart-ass.

"I got your fly pants right here, Mr. Mouth." Coral gave it right back.

"Be still, my Italian heart."

"You mean your horny heart."

The boys could see the shape of the plane in the moonlight coming in behind the compound. The lights were off, and it looked like a winged bird swooping in. It would take some flying to drop the load, fire up the engines, and hightail it out of there.

"On my mark, ten…nine…eight…seven…six…five…four… three…two….one. Showtime."

The men in front of the compound did not know what hit them; it was like a giant wave. As an added bonus, it knocked part of the front wall down. The boys scurried toward the entrance and quickly zip tied the guards who were either stunned or knocked out from the impact. They started to receive some fire from inside the building, so Chris motioned to the brothers to spread out. "Brother to my right, follow Jose in the side entrance and see if you can give us some cover from the side. We can't rush in right now. We'll be sitting ducks."

"Roger, sir." It was Sergio, the hotheaded brother.

As soon as Jose heard the water drop, he shot out the lock on the service entrance and made his way in. "Gaff, where do I turn?"

"Go through the kitchen and make a right. There is a row of what looks like rooms, start there. There is no basement, so that is your best bet."

Jose ran through the kitchen and made a right. "Kat, Lesson, where are you?"

He heard pounding on doors at the end of the hallway—with a muffled, "Here, here," behind one door and a loud pounding with, "Boss, boss," behind another door.

"Stand back, shooting the locks." Which Jose did with his Glock 45.

Kat rushed out and hugged Jose. "I knew you would come for me, papi."

Jose touched her swollen lip. "Who did this? Volkov?"

"No, papi, it was Sergei."

"I know who that is, canus vindictum."

"Every dog has its day, if I remember my Latin from high school."

"Yeah, something like that. You okay, Lesson?"

"Sure, boss, just confused."

"We'll explain later. Let's go, follow me."

Jose took them through the kitchen and showed them the side entrance. "Head in that direction. In about one hundred yards, there is a mound. Gafford is there. There's a Zodiac there, which will get us back to the seaplane. We have some unfinished business, so we will be back in about forty-five minutes."

"Do you have to?" Kat was holding on to Jose's shoulders, not wanting to let go.

"Yes, I have to. I need to see Volkov and end this."

"I don't think he is there, papi. I overheard he was going to Bimini to pick up something."

"No problem. I will get it out of someone. Besides, I have to have a talk with Sergei about slapping you around."

"Don't, Jose. It's over. You got us out. Let it go."

"Can't do that. I have to right a wrong and get to Volkov."

"Oh, Galahad. Volkov was right about you."

"Galahad? Is that a new boyfriend or something?"

"You're funny, papi. I'll explain later. Get back to me safe."

Jose kissed Kat on the forehead. "See you soon, love. Lesson, take good care of her. Get her to Gafford."

"Okay, boss."

Jose went through the kitchen and turned left toward the front of the house.

CHAPTER 64

Chris and the two brothers were at the front gate behind the partially collapsed wall and some trees. They were exchanging gunfire with what appeared to be two shooters.

It was going to be a war of attrition, whoever ran out of ammo or whoever had the wherewithal to take the other team out. That's why Chris had sent Sergio in the side to flank the team inside. "Let me know when you see the whites of their eyes, Sergio, and we'll open up on them, and you can take them from the side."

"Yes, sir. I have some help. I found some derelict named Jose coming through the kitchen at the same time."

"Watch that guy. He'll pick your pocket and say he's doing you a favor."

"Smart-asses, I'm surrounded by them."

"Nice to hear from you again, boss. You get the packages out?"

"Yes, on the way to Gafford's base."

"Good, let's take these guys out."

"On my mark, one, two, three, go!"

Chris and the brothers opened fire on the two sentries who where huddled behind sandbags in the driveway.

The two sentries fired back for about a minute when their firing stopped.

Jose's voice came over the comm, "Sentries out. Come in and sweep the outside. Let me know when all is clear."

"Roger. Good job, you two."

"Sergio, help with the sweep. I have to look for a rat in here."

"Sure you don't need backup, boss?"

"I am okay, want to do this myself."

Jose searched all the rooms and could not find Sergei. On his way out the front door, he saw one of the sentries who were zip tied by the front steps start to stir a bit. He dragged him up by his collar and sat him down. He took a knife out of its leg sheath and cut the zip ties. He put the knife back in the sheath and holstered his Glock.

Jose talked to him in Russian, "I mean you no harm. I just need to know where Volkov is."

At this time, Chris and the team came around to the front. "All clear, Chief, no sign of Volkov or his number one. We are clearing out. Shall I leave one of the boys with you?"

"No, Chris. Go and get set up to meet Coral. I will be there in ten minutes. Coral, if you copy, we'll need a pickup in twenty minutes."

"Okay, Chief, ten minutes, and we are out. You know the drill."

"Copy, See you in ten, and I won't be mad if you leave the Italian behind."

"She loves me, doesn't she?"

Jose shook his head. "Love and war, who would have thought?"

Jose spoke with the guard and found out that Volkov was not even on the island. He left for Bimini; that was all he knew.

So there it was. The exchange was in Bimini and just a sixty-mile trip to the southeast coast of Florida. He could land anywhere on the coast, Miami, Fort Lauderdale, West Palm Beach. Many smugglers brought in Cubans, Haitians, and Bahamians that way, pull them up to the shore, have them swim or wade in. Some cases, they dropped them off a mile offshore, not asking or caring if they could swim or not, with some dire consequences sometimes.

He told the guard to leave, and it would be best if he did not come back. The guard moved pretty fast out of the compound. Jose took a moment to light up a cigar. It was common practice after a mission to light one up.

He took a few puffs and started going down the steps when he felt his ankle being grabbed, and he tumbled down onto the driveway. He was mad at himself for letting down his guard; he should have known better. When he turned over, Sergei was standing over him with what looked like a long-barreled .357 Magnum.

"Well, mi amigo, looks like you are getting sloppy in your old age. Were you overconfident and thought I left?"

"You do have me at a disadvantage, I must admit." Jose tried reaching for his knife.

"Take the knife out and throw it to your left using your left hand. I can see you are right-hand centric."

Jose did as instructed. "May I stand up?"

"Nyet, mi amigo, just lie there while I bring you up to date. Volkov's plan was brilliant, kidnap the girl so you would come rescue her while he did his deal in Bimini, which should be taking place soon. Having the giant along was just bonus. Volkov was not sure the giant overheard his plans, but he could not chance it since this deal is worth over five million and will give Volkov a bigger profile in the circles he runs in."

"You mean the Vory?"

"Ah, very good, amigo. You've done your homework. Yes. The Vory."

"I am not your amigo, so let's get this over with."

"With pleasure. I will be collecting a nice bonus for killing you. Good-bye." As Sergei cocked the hammer, a red dot appeared on his chest, which stopped him in his tracks.

"You might want to do something about that stain on your chest," Jose said as he pointed to Sergei.

Sergei's eyes looked at the dot on his chest. "Wait, wait!"

Over Jose's earpiece came Chini's voice, "Sorry to let you down earlier. I hope this makes up for it."

"Only if you hurry up and squeeze that trigger, homey." Jose saw the dot rise to Sergei's forehead and his head explode a millisecond after that.

"Good shot. How many yards?"

"Only fifty, child's play for me."

"See you at the raft, brother. We'll talk later. Coral, you copy?"

"Yes, sir."

"Bring her in. You can come closer to the compound."

"Roger, see you in ten. Will get in a little closer since it appears there is no fire from the compound."

"No fire at all. That fire's been put out, thanks to you. Good job, girl, and way to think outside the box."

"Thanks, Jose, glad to be part of the team."

Chris piped in, "She can be on my team anytime."

"Buddy, keep it in your pants, will you? The girl must think you haven't been laid in years."

"Let her think that. She'll be surprised at the package."

Coral busted out laughing. "I hope the package is as big as he makes it sound."

"Okay, kids, let's make it out of here. You two get a room later, over and out."

CHAPTER 65

On the plane, everyone was relaxing in one way or another, except Jose, who was pacing up and down. "Gafford, check the coast guard for any patrols they might have out at this time. Also, does anyone know someone in Bimini we can talk to and trust?"

Lesson raised his hand. "Boss, I know Captain Billy who owns a charter boat there. When I go there on vacation, he takes me out deep-sea fishing."

"Small world. Let's try to raise him on a cell. Coral, have Papa try to raise him on shortwave or marine radio, whatever it takes. We need to know if Volkov has left yet and in what type of boat."

"Roger, sir. I estimate a three-hour flight to Bimini, and that is with the pedal to the metal. Any excess weight we can get rid of will lighten the load."

"Good idea, Coral. All I can think of is the Zodiac along with the trolling motor and battery that might help. Open the back. We'll dump it over."

"Done. Don't forget you have that excess Italian sausage back there. With the load of shit he carries, should save about three hundred pounds of weight."

"Hey, hey, take it easy on the Italian, eh?" Chris was smiling from ear to ear. He gave Jose the okay sign with his left hand then took his right index finger and put it through the ok sign.

"Geezus, we have to get you laid, man." Jose kept his mic on and went to sit next to Kat. "Listen, everyone, I do not know where this is going to wind up, but we have to intercept Volkov before he gets to Miami. I don't think he is the bomb type. He is probably selling the cesium 137 for a profit. It's the people he is selling to I'm concerned with. They have to meet up somewhere, and I think it will be out on the ocean."

Gafford cleared his throat. "JC, why don't we give Nate and his team the information? They are better equipped, have the manpower, and I am sure FDLE and Homeland are working with him or are tapped into him."

"Because it's personal," Kat and Jose said it at the same time. Jose looked at Kat and nodded.

"Listen, anyone who wants out of this part, tell me now, and there is no problem with me. Volkov tried to blow up Lesson, kidnapped Kat and Lesson, and he is bringing materials to make a dirty bomb to the US mainland strictly for profit. If I get in over my head, I will be the first to call for the cavalry, but we've done pretty good so far, and I trust everyone on this team." Jose looked directly at Chini. "Anyone want out?"

No one raised their hand. Gafford looked despondent. Kat walked over to him, sat down next to him, and put her hand on his.

"Look, Jim, I know you don't agree with violence, but you know Sir Galahad over there has to right every wrong, especially since it's personal. But sometimes violence begets violence. If you guys had not come for us, who knows what would have happened."

"Yes, Kat, but you guys were in danger. Volkov should be turned over to the authorities."

"You know Jose by now. He is cynical of the judicial system and more cynical of lawyers. He would rather make sure justice is served the right way, his way."

"It's just I feel trapped here. We are going after a bad man in a plane with armed men, and I don't like the way this might turn out."

"Be cool, Jim. Jose won't let anything happen to me, you, or Lesson. I know so."

Kat looked toward Jose and Chini, who were having a conversation off to the side. She saw both of them turn their headsets off.

Chini spoke first, "Sorry, bro. I saw the picture of Irina, and I freaked out. I did not know what to do. After thinking about it, I thought she might be dead anyway, so why strand you guys? Then I really would have felt like a shithole."

"Glad you reconsidered, just in the nick of time. You saved me. I owe you."

"No, you don't, bro. You saved me in Cuba, remember?"

"Yes, I do. That's what friends are for."

"Let's see what we have going on so far." Jose and Chini turned their headsets back on.

"Okay, kids, what do we have? Coral first."

"Papa got in touch with Captain Billy. He is going to the marina in Bimini and check on what is happening. There's been some speedboats that pulled up today. Nothing unusual for Bimini, but you never know. Also, we are making better time since we picked up a tailwind."

"Great. Coral, let us know if anything breaks. Gafford, you have anything from the coast guard?"

"Nothing out of the ordinary, and there is no need for Volkov to file a plan. Going back and forth between South Florida and Bimini is not a big deal."

Chris appeared to be asleep with his head lying on a duffle bag. Lesson had leaned into his seat and appeared to be out too. The Sanchez brothers were playing with their phones. Chini was cleaning his rifle. Kat patted the seat next to her and motioned for Jose to come over.

"Sit down, papi. Nothing we can do for an hour or so. Take a break, relax, get some rest. You must be exhausted."

"Hard to relax when the adrenaline is going, but I'll try." Jose set his watch alarm for one hour. He leaned into Kat and was snoring in two minutes.

CHAPTER 66

Captain Billy Rolle moored his Bertram 35 Sport Fisherman behind the End of the World bar in Bimini. He was a local legend who had clients come far and wide for his deep-sea-fishing excursions.

He walked in through the sandy floor, and the bartender had an icy Kalik beer on the counter waiting for him. "Thank you, Louise," he said in his Bahamian accent. "Seen any unusual activity going on about these parts?"

"Yah, mon. Some big-money boats came in last night. Don't see them cigarette boats as much as we used to back in the heyday. Three of them, out of Miami, pulled up next to a million-dollar yacht over at Resorts World."

"No race going on this weekend that I know of, right, Louise?"

"No, mon. One of them boats headed over to south Bimini. I heard from one of the workers over there that it is parked at the closed marina that is for sale."

Billy finished his beer, put a five on the counter. "Thanks. I'll catch you later."

Captain Billy went to his boat and lowered his dinghy into the water. He started the outboard motor and crossed the channel heading toward south Bimini. He took some fishing poles and a tackle box in case he was questioned. When he passed the water-taxi dock, he steered his dinghy to the canal on the left then made a right toward the marina.

As he got closer to the marina, he saw a cigarette boat tied up on the dock with a Jeep Cherokee parked next to it. There were two men on the boat, one man outside the boat who was overdressed for the occasion, and three men by the Jeep, two of them trying to load what appeared to be a metal chest onto the boat. He knew it was metal because when the sun hit it, it would shine his way.

As he got closer, he saw one of the men in the boat pull a fancy gun of some sort and point it in his direction. Billy put his hand up while still steering and said in a loud voice, "Just passin' through, mon. No harm, no foul."

A man who was on the boat looked at the well-dressed man on the dock, who nodded no at him. He then lowered the gun and pointed it toward the floor. The men from the Jeep were definitely foreign. Middle Eastern for sure, Billy thought.

Once the chest was lowered onto the boat, the well-dressed man, who had been holding a briefcase, passed it to the men who were standing by the Jeep.

The men got in the Jeep and took off immediately. Billy thought they were probably headed toward the airport, which was on the other end of south Bimini. Billy waited until he heard the big boat fire up its engine and speed away. He headed back toward his boat and would be calling Pinder shortly.

Once Billy got back to his boat, he turned on his shortwave radio and called one of his fishing cohorts, Johnnie Mac, who also ran a fishing charter on a boat named the Bimini Beast.

"Hey, Mac, I need a favor. Let me know if the cigarette boats or the big-money yacht at Resorts take off, over."

"Lots of activity going on over there. Would say they are moving out soon from what I see." Remarked Mac.

"Much obliged, owe you one next time. Just let me know when they take off. It's important." Said Billy.

"We'll see what happens. Keep you posted."

Billy called Pinder and passed on the information.

Pinder passed on the information to Coral, who passed it on to Gafford, who started checking satellite flyover schedules, checked the weather reports, and decided to wait a few minutes before waking Jose up. Gafford started writing a text that said, "coming in from Bimini, cigarette boats." He decided to wait for developments before he sent it.

CHAPTER 67

Kat had turned off Jose's headset. Coral was coming over the intercom. "Jose, do you copy?" Kat nudged Jose's shoulder. He awoke and switched on his headset.

"Yes, go ahead." Jose rubbed his eyes, stood up, and stretched.

"We are thirty minutes away. All the information has been passed on to Gafford, awaiting instructions."

"Let me get with him, and I will get back to you shortly."

"Got it, standing by."

"Okay, everyone, let's huddle up and get the latest from Gafford. Please proceed, Jim."

Gafford stood in the middle of the group. He felt nervous talking to more than one person at a time.

"There are three cigarette boats that came into Bimini last night. They docked at Resorts World next to a million-dollar yacht. One of the boats had a well-dressed man, and two armed goons were seen in a desolate area of south Bimini exchanging a briefcase for a metal chest with some men who appeared to be Middle Eastern from eyewitness reports."

"All sounds like a Volkov operation to me. Who else could it be?" Chini said while scratching his chin.

"There are no pictures, correct? But you are right. Who else could it be?" said Chris.

Gafford raised his hand. "We have eyes on them, and if they leave, we will know within minutes. Jose, don't you think it's time to notify Nate?"

Jose shook his head. "No, not yet. Nate or Homeland have no jurisdiction out here. Let's follow them and see where it leads. We have no proof. We have an idea based on what we know, but no proof yet."

"But at least if we give Nate a heads-up—"

Jose cut Gafford off, "No way. They will just clusterfuck it, especially with those Homeland boys on board. They do not need to clear anything with anyone. They can do what they want and run roughshod over any department. I know they can hold on to Volkov indefinitely, but if he rolls over and he turns in his buyers, they will cut a deal for that. Immigration will deport him back to Russia, and he will be alive and well and enjoying caviar and vodka. Not on my watch."

Gafford's shoulders slumped. Kat patted him on the back. "It's going to be okay, Jim. When have you seen Jose get in over his head?"

"It's not over his head I am worried about. It's his stubbornness, and he just can't quit and let somebody help him."

"It's either a testosterone or a Cuban thing with him."

"Probably both." Gafford laughed; so did Kat.

Jose stood in the middle of the group. "Okay, everyone, listen up. We'll be in Bimini in short time. We do not know what is going to happen, so be alert, expect the unexpected, and we might be breaking some laws along the way."

"Some more laws, you mean?" This from Chini, who elicited a laugh from everyone but Gafford.

Gafford was tempted to send the text message but decided to wait. Jose was right for the moment—what could Nate and the federales do way out here?

Jose walked over to Gafford. "Hey, buddy, how are you holding up?"

"Not bad under the circumstances. I am concerned that if we get caught doing something out of the norm, my classified friends will drop me like a hot potato."

"Nah, nothing to worry about. If something like that happens, I'll tell them we forced you to go along at gunpoint." Jose patted Jim on the back and laughed.

"Oh, geez, thanks, JC. That makes me feel much better."

"Hey, by the way, talk to me about your drone. We might be needing it in a little while." Jose knew Gafford liked to talk about his gadgets. He was hoping that would get his mind off being incarcerated.

"Sure, it's a state-of-the-art Quadcopter with infrared and high-resolution cameras. It has a top speed of one hundred miles an hour and a range of three miles. It also has a solar cell, so it can run a long time."

"That is impressive. Get it ready to go. We will use it to keep an eye on the speedboats from a distance."

"Great, been looking forward to trying it out. This would be perfect." Gafford went over to what was shaped like a guitar case and brought the Quad out. The Sanchez brothers came over to look at it, so did Chris and Chini. Gafford was like a proud papa showing off his new baby.

Chris whistled under his breath. "Sweeeeeet, that thing available for home use?"

"It probably will be soon, but not with all the extras. This is one of the first prototypes that I have modified. The manufacturer wants to see what I can do with it. They want to propose it to Defense contractors first."

"Bet you could use one of those to drop hydrochloric acid or sarin gas in a small area." Chini was imagining the possibilities.

"You bet, Chini. These babies can be modified, and unlike a one- or two-motor drone, the Quad has four motors, as you can see. So theoretically, it could carry a small cylinder, say, the size of a large can of hair spray."

"Looking forward to seeing what it can do. Is it a he or a she?"

"You know, Chris, you are the first person to ask me that. Haven't decided yet, but if it's used in a military situation, it will probably be a he."

Coral's voice came over everyone's headset and the planes intercom, "Okay, boys and girls, we have been informed that the boats are leaving Bimini now. We are fifteen minutes away, so they have a small head start. I am doing a 135 knots, so I am trying to conserve fuel so we don't get to Miami on fumes."

Jose stood in the middle of the group. "Here we go. There is no plan but to watch what happens and adjust from there. Those speedboats probably top out at about eighty-five miles an hour, so if they are booking it, they will get to South Florida in less than an hour. We have to get to them before they get within five miles of the coast because then we have no legal leg to stand on."

"Hell, we have no legal leg to stand on now," Chris said as he laughed.

"True, but three to five miles to Florida's shore, law enforcement does have jurisdiction, and I am sure Homeland has some pretext that they can go out farther than that if it is for national security."

One of the Sanchez brothers raised his hand.

"Yes, Sergio." Jose pointed at him.

"Do we shoot the boats to stop them?"

"Don't know at this time. We will see how it plays. No one shoots unless I give the order. Got it?"

All nodded in agreement.

"Gafford, get on your radar and see when you can pick up the boats leaving out of Bimini. Coordinate with Coral."

"Will do. Let me know when you want me to launch Q."

"Q who?"

"You know, the Quadcopter."

"Got it." Jose did not like not having a plan. He preferred structure and clean instructions. But this was an unusual situation, so winging it was what it had to be. He just hoped he did not put anyone in danger.

CHAPTER 68

Volkov had gone over instructions with his men: head out in the three speedboats and meet with the buyers at a longitude and latitude that was preagreed to ten miles out; do the exchange, head to Miami, and split up once they got within a couple of miles off the coast.

The cesium 137 had been divided up into two lead cylinders by the original smugglers. How they did that, Volkov did not know. He wondered if they were still alive. His buyers did not know the exact quantity they were buying; they just knew it was enough to make a dirty bomb, so Volkov was already thinking that he could sell the second cylinder for pure profit.

Volkov turned on the radio. "We have one mile to go. We should be coming up on a large ship or yacht with a yellow hull. My boat will pull up to them. You two flank my boat about fifty yards away."

On the other boats, the crew had installed .50-caliber machine guns on the bow. On Volkov's boat, there was no stationary machine gun, but two of the crew had Ingram MAC-10s, which were pretty lethal at close range. There was a rocket-propelled grenade launcher on the console just in case.

Volkov did not expect any trouble, but it was always better to be prepared than surprised. Volkov steered his boat toward the side of the ship. It was a trawler with Panamanian registry but flying a Cuban flag. Interesting, he thought.

His crew threw the mooring line over, which was secured by the crew on the ship who, in turn, threw a ladder over the side.

In a moment, a tall wiry man with full beard and a captain's hat on peered over the side. He spoke with an Irish accent, "Aye, mate, when are you coming up?"

"No, it is best if you come down and bring whoever you want with you to inspect the merchandise."

"You are crazy if you think I am going to inspect that material out in the open. I have a clean room inside where it will be safe to inspect it. Only way it's going to happen, mate."

Volkov had no choice but to give in. Guess he would have done the same if he was buying. He got on the radio. "We are going in. If we are not out in thirty minutes, you know what to do."

He motioned to the ship to throw a rope over. The rope was tied to the small chest, which was pulled up. Volkov followed up the ladder with one of his men. They reached the railing and went over. "Stay here. If I am not back in thirty minutes, you are instructed to sink this ship and go back to South Beach."

The wiry man came over and shook Volkov's hand. He was tall, had that weather-beaten face that most seamen have after years on the seas, and a mop of unruly red hair under a captain's cap. "Morrissey here. Let's have a drink while your material is checked out." They stepped into the wheelhouse. There was a decanter with two glasses on the counter. Morrissey poured what smelled like sherry and handed a glass to Volkov.

"Cheers. Hope this works out for the both of us. The folks having me pick this up invested a lot of money in that clean room. Don't know what I am going to do with it afterward. It's not every day you get asked to bring in something that requires that."

"No, I am sure that doesn't happen often, but maybe in the future, you might be asked to do it again."

"Don't know about that, mate. To need a clean room, it is either a virus or radioactive. Strange folks I am dealing with. They do not send e-mails or texts. It's all done in person through what I am sure is an intermediary, and they talk to me only inside one of their vans, which I am sure is soundproof."

"Interesting group. How did they contact you?" Volkov was curious.

Morrissey laughed. "I guess I have a reputation for bringing in anything for the right price. I've smuggled people, guns, drugs—you name it. Haven't been caught yet, knock on wood," Morrissey said this as he rapped his knuckles on the teak counter. "They just walked up to my boat. Said they'd heard I could be trusted to bring in 'sensitive' items."

Volkov took a small sip of the sherry, which he did not like. "Good to know you then. On occasion, I have the need for someone like you. Glad you can be trusted."

"Thank you. The price is always negotiable, and while this old boat might look a little sloppy on the outside, she has the latest turbo diesels on board and can cross any body of water on this planet without issues."

There was a knock, and the door opened. The crewman held up one finger.

"Just one container?" Morrissey asked.

"That is all I received. Is there a problem?"

"I was told there might be two containers."

"This material came from a long way. I am sure other deals were made. If my memory serves me right, the deal was for one container, with a bonus if it was two of them."

Morrissey had two bags by his chair. He grabbed the smallest one and handed it to Volkov.

Volkov opened the bag, looked inside, and closed it. "Men in our line of work are either trusted or not. I am sure there was no skimming off the top stacks. I trust all is well. Good luck. Hope we do business soon." Volkov stuck his hand out.

Morrissey shook hands and handed Volkov a business card. "Here is my contact information. Let me know if you need any assistance in the future."

"I might have something for you right now. Give me a minute to think about it."

"If the price is right, I'm your man." Morrissey patted Volkov on the back.

Volkov turned on his satellite phone. "Yuri, have the helicopter head our way. Have him call me when he is ten minutes away from my position."

"Yes, sir. Will do." Yuri gave the signal, which was relayed to the helicopter on the roof of Volkov's building at the end of South Beach.

Volkov called the other boats. "Go ahead, gentlemen. You know the plan. I will be two minutes behind you. I have some new business to handle."

The question came in Russian over the phone. "You are okay, boss?"

"Yes, Boris. Thanks for checking, just putting someone new to work for us, so proceed, and I will be along shortly. Stay with the plan."

Two of the boats kicked up a rooster tail of water and headed west.

CHAPTER 69

Gafford launched the Q once Coral had landed the seaplane 2.5 miles from the boats.

Jose and Gafford were huddled over Gafford's laptop. The Quad was a quarter mile away from the boats, and the video stream was crystal clear. "Too bad there is no audio," said Jose.

Gafford nodded his head. "Yes, it's on my list of customizations I want to do to the Q, although out here with the wind and the sound of the Q's motors, sound might be hard to pick up."

"I'm sure you will come up with something creative. Okay, get the name of the trawler and the direction it is headed."

"Got it. Picture will be downloading shortly. What about the speedboats? Shouldn't we contact Nate?"

"Not yet. We know they are headed toward South Florida. They are bright red, hard to miss."

Coral clicked on the intercom. "Jose, please come to the cockpit and bring Jim with you."

"What's up, darling?" Jose inquired as he sat in the copilot's seat.

"Here is the problem. When those boats take off, they will be doing about seventy miles an hour. Stall speed on this baby is seventy-eight, so I can't really fly her under eighty-five. As you can see, we will be outrunning them."

Jose was scratching his head. "Mmmmmm, going to need your help here, Gaff. This one is out of my realm."

Gafford was thinking. "Give me a minute, folks." He was tapping his hands together as if counting something. Gafford took a deep breath. "Okay, without doing any heavy lifting on my computer because we don't have the time, I am guessing we will be three to five minutes ahead of them, providing they are doing seventy miles per hour and we are doing eighty-five, so give them a ten-minute start. They will hit the coast in about forty minutes. We can be right behind them, or if you want to go ahead of them, you can throttle up."

Jose jumped in, "Can we circle and slow every three minutes to let the Q stay in range?"

Coral nodded her head sideways. "No can do. Remember, we are almost on fumes."

"Okay, give me a minute to think." Jose and Jim headed to the back.

As they headed back, Gafford spoke up, "JC, I don't think we have any choice but to call Nate."

"Dammit, I am afraid you are right. I will call him in a few minutes."

Coral's voice came over the comm sets. "Jim, I have a bogey coming directly at us, three miles out. What do you have on your screen back there?"

Gafford worked the keyboards on his laptop. He reminded Jose of the Wizard of Oz behind his curtain working all the controls.

"Coral, we do have a bogey. It's a chopper. Hang on, give me a minute to check flight plans."

"Jose, reminding you again we do not have the fuel for evasive maneuvers."

Gafford snapped his fingers. "Bingo, a chopper owned by a Volkov subsidiary, and the flight plan is to Bimini."

"Imagine that," Jose said under his breath. "Coral, just idle the right motor. Kill the left one. Chini, take a position by the door left of the cockpit, Chris take yours by the right door behind the wings. We have a chopper coming in, and I believe it has bad intentions. We are only going to get one crack at it, so it has to count. I want everyone to turn off their headsets except me, Coral, Chris, Chini, and Jim, got it?"

"Roger," said all.

"Be ready. Wait for my mark."

Coral's voice came over first, "But we'll be a sitting duck."

"Precisely. A sitting duck with enough firepower to bring down anything that gets in our way. Gaff, how far away is the bird?"

"Three minutes tops, coming in low, tree height if there were any trees out here." Jim's voice sounded a little shaky.

"Coral, turn the intercom back on. Tell everyone back there to take cover as best they can. We might be taking on some fire."

Jose went up to the cockpit and started opening the escape hatch over the copilot's seat.

"Where do you think you are going?" asked Coral.

"Topside, where else?"

"You are fucking nuts. Good luck."

"Keep the engine at idle. Might need a slight fifteen-degree turn."

"I'll do my best, and remember, we are low on fuel."

"Okay, try to get the chopper to come on your left side. That is where Chini is, and he is our best shot. I will back him up from the top." Jose went up and out of the hatch.

Coral kept the engines at idle. Now it was a matter of waiting a few minutes.

Chini was propped up against the open left door as best he could. He was used to shooting from a prone position, but circumstances being what they were, it was the best he could do. He had his long-range rifle ready. He was glad the water was like glass with very few waves.

Chris was wedged through the right door with his trusty AK-47, locked and loaded in case the chopper veered to the right of the plane.

Jose lay down on the wing with his CMMG Mk47 Mutant, which was his favorite piece in the field. It was made in the good ol' USA, which gave him some comfort.

"Gafford, let us know when the bird is two hundred yards away. Is it still headed straight for us?"

"Yes and yes."

"Coral, when Gafford gives word, turn your baby fifteen degrees to the right so the bird will be coming on your left side."

"Thanks a lot, Jose. This outfit have a medical plan?" Coral laughed.

Chris's voice came over the headsets. "Yes, we do. It's called non something. Let me think—yes, nonexistent."

Gafford's voice came over the headsets, "Here we go, folks. Two hundred yards in three...two...one."

Coral turned the plane a little to the right. Jose moved to the left; Chini adjusted to the right.

The chopper made a slight dip, which is exactly what Jose wanted so the chopper was aiming at the left side of the plane.

"On my mark...ready, set, fire!"

Chini started firing first since he had the long-range gun. Jose braced himself with his elbows and put his finger on the trigger. As soon as he saw the flashpoints coming from the chopper, he squeezed the trigger after taking a deep breath and slowly exhaling.

Jose could see the bullets hitting the water and getting closer to the plane's fuselage.

"Give it a little gas, Coral, and fire up your left engine."

Coral did as Jose asked, but she could not take her eyes off the copter. It had started to wobble. She heard some thumps on the side of the plane and knew they had been hit. All of a sudden, she heard the rapid fire above her. She saw the copter wobble violently, cartwheel, and crash into the ocean. Jose was yelling, "Yes, yes, yes," after the shooting had stopped. Coral cut the engines and went to the back to check for damage.

Jose estimated the chopper crashed about ninety yards away from them. They were extremely lucky, or the planets were aligned for them to knock that bird down. Jose stepped down through the hatch and headed toward the back, where there was some commotion going on.

Chini and Chris were already there. Kat was attending to Lesson, who had a bloody shirt that Kat was ripping off him. The Sanchez brothers were attending to Sergio, who was writhing in pain and holding his shoulder.

Coral stepped up to Jose. "Some shrapnel hit the both of them. Sergio has a broken clavicle, but your boy Lesson there took it in the rib cage. Don't know if it is deep or not, but I don't like the amount of blood."

"Get us going. We'll sort this mess out."

Coral took off for the cockpit.

Jose walked over to Lesson. Kat was feverishly trying to put some gauze on his rib area. Her hands were bloodied, and she could not stem the flow. He put his hand on her shoulder. Lesson looked pale and was sweating; Jose knew this was not a good sign. He leaned down and grabbed Lesson's hand. "You hang in there, amigo."

"I'll be fine, boss, no worries," Lesson said in a weak voice.

Chris had the field kit out. He gave Kat more gauze and passed some to the brothers. He looked for an arm sling and threw it at the brothers. "Put that on him and apply pressure to the wound, tape it up, which is all we can do for him now."

He then raised Lesson's feet up and covered him with a blanket as best he could. "We'll take turns applying pressure. Let me know when you get tired, Kat."

Kat nodded at Chris. He could see Kat's eyes were welling with tears. Gafford was sitting and looked nauseous and was as white as a ghost. Jose walked up to Gafford. "You okay, bro?"

Gafford looked up to Jose. "I don't do too well around blood. I think it's time to call Nate, don't you think?"

Jose took off his cap and ran his hands through his hair. "Can you put a tracer on the boat?"

Gafford rolled his eyes. "Come on, man, already did that before I brought the Q back. Unless you can talk me out of it, I am calling Nate."

"No need to. I'll call him, better me than you."

CHAPTER 70

"Motherfucker, son of a bitch, Judas H. Priest! Let me get this straight. You and your friends went off half-cocked to another country to save your girl and your friend, you've chased a criminal who might or might not be smuggling radioactive material across the Gulf Stream, and now you decide to call? At what point did you decide you were in over your head? I'd like to fucking know." Nate was exasperated.

"Nate, calm down, man. There is plenty of time. There is nothing you could have done in international waters anyway."

"Yeah, you think? I now have less than a half hour to coordinate three agencies, including the spooks at Homeland, to try to catch three boats that could come in anywhere from Key West to Palm Beach. That's a three-hundred-mile coast to cover. Never mind about a dozen jetties and inlets. Thanks a lot, pal."

"We, I mean, you are in better shape than you think. Gafford had tagged the three boats with electronic signatures, which he can pass on to you, which will make it easier to track them."

"Have him send my sitrep team all the info he has like right now. I will text you the e-mail for them. In the meantime, if you fuck this thing up, I will promise you an obstruction charge and whatever else I can think of. Stay clear and stay out of the way."

"I will do what I can, but I will not lose sight of Volkov's boat until I see you guys have him in your sights."

"Stay out of the way, JC. I mean it."

"Later, Nate. I'll be in touch."

Nate called Susan and gave her the particulars, just saying a confidential informant had passed on some information on the boats and where they were coming in from.

"Okay, Nate, as soon as you get any more info, let me know. I have birds in the air and boats on the water. I will have them spread out as best as possible, but it's a lot of area to cover."

"I should have a description or an electronic signature on them soon. Will pass on what I get. I will call the Homeland guys too."

"Good luck with that, amigo. Hope they don't crawl up your ass too far."

Nate chuckled. "There's not too much room in there between my boss, the mayor, and the governor."

"At least the head of Homeland hasn't called you yet."

"Not yet, but I will make a little room for him just in case. Talk soon, Susan. Thanks for the help."

CHAPTER 71

Jose walked up to Gafford and showed him his phone's screen. "Gaff, can you send the electronic tags on the boats to this e-mail? That way, Nate's wonks can follow the boats."

"Umm...no, I can't, JC. This is stuff my peeps have...let's say... procured from government sites without...authorization. We—and by that, I mean me and my friends—can get in a lot of trouble."

"So you and your hacker friends who might or might not work for the government are using pirated programs that are classified, correct?"

"That pretty well sums it up."

"Fuck me. Okay, send them the videos from the quad copter. That way, they will at least have a visual." JC touched his headset. "Coral, what is our ETA to the coast?"

"Fifteen minutes tops, twelve to the three-mile line. Boats are a couple of minutes ahead, give or take."

"Thanks. Follow Volkov's boat only. You have the info on your radar, right?"

"Copy. I have him tagged dead center. Remember, I am flying a plane and not a boat, so it's not like I can maneuver in tight spots."

"I have a plan. Give me a few minutes."

JC's cell phone rang; he saw it was from Nate and let the call go through to voice mail. He turned to Kat. "How is he doing?" He nodded at Lesson, who appeared to be in and out of consciousness.

"He is hanging in there, papi. We've stanched the flow, but we have to get him to a hospital. He's lost quite a bit of blood."

The cell phone rang. It was Nate again.

JC answered, "What's up, brother?"

"Don't give me that brother shit. Where are the electronic bull's-eyes on the boats? My team has not received anything yet."

"You will be getting video on the boats shortly. That's all we can send, some type of technical horseshit even I don't understand."

"Better be right, son. I will lock you up, and I've done it before."

"Yes, you sure have. Now, if you want some suggestions, I would have the Port of Miami blocked where the cruise ships come out of. I would have Government Cut sealed off on the south end, and I would have the entrances to Star Island blocked off."

"Sure, I'll just snap my fingers and make that happen in the next, what, ten minutes or so? Thanks for the info, Captain Obvious. I'm already working on it, thanks to the help from the FDLE and Homeland. Stay out of the way or suffer the consequences."

"Homeland and FDLE, you are moving in the high circles. By the way, I need a favor. I have two injured on board, and I'm going to need them medevacked once we land."

"Sure, just give me the location once you do. I'll do what I can. Airspace over Miami is going to be a clusterfuck as it is as Miami International is already screaming about the rerouting we asked for since the president is flying in tonight."

Jose was absorbing what Nate had said. "The president?"

"Yes, he is having a meeting with the Organization of American States. Good timing, huh? That's why the Homeland grunts have been hanging around."

"Yeah, I guess they have to get a little up to date with what's going on."

"Sure. As soon as you stop rescuing maidens and being the white knight, you do that."

"Come on, Nate. You would have done the same if you were in my shoes."

"Probably would, hate to admit it. Just keep it clean. I have no pull with the federales."

"I'll do the best I can, my friend. As always."

"Yep, that's what I'm afraid of. Adiós."

Jose walked up to the cockpit. "Coral, full speed ahead. Blast past the boats and call Pops to have an ambulance and Mother ready for us when we land."

"I am afraid to ask why. Papa's right. You are a crazy Cuban."

CHAPTER 72

At the Metro-Dade situation room, there was only SRO available. With Nate's team, Susan's team, and the Homeland agents, it was a little tight. They had the three speedboats on the screen. The Homeland folks linked their SAURON satellite system into Metro's feed, so they were watching in real time.

Susan spoke first, "We have most of the probable routes covered. It should be fairly easy to track and grab the boats. We have coast guard cutters and choppers within a half mile of the coast. Let's guide them in to the port. There's little room for them to wiggle out of there."

Nate had taken off his jacket and had rolled up his sleeves. "I have my Marine Patrol close to shore at different inlets with a few choppers on standby."

The Homeland men had headsets attached to their phones, and whenever they talked into their mics, they would talk softly so they would not be heard by those nearby.

"We should have visuals from the choppers shortly." Susan was as cool as a cucumber; she was leaning up against a wall like she was waiting for a bus.

There were three beeps, and on the screen, the boats had circles on them, which meant they were locked in to the chopper's target acquisition system. One boat was about half a mile behind the front two.

"Not that we are going to lose any of them, but glad they are locked in. Good job, everyone. Now let's guide them in close to the cutters so we can do a search." Nate felt relieved already.

Smith from Homeland walked over to Nate. "Detective, I need a word with you."

"Sure, shoot. What's the word from your superiors?" Nate loosened his tie.

"How do you know it's from my superiors?"

"Come on, son. This is not my first rodeo. Every time I have dealt with feds, they are led around by a leash from Washington, Langley, or wherever. They can't wipe their ass unless they get an order from upstairs."

Smith's face was red. Nate did not know if he was mad or embarrassed. Smith cleared his throat.

"Well, sir, my superiors want anyone taken into custody to come with us and any material confiscated also."

"Of course, you Washington boys would want that. However, the principal in this operation, Mr. Volkov, is under suspicion for blowing up an apartment in my jurisdiction, and we are not finished with that investigation at this time."

"You can have any material we confiscate, but to take Volkov into federal custody is going to require a federal judge to authorize that."

"I'll relay your concerns on to my boss. I'm just passing his request on, sir."

"You do that, son. I know it's tough being on the bottom of the food chain in the cesspool called Washington. I feel your pain."

"Thank you, sir, much appreciated."

"And stop calling me *sir*. Detective or Nate will be fine."

"Just my upbringing, sir—oops, there I go again. Sorry, sir—damn it!"

Nate patted Smith on the shoulder. "At ease, son. Let's go get some bad actors."

Susan waved Nate over. "Looks like the interception of the first two boats will be in a few minutes. We should be ready to move soon."

"Let's go. I have a boat downstairs. Come on, folks, follow me." Nate pointed toward Smith and Wesson and Susan.

Nate's phone rang; it was Jose. "Hey, brother, we are pulling up to Pinder's. Can you get a couple of units to run some interference for the ambulance taking my two guys to Jackson Memorial?"

"Jose, I have everyone stretched out, but I can spare one unit. I will have them meet you at the end of the causeway, and they will clear a path to the hospital for you."

"Okay, much appreciated."

"Will keep you posted on what we find."

"Thanks, Nate. Will keep you posted too." Jose hung up.

Nate wondered what Jose meant by that.

CHAPTER 73

Coral had no sooner taxied and shut off the engines than there was a flurry of activity around the plane. The Sanchez brothers had family waiting for them. Pinder had called for an ambulance.

The Sanchez gang didn't waste anytime and whisked the hurt brother into a jacked-up SUV, which immediately burned rubber and was headed hopefully toward a hospital.

Lesson was gently placed on a stretcher by the EMT who took over for Kat, who by now was soaked in Lesson's blood.

Jose took a hold of the EMT driver's arm. "There's a Metro unit waiting for you at the end of the causeway. Get him there as fast as you can."

"You got it, man. Been apprised of your situation."

"Thanks. You need anything for your ride, come see me at Jose's Cruisers."

"No problem. Like I said, I've been informed of your situation. I'm tight with the Sanchez clan. Later, ese." He gave Jose the gang hand signal.

Small world, Jose thought.

Coral walked over to Kat. "Come, child, my apartment is out back. Let's get you into a shower and some clean clothes."

Jose walked to Kat and gave her a kiss on top of her head. "Good job, honey. You might have saved Lesson."

"I hope so, papi. He doesn't deserve that fate."

"Fate, that which is only written for the gods to see."

"Oh shit, don't get all metaphysical on me now, papi." Kat punched him on the arm.

Coral punched him on the other arm. "Yeah, mon, don't you have some unfinished business?"

"Yeah, and I'm itching for a fight."

"Careful out there, baby. Let the professionals do their job." Kat reached up and kissed him on the lips.

"Hey, you know I am a professional agitator, so I'll get to work."

Coral grabbed Kat by the arm. "Aw Lord, let's get you cleaned up, girl, so you can continue this lovefest later."

Jose walked to Mother, where the boys were reloading and stocking up on supplies.

"Hey, guys, we will be on stand-down till we see what happens when the gendarmes pull the boats over for the search. Jim, do you still have the boats on your screen?"

"Sure do. What do you want to know?"

"Let me know when they are stopped and what happens after. Can you break into Metro's scanner?"

"Already have. Lot of chatter, looks like they are pretty well coordinated between the coast guard, FDLE, and the feds. No pissing contest going on or anyone stepping on others' toes. Hold on a sec. Okay, the first two boats have stopped. They are about half a mile out."

"Keep listening to the scanner. Anything at all changes, let me know right away." Jose walked over to the group.

Chris was first to talk, "What's the lowdown, Jefe?"

"Boys, now that we are back in the states, we have no jurisdiction or legal leg to stand on if we go after Volkov, so anything we do will be against the law. I do not expect any of you to follow what I do since I will probably be bending the law in one way or another, so I don't blame you if any of you want to bail."

Chini smiled and chuckled. "First of all, this is not our first rodeo with you. Secondly, where else are we going to get the adrenaline rush we are used to and look for in most of the things we do? And last, we get tired of hearing this all the time."

"Chini is right, JC, on all counts. One for all, all for one. Just keep in mind, both of us have PI licenses, so let's not do too much bending of the law."

"Like I said, Chris, bail anytime you need to."

Gafford was playing with his laptop. "Okay, guys, the two boats are still stationary, but the third boat is moving faster and just took a right turn and is speeding up."

"Is he outside the port entrance?" Jose was trying to think ahead.

"Yes, he is. Why would he be speeding up if he is soon to be going into the channel that brings him into the port?" Gafford sounded perplexed.

Jose had the palm of his hand on his forehead and muttered, "Think...think." He slapped his forehead. "Let's go. Everyone in Mother. I know where he is going."

The older Sanchez brother who stayed behind spoke up, "Coming with you, JC?"

"No, I want you to stay here and guard this place. Anyone coming by that looks suspicious, take them and hold them," Jose said as he was jumping into Mother.

"Where to, JC?" Gafford said as he slipped into the driver's seat.

"Volkov's office in South Beach. Let's roll."

CHAPTER 74

Nate's boat pulled up next to the cutter that had stopped the first boat. The cutter's captain was at the railing and was shaking his head.

"What do you have, Captain?"

"Nothing at all. They have a tripod on the front of the boat where I imagine they can load a machine gun onto, but if they had one, they threw it overboard before they got close to the coast."

"Did your Geiger counter pick up any radiation?" Nate was getting exasperated.

"Nothing, not even a damn tremble on the needle, same thing on boat two. We have nothing to hold them on at this time."

Agent Wesson stepped up and identified himself. "Captain, confiscate the boats and take the occupants to your base station on Miami Beach and wait for further instructions. If they ask for an attorney or any attorneys show up, tell them to contact Homeland Security in Washington."

"Will do, aye." The Captain looked at Nate while raising his eyebrows.

"What about the third boat?" Nate was trying to think ahead.

"Interestingly enough, the third boat is speeding up, so they haven't tried any evasive maneuvers so far. We'll pull him over as soon as he gets in the channel."

"Let's head over there. I want to be at the interception. Captain, please have your team hold boarding till we get there."

"Consider it done, Detective. FDLE and our top brass told us to give you whatever you needed."

"Captain, if you can make me young and rich, I would be perfect." Nate laughed at his own joke.

"I am afraid that is out of my jurisdiction and powers, Detective."

"No problem. You find a magic lamp, save a wish for me."

"It better have three wishes because I will use the first two, one for the Dolphins to make the playoffs and two for my ex-wife to find a rich boyfriend."

"Damn, that's a good one, Captain. Every time my ex decides to redecorate her condo, my asshole gets wider and my wallet gets smaller."

At this time, an ensign walked up to the captain and spoke out of Nate's earshot.

The captain nodded to the ensign and waved him away. "Well, you better get going. I've just been informed that the third boat is taking a right angle and heading toward South Beach. One of our patrol boats is heading for it now."

"Thank you, Captain. We will go after him too. We'll get there first. Hopefully, we'll meet back at your station after this." Nate motioned to the bridge to get going and walked over to the Homeland agents. "Gentlemen, it looks like we are going after the last boat, which has decided to go in a different direction, so let's concentrate on getting this right. If we find nothing on this last boat, start thinking about what plan B might be."

Smith spoke first, "We can hold most anyone indefinitely on a terrorism premise. Eventually something will have to give, so we do not tie up resources on someone who has nothing or won't talk."

Wesson spoke up, "Yes, they don't allow for waterboarding anymore, not that we used it anyway. Those were the spooks at the CIA." He smiled as he said this.

"Remind me never to say anything remotely terroristic around you guys, okay?" Nate headed up to the bridge.

Jose turned toward the back of Mother, where Chris and Chini and Gafford were sitting. "Here is what I think is happening. Volkov sent the first two boats to throw off the scent. So everyone tracking them thinks the third boat is going into the port. We are the only ones that know that Volkov's complex with the bar and the offices has boat docks under it."

Chris spoke first, "So he is going to pull right under his building, unload what he has and could hide it anywhere, or ship it right out by taxi, messenger, Uber. or even have one of his staff drive right out to any location."

Gafford spoke, "Shouldn't we contact Nate then?"

"They are concentrating on the ocean and have all their assets geared toward that. We can get there quicker. I will let Nate know what we are doing."

Jose dialed Nate's number. "Hey, pal, we are heading over to Volkov's complex. I have a feeling about something, and we can get there quicker than you can."

"Don't pal me. Is there something you are keeping from me, keemosabe?"

"No, just a hunch I am following up on. I will keep you posted."

"Stay out of trouble, JC. Last time you had a hunch, I believe you spent some time in lockup as a material witness. Call me, don't be a hero."

"Me, a hero? Come on, brother, that's not my style."

"Shit, you are such a media whore you practically get a hard-on when you see a reporter holding a microphone."

"That's because I enjoy seeing things smaller than my privates. Besides, I have to be a shameless promoter for both businesses. Need clients for the PI work and need those rich folks that want to blow money on their cars."

"All right, don't be talking dick size to a brother. I don't want to put you to shame and send you back to Little Havana with your tiny tail between your legs."

"Hey, bro, the Little Havana I grew up in is long gone. There's nothing but Nicaraguans and Central and South Americans there now. It was known for Cuban sandwiches back then. Now it's arepas and fritangas."

"Don't change the subject on me. I know you studied psychology, Buddhism, and shit, but don't yank my dick and tell me you're checking my pulse."

"Not dicking you around, Nate. Besides, we are almost there."

"You fuck, no wonder you were yapping and yapping. Don't do anything stupid." Nate hung up and called Miami Beach PD.

"Good afternoon, this is Nate Devine from Metro-Dade Homicide. Can I speak to your watch commander?"

Nate asked for a courtesy check on Volkov's building with a request to be called if anything unusual was going on. He also called his watch commander and asked for a patrol car and one of his choppers to head to Volkov's address. Now it was a race to see who would get there first.

CHAPTER 75

Volkov's building was the southernmost one on South Beach. It was built by the old Miami Beach dog track parcel that had long ago ceased to be relevant among all the glitz and glass that had rapidly been built around it after the renaissance, which was helped by the success of the *Miami Vice* television show of the mid-eighties. Art deco hotels that had been languishing in repairs and had elderly tenants on the front porches just passing time, waiting for their turn to go, were now worth a lot more money.

Volkov's condo had docks for the owners, most of whom owned boats from cigarette speedboats to million-dollar Bertrams. The marina was staffed twenty-four hours a day, so Volkov had called ahead to inform them that his boat was coming in and he needed a full service and cleanup on it as soon as it pulled in.

Jose had made a right turn from the causeway onto Alton Road when Jose slowed down for a moment.

"Here's the plan, boys. When we get to the marina, I want Chris and Chini to head in on foot and go around the restaurant and head to the docks from that side. Gafford will pull up to the docks, and the both of us will head to the slip to meet the boat. What we'll do there depends on the circumstances and how they react. No long guns, just handguns, and don't show unless they pull first."

Gafford nervously spoke up, "You want me to go along with you?"

"Jim, we have no choice. It's just us four. I don't suspect there will be any gunplay, and you don't have to carry if you do not want to."

"I would rather not, JC. You know how I feel about guns."

"No problem, just tag along. Four of us showing up will look better than three. Where does your tracking program show they are at?"

"Just coming in. They should be pulling up to the marina in minutes."

Chris raised his hand. "What do we do, hold them? What if they resist?"

Jose shook his head. "I don't think so, unless they get desperate. Let's just slow them down and stall until Nate brings the cavalry. Use common sense."

Chini stood up and loaded a mag into his Glock 21. "I got your common sense right here."

"Easy there, cowboy. What, not enough adrenaline so far?" JC punched Chini on the arm.

Chini smiled like the Cheshire Cat. "You know adrenaline is like cocaine. You want more till it wears you down and out, exhausted."

Chris punched Chini on his other arm. "Come on, you sick fuck. Let's go back up Gilligan and the professor here," he said while pointing at Jose and Jim.

Jose opened the side door on Mother. "I'm surrounded by comedians. Get out, you two."

Gafford eased into the marina's parking lot. He had transferred the tracking program to his cell phone. They started walking down the dock toward the marina office and fuel depot.

"This is pretty good timing. We should be arriving at the same time."

Jose pointed toward the port. "Well, if that isn't a boat with lights flashing about half a mile away. Nate and his group has been hauling ass."

At this time, a helicopter appeared overhead with a searchlight on. It was a Metro-Dade unit. It was shining its light at the marina office and Volkov's boat, which had just pulled up.

The crackling of speakers was heard from the chopper, "Everyone stay where they are until you are told otherwise."

Jose could see the silhouette of a person leaning from the side door of the chopper with what looked like a semiautomatic rifle.

As Jose and Gafford walked up to the boat, Volkov was sitting in the back of the boat, drinking a glass of champagne.

"Gentlemen, what brings you here? Would you like a glass of champagne? It's Krug, one of the finest." Volkov raised his glass.

"I didn't come here to drink out of a two-thousand-dollar bottle of champagne. I came to settle a score with you about kidnapping my lady and friend, blowing up my friend's apartment, shooting at our plane, and if anything else like smuggling pops up—well, the more, the merrier." Jose was staring at Volkov with fire in his eyes.

"Nyet. I am glad you know your champagnes, Castillo, but you are wrong on everything else. I did not kidnap your girl and your friend. You sent him to pick her up at the airport. I merely had a job for her that I wanted her to see. Your friend the gentle giant escorted her. As far as blowing up any apartment, I do not know what you are talking about. And smuggling? Whatever do you mean?"

"We shall see. There are some friends of mine pulling up right behind you."

"Ah, more to the party. Well, I should have more champagne brought up. Looks like an interesting party is about to commence. Maybe some caviar is called for. Petrov, bring more champagne and glasses please."

As Petrov moved toward the galley door, a red dot appeared on his chest.

"Bet he can knock off his shirt button even from up there." Jose motioned to the chopper. Gafford stepped away from Petrov.

Petrov stopped in his tracks.

"Smart move, son," Jose said in perfect Russian.

"Ah, better to wait anyway. We have more guests coming." Volkov waved at no one in particular.

Nate and the two suits were hustling up the dock doing double time, followed by Chris and Chini, who were leisurely taking their time and smoking cigars.

Jose turned to Gafford. "Like Pat Riley says, it's showtime."

Gafford looked perplexed. "Who's Pat Riley?"

CHAPTER 76

Nate had separated everyone in the marina's office. There were armed FDLE agents stationed every five feet around the office. There was a hazmat team going over Volkov's boat, and a Homeland rocket scientist who had some unusual equipment with him. Jose overheard he was with Homeland's NRT (nuclear response team). The chopper was still overhead. The coast guard station was across the way, and all lights were pointed toward the marina.

Volkov and his men were in the interior office. Jose and his gang were in the lobby. They could look through the windows and see everything that was going on. All guns had been confiscated as well as cell phones. They could not hear what was going on outside, but Jose was adept at reading body language, and he did not like what he was seeing. The Homeland agents were talking into their headsets and pacing. One had his hand on the back of his neck, and the other agent had his hand either on his forehead or on top of his head, and they appeared to be having animated conversations. Nate was on the phone yelling at someone and was scratching his head or rubbing his goatee. Jose wondered what was going on. Everyone had been interviewed twice; they had been in the office for over an hour.

Nate came in and unzipped his windbreaker. "Have a seat, gentlemen. This will take some explaining. I do not want anyone to talk until I am done. Everyone get that? Especially you, JC."

Jose felt that a five-hundred-pound shit hammer was coming around the corner.

Nate cleared his throat. "Here is the deal. There is nothing on board any of Volkov's boats, nothing at all, not a speck of anything radioactive, drugs, nothing we can hold him for. No laws were broken, and I can't take your suspicions and arrest him. JC, sit down and let me finish."

Jose had gotten up and was pacing and muttering, "Son of a bitch, how can that be?"

"As far as the kidnapping, it's going to be a touchy subject. He insists it was a business deal, and at no time did your girl and Lesson request to be let go."

Jose had his hands balled up into fists. "Nate, how can you request to be let go when you are being held at gunpoint and taken out of the country?"

"He says it was a trip to hire Kat to take pictures of his compound and that Lesson was in his employment helping out, so it's going to be a he-said-she-said situation. And let me remind you, it was out of country. We have no jurisdiction. And Volkov added that they were going to bring them back before you staged your rescue mission."

"Bullshit, Nate, you know it! What about the exchange? We saw it. We have it on tape. Gafford forwarded that video to you?"

"All we see is a metal box going to the ship. Unfortunately, that box is not on board any of the three boats."

"What, no box? They must have thrown it overboard, but how could they bring the cesium in them…" Jose's thoughts trailed off. "Nate, when will we be released?"

"Any moment now. Volkov has requested we leave a unit by the front door. He is concerned you will come back to harm him. I suggest you do not come back anywhere near here for a while."

"Okay, got it, but we need our phones and Jim's laptop back right away."

"Will do, but remember to stay away from here. We have enough going. I don't need to spread my team so thin. We will have to fill out a lot of reports after this fiasco."

"Let's go, guys. We'll talk when we get to Mother." Jose shook Nate's hand. "Thanks for not grilling us for hours. Appreciate that."

"No problem. As you are straight with me, I will be with you. Now stay out of trouble."

"I'll do the best I can, promise."

"Well, I have heard that before. Hope you mean it this time." Nate slapped Jose on the back.

CHAPTER 77

As they stepped out of the marina office, Chris was the first to speak, "What now, Chief? You seemed in a hurry to get out of there."

"Let's get out of earshot and into Mother. We have her equipped with a jamming device in case anyone wants to listen in on our conversation." Jose was walking briskly like he had no time to lose.

As soon as they all got into Mother and Gafford flipped on the jamming device, Jose spoke up, "Jim, go back to your video and get the name of the trawler. We need to find out where it's headed."

Gafford centered his horn-rimmed glasses, which reminded Jose more of how much he resembled John Lennon. "I can do better than that. I tagged it electronically through its GPS system. I also can access the database of the company the ship is registered with in case there is a log or a port-of-entry log." Gafford had already started to run his fingers over the keyboard like a piano virtuoso.

"Man, I love your resourcefulness. You are better than Dr. Watson."

"Doc Watson, who the hell is that?" Chris asked.

"You know, Sherlock's assistant, helper, comrade, right-hand man."

"Oh, goody, here we go with the literary references. Class is in, Dr. Castillo in charge."

"Might be a good idea to pick up a book once in a while. Might do you some good, pal."

"Sure, I will be doing that real soon. Any suggestions?"

Chini jumped into the fray, "How about *A Confederacy of Dunces* by John Kennedy Toole? It could be the title for this fiasco we are in, as Nate put it."

Jose was laughing. "Very good, Chini. I am impressed with your choice."

"Yeah, I get to read a little during assignments. It's mostly reconnaissance work anyway."

Gafford snapped his fingers. "Guys, guys, got it. The ship will be pulling into the Port of Miami in a few. There is a port-of-entry request, and based on the GPS coordinates, it is headed into the channel soon."

"Okay, here is what we are going to do. Chris and Chini, you guys stay here in case the trawler makes a detour in here, which I doubt they will with all the heat. Jim and I will head to the port and see what happens from there. Stay in touch by cell phone since our comm system will probably be out of range. Call a taxi or Uber and have them wait on you in case you have to move fast."

Chris and Chini jumped out of Mother as Jim and Jose got seated with Jose driving. Jose looked at Gafford. "Fasten your seat belt. It's going to be a bumpy ride."

Gafford was already holding on. "Great, any more excitement for the evening?"

Jose grinned as he put Mother in gear and floored the accelerator. "Just the start, baby. Just the start, I am sure."

Gafford did not want to ask but did anyway, "Should we notify Nate?"

"After what has gone down, do you actually think he will listen to anything I have to say or suggest? If we find what we are looking for and put our eyes on it, then we will contact him."

"Just trying to check all our angles. We could be up against anything."

"Here is what I think, Jim. Volkov left the cesium on the trawler in case he was being followed, which he was right about because he sent the chopper after us. So he cut a deal with the trawler to bring it in. Genius, if you ask me."

"So all we have to do is get to the trawler first?"

"Well, Jim, maybe, maybe not. We have to see who and what is there to meet and greet. I am not sure what their plan is. Maybe the best way is to intercept on the way out of the port. There are not a lot of ways out or in by vehicle. There are no helipads there, and putting it on another boat would be foolish and counterproductive. If I were them, I would drive it out, so many places to go to once they hit Biscayne Boulevard."

"You are right, JC, north or south on US1, the east-west expressway, and I-95, or even back to the beach."

"Yes, indeed, my friend. Now see on your laptop where the trawler is headed to. I bet it's going to the south side of the port where Seaboard Marine is. That is opposite the side where the cruise ships are, where that trawler would stick out like a virgin at a Hells Angels' bike rally."

"There it is. You are right, it has pulled into the Seaboard side docks."

"Good, we are almost there. I know where we can park and observe. Get the night-vision gear out. We'll need it." Jose steered Mother through the Miami Tunnel. It took about ninety seconds to come out the other side.

Jose pulled up behind one of the cargo buildings. The port was open around the clock with trucks pulling containers in and out constantly, with most of the work being done during daylight hours. The cruise ships were a hub of activity Friday through Sunday with very little action from them during the week.

Gafford had already started video recording while Jose was observing through the night-vision binoculars. Two shipmates were at each end of the trawler, securing lines. One mate was hosing down the stern while there seemed to be some activity in the wheelhouse.

Jose's phone rang, and he saw it was Chris calling. "What's up, boss? Nothing going on over here. No trawler, just a delivery van leaving. Where do you want us at?"

"All good. Follow that van and see where it goes. If it goes north or east, ditch it and get to the port. If it heads in the port's direction, stay on it."

"Ten-four, be in touch."

Jose was thinking about letting Nate know what was going on. He speed-dialed Nate.

"Nate, I need a few minutes of your time, and I need you to be flexible here. I am at the port watching the trawler that Volkov met out at sea. I am pretty sure the cesium is on it. If I see the metal chest or anything than can house it, I will take a picture or video and send it to you."

Jose could hear Nate breathing on the other end.

"Nate, are you there?"

"I am here. Let's take this slowly and stop me if I miss anything. Somehow you put two and two together and figured out that Volkov left the cesium on the trawler in case he got stopped on the way in."

"Right, but—"

"But nothing. Wait until I am finished, or I ask you a question."

"Yes, sir."

"Screw you with the 'yes, sir.' So you somehow happened to know when the ship was coming in by osmosis, tea leaves, or divine intervention."

"No, when we were following Volkov, he met up with the trawler, and Gafford tagged it just like he did with Volkov's boats, which I believe he sent you, which helped with your interception of said boats." Jose knew Nate was going to bust his chops.

"Ah, you did not mention the other boat. Any reason why? And stop sounding like a lawyer."

"Just thought the main catch would be Volkov, did not think a trawler with a Cuban flag would be of interest out in international waters. I am glad we tagged it, though, or we wouldn't be here."

"This electronic tagging business is pretty fancy for a PI working out of auto-restoration shop, if you ask me."

"Come on, Nate. You know Gafford is a gizmo wonk. Besides, we never would have gotten this far without his help."

"Whatever. Get me proof of something this time. I am sending a unit to where you are at, and I will be right behind them just in case this is not another wild-goose chase."

Jose saw a call coming in from Chris. "Nate, I am putting you on hold for a second. I have a call from one of my guys that was watching Volkov's place." Then he spoke to other line, "Hey, Chris, what's up?"

"Boss, the van is heading toward the port, heads-up."

Gafford tapped Jose on the shoulder and pointed at the ship. There was the metal chest being transferred from the ship to the dock. There was a wooden pallet with a contraption on it that looked like a tripod with a hanging cylinder on it. Jose wondered what that was.

"Stay back and stay near the exit. Will call you shortly."

"Got that, Jim?"

"Yes, picture and a video. Should I send it to Nate?"

"Please do." Jose went back to his phone. "Nate, you still there?"

"Sure, where else would I go to? The president? He's in good hands. I'm filling out reports on the Volkov fiasco and getting ready to head to you."

"Well, stop what you are doing. Gafford just sent you video of what was unloaded off the ship, same box we saw Volkov take on that ship. Call me when you get close. Have to go."

A white van pulled up to the dock, and a tall, thin wiry man went into it. His men put the box in the back of the van and the small pallet with the tripod contraption in the side door.

Jose's phone rang within a minute of the sent information. "Okay, so the box is real. Don't screw the pooch on this one." Nate sounded exasperated.

"What, no thanks for being a supersleuth and following my gut instinct?"

"Come on, Jose. I have no time for this. Everyone is headed to Miami International because the president's plane is about to land, and it's me and one street unit here, that's all."

"I will do what I can, but I suggest we block the exit out of the port. Start with Port Boulevard. That will only leave the tunnel to get out of, and we'll have them like rats in a cage there. Gafford will send you a picture of the van. We will be behind it, so keep in touch. Don't know if the cell phones will work in the tunnel or not. Two of my boys are there already. I have them stationed by the exit."

"Thanks, Jose. That is a good plan, considering we have short time and low manpower. I'm heading your way."

CHAPTER 78

Nate turned toward the port exit just as he was being hailed on his radio by the patrolman who had arrived two minutes before him.

"Detective, this is Patrolman Lopez. There are two guys in a taxi blocking the exit to the tunnel, and they don't look like taxi drivers. They have jackets on in this hot weather, and I suspect they are packing under those jackets."

"Thank you, Officer. Does one of the guys look like Bruce Lee and the other like Marlon Brando?"

"Well, sir, they kind of do, now that you mention it."

"They are okay. I will be there in seconds. Hang tight."

Jose pulled out from their spot and started following the van. The van was going the speed limit but started slowing down about halfway into the tunnel. Jose could see why: the lights from a police car was flashing off the walls of the tunnel on the exit side. The van came to a complete stop just past the halfway point in the tunnel.

As he got about forty yards from the van, Jose turned Mother sideways, blocking both lanes. He saw a police cruiser that was stopped, a taxi, and Nate's Charger slowly moving toward the van from the other side. All three vehicles were blocking both exit lanes.

"Come out with your hands up," was what was heard over the police cruisers PA system.

"Gafford, go to the safety walkway to your right and lie down on it and point this gun toward the van, but do not shoot. Do not take the gun out until you are prone on the floor, and don't worry, it's not loaded."

"Okay, Jose. What do I do after?"

"Just stay out of harm's way. We got this."

Gafford walked to the back of Mother and carefully made his way to the stairs that led to the walkway.

Jose had a handgun in his ankle holster that he decided to keep for the moment. He moved close to the walkway on the other side of the road while plugging in his phone's earpiece. There was a commotion in the van, and a shot was fired. The tall, thin wiry bearded man staggered out of the driver's door and fell on the pavement.

Some unintelligible yelling was coming from the van. Jose's phone rang; it was Nate.

"What the fuck is going on? Is it safe to move in? We can't see too well since the van's lights are pointed right at us."

"Hold on. Something has to give."

The van's back door and the side door opened simultaneously. Volkov ran out the back with something tucked under his jacket. He was headed toward the walkway on the right when he saw Gafford getting to the same side about fifty yards away. There was an emergency-escape cross passage about ten yards from Volkov. Volkov slipped a gun out of his jacket and shot in the direction of Gafford. He saw Gafford dive to the ground and not move.

"What's going on, JC? We are blind over here. Who took that shot?"

"It was Volkov. He's trying to escape."

Jose was going to go after Volkov when he noticed a man had jumped from the side door of the van and was holding a cylinder in one hand that had a wire that ran to his other hand. Jose guessed it was a trigger.

"Okay, something is about to give. Nate, tell my guys to position themselves right away. This guy by the side of the van appears to have a bomb. It's a cylinder, and it's wired."

"Can you take him out, JC?'

"No way, my man. He's looking right at me."

All of a sudden, a great whirring noise came from both ends of the tunnel.

"What the hell is going on, Nate?"

"Your guess is as good as mine, brother."

There was a crackle over both their phones, and Agent Smith's voice came through.

"Gentlemen, we have been monitoring your situation, and we are taking some action that might alleviate some collateral damage."

Nate spoke first, "What the hell, have you been eavesdropping on our conversation? Tapping a police officer's phone? Isn't that against the law or at least take a court order?"

Agent Smith continued, "As a precaution, we are closing the hurricane doors on the tunnel. We cannot take any chances that that there might be a dirty bomb, so we do not have time to guess. As we speak, the five escape hatches are going to be shut, so there is no way out. I am sorry to do this to you, but I must sacrifice you for the greater good. Do the best you can. We will be watching the CCTV cameras, but if you disarm the perpetrator, please send proof by picture or video. Then we will reopen the doors. Good luck. And by the way, Detective, the NSA and Homeland have expanded powers since 9/11."

"Man, those fuckers from Homeland work fast. Heartless too." Nate sighed.

"Hey, we are still listening, Detective."

"You are? Then fuck you. Now get off the line so that those of us down here can get something done." He turned to JC. "Play the good guy, JC. I will see what we can do back here."

"I hear you, brother. Let me get close in to this guy. Are my guys in position?"

"Yes, they are. What do I tell them?"

"Tell them to take the shot if they have it. Try to hit the trigger hand and a head shot. If anyone can do it, it's those two. I will try to buy us some time, but I am going to have to lay down my gun and make nice."

"Piece of cake for you, JC. You can charm the pants off anyone with your arrogant attitude, churlish demeanor, and winning smile."

"Wow, Nate, you have been reading a thesaurus and a book to make people feel better about themselves or what?"

"Yeah, something like that, brother. Good luck, hope you can do something here. I would hate to die in this tunnel."

"I'll do my best as always. Roger and out."

As Jose walked toward the van, he put his hands in the air.

CHAPTER 79

The Miami Tunnel was first proposed in 1983 to alleviate the traffic going into the port in Downtown Miami. Between the burgeoning cruise ship traffic and the steady flow of the cargo container industry, it became evident that something had to be done. Some politicians like Congressman Claude Pepper and Miami mayor Maurice Ferre had the foresight to propose such a plan back then.

Federal transportation authorities finally started to warm to the idea of the tunnel around 1999–2000. The official go-ahead was given on October 15, 2009, after a public-private partnership was created with Meridian Infrastructure Finance, construction firm Bouygues Travaux Publics, the State of Florida, the City of Miami, Metro-Dade County, the Department of Transportation, and other entities taking charge of the project. It would be South Florida's biggest construction project to date with a final budget of one billion dollars. It opened to local traffic on August 3, 2015.

The tunnel is almost one mile long, and at its deepest point, it will be one hundred and twenty feet under sea level. There are ninety-one CCTV cameras in the tunnel as well as five emergency cross-passage hatches built every seven hundred feet. The fifty-ton floodgates or doors are made to keep the tunnel watertight up to a category-three or more hurricane. They were not tested for bombs.

As Jose started toward the van, Chini and Chris had positioned themselves one at the hood and one at the trunk of Nate's Charger. Chris had a PPQ M2 Walther, and Chini had a Ruger Redhawk .44 Magnum aimed at the man who was standing by the van. They would have liked a long gun, but that is what they were carrying at the time. The front door to the van was open and partially blocking the man from their position. All they could see was the torso and head through the window opening and his feet through the bottom.

Chris whispered to Nate, "Please tell Jose to get the man to move away from the door."

Nate talked softly into his headset, "Jose, move the guy away from the door. The boys need a clear shot."

Jose was within twenty yards from the man when the man started yelling, "You no cop. Who are you? What you want?" The man looked nervous and was sweating. He had an accent that Jose could not place.

"I am not a cop. I don't want any trouble. I was just behind you and had to stop when you stopped. After I heard the gunshots, I wanted to see if anyone needed help."

"You have a gun?" The man was jittery; he kept looking around.

"Yes, I do. It's in my ankle holster. I am going to bend down, take it out, and slide it to you if that is what you want."

"Right away, mister, right away, or I blow us up." The man took a step forward but not sideways.

Jose talked into his headset, "Guys, I am throwing my gun to his right, my left. As soon as he moves, take him down. Don't worry about me. I will be diving to my right."

"Who you talk to, mister? I want gun now!"

"You want it? You got it." Jose was on one knee, reaching for his ankle holster. He gingerly grabbed the handle of his Ruger LCP and slid it about four feet to the right of the man.

The man had the cylinder under his right arm and was holding the trigger in his left hand. The man shuffled over to the gun, placed the cylinder on the ground, reached for the gun; and as he started moving up, he raised the barrel and was pointing it in Jose's direction.

Jose had not taken his eyes off the man and expected as much. He was vulnerable, no gun, nothing to hide behind, so he did as planned and started to tuck and roll to his right. The man got off a shot before he was halfway up. Jose felt a sting on his calf. As soon as he stood all the way up and squared himself to Jose, the man's head exploded like a watermelon at a Gallagher concert. The noise from the shots was deafening.

Nate, Chini, Chris, and the patrolman were running toward the man. They surrounded him, and Nate was taking a picture with his phone of what was left of the man. He took a close-up of the cylinder and the trigger and sent them to Smith and Wesson.

"Nice shot, you guys. There's no head or neck left on this guy." Nate turned and high-fived the boys. "Excuse me, I have some calls to make."

"Who do you think got him, you or me?" Chris was blowing on his shooting hand.

"Stop taking all the credit, man. Based on what's left, I think we both got him."

"Hey, guys, over here. Remember me?" Jose was still on the ground. There was some blood under his leg.

"Oh shit, JC. We almost forgot about you," Chini said as they hustled over to Jose.

"Some friends you are, celebrating and forgetting about me." Jose was wincing as he held his calf. There was blood on his hand.

Chris took his shirt off, ripped the sleeve off, and tied it around Jose's calf. Chini helped Jose up. "How does it feel? Any muscle or bone damage, Chief?"

"If it was bone, he would be squealing like a pig, right, paisan?" Chris slapped Jose on the shoulder.

"You know, I don't squeal like a pig, compadre. Did you forget the shrapnel I took on my right shin in Nicaragua?"

"That didn't count, man. You had so much rum in you that night a tank could have run you over and you would not have felt a thing."

"The guy's shot hit the asphalt broke up, and I have a surface wound, that's all."

At this time, Gafford came around the back of Mother.

"Thanks for coming to look for me, guys." He stopped in his tracks. He looked at Jose, looked at the headless body on the ground, and promptly threw up.

"Holy smoke, JC, is he one of those people that faints at the sight of blood?" Chris was gawking at Gafford.

"I guess so, or maybe he's seen his first body—beats me." Jose was leaning on Chini, but he moved away and made himself walk to see how his leg felt. It felt okay.

Nate was walking toward the group. "Okay, girls, the party is over. What do we have here, a MASH unit? You okay, Jose? Gafford okay? You are bleeding. He's not. I will call for an ambulance. Get ready, the feds are coming. FDLE, ATF, FBI are all coming. Be prepared to get asked the same questions till the sun comes up."

Jose snapped his fingers. "I am okay, just a superficial wound. Where's Volkov? Did he make it out the escape hatch before the feds closed them?"

"Damn, with all the excitement, we forgot about him." Chini hit his forehead with the palm of his hand.

"He headed toward that emergency escape tunnel over there." Jose pointed at the door leading to the hatch that was closest to them.

"Chini, you and I will go to the two closest escape tunnels, take it all the way up, and if there are any rooms or doors between here and the top, open them. We'll meet up top. Nate, please call your fed pals and ask them if anyone came out of the hatches before they shut them down or in the last few minutes. Chris, take Mother and go back toward the entrance."

The motors that moved the hurricane doors started humming. Gafford started to stir. He was holding his head.

"Welcome back to the real world, sunshine," Chris said as he helped Gafford up.

Gafford put his horn-rimmed glasses back on. "Dudes, I've never seen so much blood."

"Chini, let's go." Jose reached down and retrieved his gun, which was still in the bomber's hand. He checked to make sure there was a bullet in the chamber and started walking toward the emergency exit.

CHAPTER 80

The emergency exits in the tunnel were built so if there was a problem, it would take you to the other side of the tunnel. Since the current situation was on the exit side, by taking the emergency hatch out, Volkov was now on the entry side. He could take the walkway toward the front, but it would leave him exposed when everyone showed up. He could walk back toward the port and cargo area, but that would not give him an exit unless he called his men and they came by in one of the boats. That would surely attract attention to him. He decided to head to the cargo area to see how he could get out of there.

Jose and Chini headed to the two closest exits, hoping to cover more ground. Jose's phone rang; it was Nate. "Hey, brother, I checked with the feds, and no one came out of the tunnel prior to them closing the doors."

"Thanks for the heads-up. That means he is still in the tunnel and probably heading back to the trawler. Give them a description of Volkov. He was wearing a light-colored suit and carrying something under his coat. Bet it's a cylinder with something nasty in it."

"Hope so, man. We've been chasing for that thing all night. I'll station a unit on both exit and entry side over here."

"Good, because we are heading back toward the cargo area. Talk soon."

"Don't do anything stupid, Jose."

"Who, me? Never. You know I play by the book."

Nate laughed. "The problem is it's your book, and only you know the contents, and it's based on some twisted logic. Eastern philosophy and Don Quixote ideals and old-school morals that only you can decipher."

"I never thought of it that way, but a good analysis, Nate. Maybe you have a future calling as a psychiatrist."

"Ha! That would be ironic after all the hours I paid a shrink for my ex as a result of our divorce settlement."

"Based on what you pay that gal for shrinks, interior decorators, and plastic surgery, it would have been cheaper to keep her."

"You are right, bro. Hindsight is twenty-twenty, If I knew then what I know now, I might have forgiven her peccadilloes."

"Nate, I am really impressed with your vocabulary lately. Are you sure you are not taking remedial vocabulary classes or dating a teacher?"

"Very funny, Jose. I have been reading a lot lately, something I have always wanted to do but never seemed to have the time. I just went home one day last week and unplugged the cable box and had my service shut off. For news, just a good old radio and a computer. That way, I can read the news at my leisure and don't have to hear talking heads with their agendas or a particular cable channel's propaganda."

"I never would have guessed you for that. Like I said, I am impressed."

"I see enough crap in my job. You know that I don't want to go home and see more mass shootings, murders, abuses brought into my living room 24-7. Let's get going, man. Let's go catch a bad actor."

"Going, man. Let's wrap this up." Jose headed toward the cargo area. Nate headed toward the entrance.

Chini came out of the tunnel and saw Volkov heading toward a maintenance vehicle that was stationed by a cargo crane. He picked up his speed and made sure he had a full clip in his mag.

Volkov reached the truck and pointed his gun at the driver, who was in the process of filling out some paperwork. "I need your truck. I am being chased by armed men, and I am in danger."

The man put his clipboard down and calmly stepped out of the truck while keeping his eye on the gun the whole time. "Take what you need, sir. I don't need any trouble."

Once the driver was five feet from the man holding the gun, he saw the gun being pointed at him. He started to run to no avail. Volkov aimed and shot the man three times in the back.

Chini saw what was happening and fired at Volkov, but he was too far away to be accurate with a handgun. Volkov swung toward Chini and fired in that direction, jumped in the truck, and floored it toward the tunnel.

Jose was thirty yards behind and ten yards to the left of Chini. He saw what was happening and picked up his pace. He was pulling his gun out and taking a bead on the maintenance truck, which was speeding up and leaving a trail of spray in its wake from the water on the ground. The moon was high in the sky behind the truck, and it made for a surreal picture in Jose's mind. It appeared to him that it was happening in slow motion. He saw Chini take a shooting stance. He ran up closer to Chini and was about twenty yards to Chini's right near some containers that were stacked ready for the cranes. It was them against Volkov and the truck.

Volkov leaned out and shot at Jose and Chini but ran out of ammo after six shots. He floored the truck and was deciding who to take out, Castillo or the other shooter, when he saw the shooter go to one knee, drop his gun, and reach for his shoulder.

"Damn it, I'm hit!" Chini had dropped to one knee, and Jose saw him holding his right arm.

"Slide your gun over and roll away, man. He's coming. I got this." Jose had a full clip in his Ruger but wanted the firepower of the Magnum.

Chini slid the .44 over and started running toward some containers that were about fifty feet away on the other side of the dock when he heard the roar of the Magnum once...twice...and a third time, which was the last because he knew there were only three bullets left in the cylinder.

Jose grabbed the .44 from the floor, opened the cylinder, and saw there were only three bullets left. He knew they had to count. He took a shooter's stance and fired at the truck's grill, one at the driver's side of the windshield and one at the left front tire. He saw sparks and smoke coming from under the hood, so he knew he hit the radiator at the very least. He saw Volkov was behind the wheel, so he had missed him. And he saw the left front of the truck start to dip and wobble, so he knew he had hit the tire. He quickly did the math, and he had hit two out of three targets, but not the one he really wanted to. He looked where he could take cover when he saw the truck's left front tire collapse and the truck start to slide and shake in his direction.

Volkov saw the bullet come through the windshield, felt the bullet whizz right by him, and break the glass behind him. He was struggling with the wheel as the truck was pulling to the left and shaking apart. He smelled something burning and saw that the floorboard was starting to smoke. He stepped on the brake, and nothing happened. He used the emergency brake, and that made the truck go into a tailspin. It reminded him of the Tilt-A-Whirl rides at carnivals; he didn't like them much at all. He decided to take his chances and jump out of the speeding truck, but the door was jammed. The truck was out of control and was headed for a row of containers on the left.

Jose ran as fast as he could toward the containers that were maybe forty feet away. The out-of-control truck was careening toward him. He dove toward the closest opening he could see when he saw the truck start to tailspin and was only thirty feet from him.

Volkov saw that the truck was heading toward Castillo, and he thought briefly about what a good ending this could have. He decided to leave it up to fate. He stopped fighting the wheel, sat back, closed his eyes, decided to let destiny take over, and started laughing.

Jose had slipped in between containers and was watching the spinning truck head right for him. He saw Volkov sitting back in the seat with his eyes closed in an almost peaceful state. He thought maybe he hadn't missed him when he saw Volkov open his eyes and appear to be laughing before the truck plowed into the container to the left. There was an earsplitting crash with parts showering the area. A burning smell immediately permeated the air.

Jose squeezed from between the containers and headed to the truck's carcass, which had landed twenty yards away. The cab was on its side with fire coming from the front and smoking from the back. Jose crawled to the mangled cab and saw Volkov was stirring.

"Give me your hand so I can pull you out." Jose reached in, but Volkov pulled away.

"I am afraid not, my friend. My legs are trapped, and I can't feel anything below my chest. If the smoke and fire don't kill me, I refuse to live as a scarred invalid in a wheelchair the rest of my life."

Jose was deciding whether to go in and do what he could. "You are sure this is what you want? With your money, you can be comfortable."

"I will let you in on a secret. I was diagnosed with cancer, and we've tried everything, but it's inevitable. You see, I lived near Chernobyl, so it was only a matter of time before the Grim Reaper, as you call it, came knocking at my door. So this will be a Pyrrhic victory my friend. I will deny the Grim Reaper his prize."

Jose thought for a moment. "But he is getting you anyway."

"Yes, but by my doing, by my hand. I am in charge of my death." Volkov started to cough up blood.

Jose backed up a little and looked at Volkov. "So this is it? This is how you want to go out? Guess this is better than the ignominy of having your ass wiped by a stranger or losing control of your bowels."

"See, my friend, we are from different worlds, but we think alike. If anyone could understand me, it's a fellow traveler who has seen the best and the worst sides of this unique world we inhabit. I know you've seen it. It's in your eyes."

Chini had rushed in and started to help, but Jose waved him off. He looked at Jose like he was a madman. Jose shook his head. The fire has started to get hotter and bigger under the hood.

Jose reached into his ankle holster and started to hand the Ruger LCP to Volkov when Chini grabbed Jose's arm. Jose shook him off and finished handing the gun to Volkov.

Volkov reached for the gun. "My friend, you have been a worthy adversary. Spasiba."

"You are welcome." Jose grabbed Chini by the arm. "Let's go. We are done here. Let's get some attention to your wound."

As they walked away from the fiery wreckage, they heard one shot and then the sound of sirens coming from far away.

CHAPTER 81

Homeland's NRT team had used a robot to extract the cylinder from the charred cab. They had set up a perimeter fifty yards from the wreckage, and they were relieved when the robot did not pick up any radiation on its first pass by the cab of the truck.

Metro-Dade's medical examiner was standing by, ready to pull the body from the wreckage once the fire department had finished with the Jaws of Life operation. At the Seaboard Marine offices, all the departments involved had set up their people. Calls, faxes, and e-mails were being sent and received at a rapid pace.

Daylight had come. The bright sun was shining on the Atlantic Ocean like a floodlight. It would be soon before Jose and his crew would be let go after being interviewed by Homeland, FDLE, Nate, and the FBI in that order.

Jose had talked to his crew and told them not to mention anything about what happened in Roatán.

Since it was bustling at the port, some smart lunch truck drivers saw the group around the wreckage, reloaded their trucks, and came back to park nearby. That is where Jose and his group were standing by having coffee and pastries when Nate came up to talk to them.

"Okay, gentlemen, we are done with all of you for the moment. Just inform us if you are planning to leave town and give us a contact number. As far as we know, there might be a reward for the strangler case, so I will keep in touch with you. Jose, I need a word with you privately."

Jose and Nate stepped away from the group. "Listen, I appreciate the heads-up on the possible smuggling. I couldn't figure out who was doing it, but it had to be you."

There was a look of confusion on Jose's face. "Sorry, bro, but it was not me. But now that you mention it, there was someone on my team that was a bit skittish about the entire goings-on." Jose looked toward Gafford.

Nate patted Jose on the arm. "Take it easy on him, will you? It was probably his first time in the field."

"Well, it was a rough go, after all. He did get shot at while doing surveillance in Mother, and I'd tell you about Roatán, but you might hold that against me in the future."

"Dammit, man, I don't care what you did down there in a banana republic as long as you toe the line in my jurisdiction."

"You know, Nate, one of these days, I will listen to that. What's the story on the canisters?"

"Both accounted for. Danger is over. Get your team home. Look like you guys have been through hell. Is Chini okay?"

"Yes, just got winged by Volkov, but nothing serious. He's taped up and will be fine. It's been interesting, to say the least, never a dull moment. Heading to the hospital to see how Lesson is doing. Will stay in touch." Jose fist-bumped Nate and headed toward the team.

"Come on, guys. Let's head back to the shop, and we'll start cleanup. I will head to the hospital and check on Lesson."

Chris was the first to speak up, "Hey, JC, what did we get out of this? Brownie points with the feds? Goodwill with Metro-Dade? Personal satisfaction?"

"Well, let's see my friend. Personal satisfaction, check. Camaraderie with old pals, check. Adrenaline rush, check. Travels to exotic locales, check. Meet and shoot interesting people, check. Get to see a professional in action, check."

Chris jumped in, "Get a bushel of bullshit from my pal, check."

All laughed except for Gafford, who was still looking a bit stressed.

"Hey, Jim, how are you holding up, man?" Jose patted Gafford on the shoulder.

"Stressed, dude, We've been interrogated and surrounded by cops for three hours. I haven't been able to light up and relax."

"Well, hell, no wonder you are jumpy. Let's go. You can light up in Mother."

Jose figured he would bring up what Nate said about the messages after Gafford calmed down. Everyone piled into Mother, and Jose steered out of the port toward Little Havana.

CHAPTER 82

Jose had a shower built at the shop, so when he finished working on a car, he didn't have to go upstairs to clean up. It came in handy with the four of them needing a shower. Jose and Gafford took turns downstairs while Chris and Chini took turns upstairs in the master bedroom. Jose had started the coffee and was smoking a Black & Mild wine in the shop's office, waiting for Gafford to finish. He wanted to talk to him before they went up to the kitchen.

Gafford came out of the shower looking refreshed and relaxed. He borrowed one of Jose's T-shirts, which happened to have the University of Miami slogan, "The U invented swagger," which Jose thought was ironic at best.

"Hey, Jim, I need a minute of your time before we head up."

"Sure, JC. What's up?" Gafford took a seat by the client's side of Jose's desk.

Jose had his feet up on the desk. He had pulled an Amstel Light from his vintage soda machine. "Jim, we make a good team, and I trust we'll continue to work together, but there has to be absolute trust in order to work as a team."

"Oh, for sure, dude. I couldn't agree more."

"Okay, so in the future, no messages, notes, or hints to law enforcement in any case we are working."

It took Gafford a few seconds to comprehend where Jose was coming from. Then he sat straight up with a red face. "Oh, dude, Nate must have told you…"

Jose nodded. "Didn't you think he would?"

"Sorry, dude. I was a bit scared out there and wasn't sure where it all was headed."

Jose nodded again. "Just so we are clear, I never, ever put anyone in jeopardy without letting them know where they stand and giving them the option of bailing. If there is the possibility of harm, I will let them know, and I will not force anyone to go or do something they don't want to. I did not know what we were going to be up against in Roatán, so I needed all hands on board."

"No problem, JC, I understand. Sorry, I was a bit skittish. It was my first time being 'out there,' as you say."

"Great. Glad we are on the same page. Let's go up and get everyone going. I am sure everyone wants to go home."

Chris and Chini were already sitting at the kitchen table. Chini was having a cup of coffee, and Chris had made espresso.

"What's your poison, gentlemen?" Chris said as he held up one cup of coffee and one demitasse cup.

"I'll have the espresso. Give Gafford the coffee. Last time I gave him espresso, he was bouncing off the walls." Jose pulled up a chair. "Listen, guys, I have to get to the hospital, so make your flight arrangements, and Gafford can take you to the airport. I appreciate all your help, and if there's anything you need, let me know. I will keep you posted if there is any reward on the strangler case. After all, we all worked on it one way or another."

Chris had to be the first to pipe up, "Paisan, unless it's a million dollars, don't worry about me. I feel I am overpaid anyway by the studios to babysit these actors."

"Take my cut, if any, and apply it to your favorite nonprofit. Or if you want to buy a project car, I'll go in halves on it with you."

"Well, Chris, on one hand, you are altruistic, and on the other hand, you are capitalistic. So I decide which way to invest?"

"Yep, Homes, I leave it to you. Charity or capitalism, I am good with either."

"All right, my brothers, I am out of here. Thanks again. Love you all." Jose hugged Chris and Chini and headed to the hospital.

CHAPTER 83

Jose sent Kat a text that he was on the way; he was surprised when she did not respond. It was only a ten-minute drive to Jackson Memorial from the shop, so he stepped on the gas.

Arriving at Jackson Memorial, Jose remembered growing up in the surrounding neighborhood as a child. A lot had changed, he thought, as he hurried toward the main building. In the fields where he used to play baseball or football with his friends now stood Miami VA hospital, University of Miami medical center, and the city of Miami civic center. The Miami Stadium, where he used to watch spring baseball, had been razed long ago for public housing. Progress, unstoppable in the name of the almighty dollar, Jose pondered. He knew Miami was an international city, a tourist hot spot, a cultural pastiche of Latin, Caribbean, South and Central American influences, but he remembered fondly how sleepy Miami was when he was a kid and how much it had changed since then.

Jose's phone buzzed with a text notification. It was from Kat: "Come to the operating room waiting area on the fourth floor, main building." He got off the elevator and turned right where the waiting room was. He'd been there before, more than he wanted to remember.

He walked in and saw Coral hugging Kat while both were crying. Jose's heart sank, and he feared the worst. Kat looked up, and her eyes were swollen from the tears. Kat ran over to Jose and hugged him.

"Oh, papi, he did not make it. The doctors tried for hours, but they said there was too much internal damage. I am so sorry. He was a gentle soul."

Jose felt as if he'd been gutted. Coral had come close to them, and Jose was now hugging both of them.

Jose cleared his throat. "Sit down, girls. I want to talk to the doctor. I'll be right back."

Arriving at the nurse's station, Jose asked for the operating physician. He was told he would be a few minutes as he was wrapping up his notes on the operation.

Shortly thereafter, a small Asian-looking man came out of the doctor's lounge and walked toward Jose. He did not offer his hand to Jose. He remembered most surgeons protect their hands as much as classical pianists do.

"Hello, sir, I am Dr. Chen. How can I help you, and are you family of the deceased?"

"I am Jose Castillo, and I am the only friend or family that he had."

"I won't beat around the bush, but the deceased had a lot of internal organ damage due to shrapnel. He lost a lot of blood. I only wish we would have gotten to him sooner. His chances of survival would have increased exponentially."

Jose felt like he had been kicked in the gut. "That's pretty to the point, Doc. So had I gotten him here sooner, there would be a better chance for him to have survived, is that right?"

"I am afraid you correct. I am sorry. The burden of his life rested on your shoulders."

Jose did feel the weight of the world fall upon his shoulders. "Did you tell the ladies that?"

"No, I did not. They did not pass themselves off as family, so I was discreet. Again, my condolences."

"Thank you, Doctor. I appreciate everything you and your team did."

Jose went back to the waiting room and collected Coral and Kat, who were still crying.

"Come on, girls. Let's get Coral back home, and we'll head over to my place and collect ourselves."

He wrapped one arm around Coral and one around Kat's shoulder and headed toward the elevator with a heavy heart.

"Papi, is there any justice for Lesson in all of this?"

"Baby, I have to bring you up to date. Volkov is dead. I will explain everything once we get a chance to decompress."

"How did he die? Did you kill him?"

"Only indirectly, baby. He was trying to run down Chini and me, and he created his own demise. I could have saved him, but he refused help. It's a long story, and I promise to explain it all once things calm down."

Coral, who was usually quiet, spoke up, "At least all our efforts were not in vain. I am assuming the cesium was secured since I haven't heard anything, and one bad man off the planet can't be all bad."

"It's all good, Coral. The results weighed in our favor for the greater good. The only regret I have is Lesson. I should have had sending him to the hospital a big priority."

"Too much going on, man. You did the best you could. Papa says that is your mantra: do the best you can and have a clear conscience that you did."

"Thanks for that, but hindsight is twenty-twenty."

"You said it, in hindsight. If we knew what was going to happen, we could change things, but that is not the way the universe works, my Cubano brother. Hey, by the way, let me have the phone number for your Italian goombah friend. I am going to call his bluff and ask him out after all the flirting and drooling he did over me."

"Will do. I take no responsibility for what happens, okay?"

"No problem. As we say in the islands, no problem, mon, we're adults. I'll be gentle on him, promise."

"Please take it easy on him. He's had his heart broken a few times."

"Haven't we all, my friend? Haven't we all?"

Jose pulled up to Pinder's place. "There you go, darling. Tell Papa to send me any bills for this adventure."

Coral gave Kat a kiss and Jose a hug. "Nice to have met you. Sorry it was under these circumstances, but glad I did. You kids take care, and Jose, you go out of your way to make this lovely kitten feel special."

"Consider it done, darling. Great flying out there, by the way."

"Hey, it's what I do. Call me anytime you need our services."

"Take care. Good luck with Chris."

CHAPTER 84

Kat was steering her Beneteau Oceanis sailboat named Tranquility into the marina at Ocean Pointe in Key Largo while Jose was manning the ropes to secure the boat to the dock. It was their getaway from the rat race. Jose had bought a time-share there during the last real estate crash. It was on the Atlantic side of the Florida Keys—quiet, unobtrusive, out of the way, and with easy ocean access. After checking in, they unpacked, made some cocktails, and sat in the balcony enjoying the ocean view while Kat smoked her Nat Shermans, and Jose smoked a Black & Mild.

It had been a busy week with additional questions from the Homeland folks about Volkov and the cesium, reporters trying to get an exclusive on the strangler story, and Lesson's funeral, which was only attended by Jose, Kat, Coral, Nate, and Lesson's landlady. Gafford did not want to go to the funeral; he said he did not believe in them.

"You know, handsome, you need to stop beating yourself up about Lesson. The what-ifs are going to drive you crazy. You did the best you could under the circumstances, and as you always have told me, the best you can do is the best you can reach for."

"I know, honey, and I appreciate it, but I always hold myself to a higher standard. I should have used common sense and made Lesson's health and safety a priority."

"My Galahad, you always take on the problems of others. It's what you do, but you can't beat yourself up when you fall short. You are only human and can only do so much. Appreciate what you have done for others and stop beating yourself up for the what-ifs, okay?"

"What's this Galahad business you keep calling me lately?"

"Oh, baby, it's something Volkov mentioned while we were his 'guests.' He said you were like a knight tilting against the windmills, a throwback to the Dark Ages."

"Okay, so now I am a swashbuckling arbiter of justice? Or a Neanderthal or something?"

Kat laughed. "There you go with those fancy words. No, darling, I think he admired your resolve and old-fashioned way of justice and of doing the right thing. Speaking of Volkov, what happened?"

"Well, darling, he tried shooting and running over me and Chini, and he failed. He wrecked the truck he had jacked and, in the process, got himself trapped in the collapsed cab. I could have pulled him out, but he said he couldn't feel his legs, and he admitted he had terminal cancer, so he decided to take matters into his own hands—literally."

"Did you facilitate his request?" Kat looked at Jose right in the eyes.

"Of course. I was not going to let him burn to death, so I gave him a way out. I understood where his mind was at."

"There you go. You just proved what Volkov said about you to the nth degree: do the right thing and justice at the same time." Kat stroked Jose's arm and blew him a kiss.

"You better do more than blow me a kiss, young lady. We've been apart for a long time."

"Don't you worry there, cowboy. I am going to the rodeo all weekend, and guess who I'm riding?"

"I hope this bull right here, my lady."

"Bingo, Daddy." She smiled that smile that made him glad every day he had made the right decision with her.

Jose got up to freshen their drinks. They sat admiring the cool blue of the ocean waves and the harmony of the palm trees swaying in the breeze.

"Well, pumpkin, let's take these next two days to recharge our batteries. I'll finish the Cobra when we get back, and maybe we can plan a vacation abroad somewhere," Jose said as he kissed Kat on the forehead.

"Sounds like a plan, Papa. I like that. Let's get away and let's make some memories of our own."

EPILOGUE

Jose Lopez had always looked out for his little brother. When their father left their mother, the boys were only twelve and nine years old. Jose had to become the man of the family; there was no other choice. Whether it was protecting Julio from the neighborhood bullies around their favela or getting him out of whatever scrape he got himself into after he was older and started developing a temper. He had promised his mother on her dying bed that he would look out for him no matter what.

During the years, there were countless situations Julio got himself into that Jose had to bail, cajole, bribe, or maneuver to get Julio freed or out of trouble. He noticed Julio had a propensity for beating up girlfriends, and his first wife had left him after a particular vicious beating. She had charged him with rape, but she dropped the charges before it went to trial. Julio had said that no wife can charge her husband with rape since it was her duty to please and satisfy her husband. This type of thinking troubled Jose.

Jose was thinking about all of this as he sat waiting to see Julio, who had been locked up after an altercation at a bar. There was no bail currently set since Julio had a prior history of assault. The local state attorney was not in the mood to play ball and had requested no bail until they could see a judge in the morning. Julio had used his one call to get Jose to come to see him at lockup; he said it was very important.

As Julio was led to the cubicle, he had that wild-eyed look that Jose had seen too many times.

"I will have bail for you in the morning as soon as the judge sets it, so a night in here might cool you off, my brother. Is your car at the bar?"

"Listen, ese, to what I am going to say very carefully. Forget about the bail for now. What you have to do right away is get the car from the bar. I have a spare key under the front bumper. You know that motel that I go to once in a while, the one on Eighth Street?"

"Yes, you called me there last year when you had a fight with your wife."

"Yes, that one. Now pay attention. In the ashtray of the car, there is a key to a room in that motel. You need to get there ASAP and clean the room and get whatever is in there out of there, or everything I have done until now will seem like child's play."

"What have you done, my brother?"

"I will explain after I get out tomorrow morning. Promise on Mama's grave."

"Okay, okay, but I am promising *you* on Mama's grave that this is the last thing I will do for you ever. Are we clear?"

"Si, mi hermano. You do this, and you don't have to do anything else to get me out of trouble. Now go. Go do your little brother one last good deed, and I promise I will never get in trouble again."

"Okay, Julio, I am going to hold you to that promise."

"Gracias, brother. Now go, go, go and make it happen. See you when you get me out in the morning."

"I am on it. Don't worry, what could possibly go wrong? See you in the morning."

CPSIA information can be obtained
at www.ICGtesting.com
Printed in the USA
LVOW07s0426040817
543805LV00003B/124/P